The Daughters of

Sarah Stickney Ellis

THE

DAUGHTERS OF ENGLAND.

THEIR

POSITION IN SOCIETY,

CHARACTER AND RESPONSIBILITIES.

BY

MRS. ELLIS,

author of "the women of england," "sons of the soil," hints to make," and summer and winter in the pyrenees."

NEW-YORK.
D. APPLETON AND COMPANY.
1842.

CONTENTS.

PREFACE.

There can be no more gratifying circumstance to a writer, than to find that a subject which has occupied her thoughts, and employed her pen, has also been occupying the thoughts of thousands of her fellow-beings; but she is gratified in a still higher degree to find, that the peculiar views she entertains on that subject, are beginning to be entertained by a vast number of the intelligent and thinking part of the community, with whom she was not previously aware of sharing, either in their sympathy, or their convictions.

Such are the circumstances under which "The Women of England" has been received by the public, with a degree of favour, which the merits of the work alone would never have procured for it. And as no homage of mere admiration could have been so welcome to the author, as the approval it has met with at many an English hearth, she has been induced to ask the attention of the public again, to a farther exemplification of some subjects but slightly touched upon, and a candid examination of others which found no place, in that work.

The more minute the details of individual, domestic, and social duty, to which allusion is made, the more necessary it becomes to make a distinct classification of the different eras in woman's personal experience; the Author, therefore, proposes dividing the subject into three parts, in which will be separately considered, the character and situation of the Daughters, Wives, and Mothers of England.

The Daughters of England only form the subject of the present volume: and as in a former work the remarks which were offered to the public upon the social and domestic duties of woman, were expressly limited to the middle ranks of society in Great Britain; so, in the present, it must be clearly understood as the intention of the writer to address herself especially to the same interesting and influential class of her countrywomen. Much that is contained in that volume, too, might with propriety have been repeated here, had not the Author preferred referring the reader again to those pages, assured that she will be more readily pardoned for this liberty, than for transcribing a fainter copy of what was written in the first instance fresh from the heart.

It seems to be the peculiar taste of the present day to write, and to read, on the subject of woman. Some apology for thus taxing the patience of the public might be necessary, were it not that both honour and justice are due to a theme, in which a female sovereign may, without presumption, be supposed to sympathize with her people. Thus, while the character of the daughter, the wife, and the mother, are so beautifully exemplified in connection with the dignity of a British Queen, it is the privilege of the humblest, as well as the most exalted of her subjects, to know that the heart of woman, in all her tenderest and holiest feelings, is the same beneath the shelter of a cottage, as under the canopy of a throne.

Rose Hill, January 10th, 1842.

CHAP. I.
IMPORTANT INQUIRIES.

If it were possible for a human being to be suddenly, and for the first time, awakened to consciousness, with the full possession of all its reasoning faculties, the natural inquiry of such a being would be, "What am I?—how am I to act?—and, what are my capabilities for action?"

The sphere upon which a young woman enters on first leaving school, or, to use a popular phrase, on "completing her education," is so entirely new to her, her mind is so often the subject of new impressions, and her attention so frequently absorbed by new motives for exertion, that, if at all accustomed to reflect, we cannot doubt but she will make these, or similar questions, the subject of serious inquiry—"What is my position in society? what do I aim at? and what means do I intend to employ for the accomplishment of my purpose?" And it is to assist any of the daughters of England, who may be making these inquiries in sincerity of heart, that I would ask their attention to the following pages; just as an experienced traveller, who had himself often stepped aside from the safest path, and found the difficulty of returning, would be anxious to leave directions for others who might follow, in order that they might avoid the dangers with which he had already become acquainted, and pursue their course with greater certainty of attaining the end desired.

First, then, What is your position in society? for, until this point is clearly settled in your own mind, it would be vain to attempt any description of the plan to be pursued. The settlement of this point, however, must depend upon yourselves. Whether you are rich, or poor, an orphan, or the child of watchful parents—one of a numerous family, or comparatively alone—filling an exalted or an humble position—of highly-gifted mind, or otherwise—all these points must be clearly ascertained before you can properly understand the kind of duty required of you. How these questions might be answered, is of no importance to the writer, in the present stage of this work. The importance of their being clearly and faithfully answered to yourselves, is all she would enforce.

For my own purpose, it is not necessary to go further into your particular history or circumstances, than to regard you as women, and, as I hope, Christian women. As Christian women, then, I address you. This is placing you on high ground; yet surely there are few of my young countrywomen who would be willing to take lower. As women, then, the first thing of importance is to be content to be inferior to men—inferior in mental power, in the same proportion that you are inferior in bodily strength.

Facility of movement, aptitude, and grace, the bodily frame of woman may possess in a higher degree than that of man; just as in the softer touches of mental and spiritual beauty, her character may present a lovelier page than his. Yet, as the great attribute of power must still be wanting there, it becomes more immediately her business to inquire how this want may be supplied. An able and eloquent writer on "Woman's Mission," has justly observed, that woman's strength is in her influence. And, in order to render this influence more complete, you will find, on examination, that you are by nature endowed with peculiar faculties?with a quickness of perception, facility of adaptation, and acuteness of feeling, which fit you especially for the part you have to act in life; and which, at the same time, render you, in a higher degree than men, susceptible both of pain and pleasure.   These are your qualifications as mere women. As Christians, how wide is the prospect which opens before you—how various the claims upon your attention—how vast your capabilities—how deep the responsibility which those capabilities involve! In the first place, you are not alone; you are one of a family—of a social circle—of a community—of a nation. You are a being whose existence will never terminate, who *must* live for ever, and whose happiness or misery through that endless future which lies before you, will be influenced by the choice you are now in the act of making.

What, then, is the great object of your life? "To be good and happy," you will probably say; or, "To be happy and good." Which is it? For there is an important difference in giving precedence to one or the other of these two words. In one case, your aim is to secure to yourself all the advantages you can possibly enjoy, and wait for the satisfaction they produce, before you begin the great business of self-improvement. In the other, you look at your duties first, examine them well, submit yourself without reserve to their claims, and, having made them habitual, reap your reward in that happiness of which no human being can deprive you, and which no earthly event can entirely destroy.

Is it your intention beyond this to live for yourself, or for others? Perhaps you have no definite aim as relates to this subject. You are ashamed to think of living only for yourself, and deem it hard to live entirely for others; you, therefore, put away the thought, and conclude to leave this important subject until some future day. Do not, however, be deceived by such a fallacious conclusion. Each day of your life will prove that you have decided, and are acting upon the decision you make on this momentous point. Your conduct in society proves it, your behaviour in your family, every thought which occupies your mind, every wish you breathe, every plan you form, every pleasure you enjoy, every pain you suffer—all prove whether it is your object to live for yourself, or for others.

Again, is it your aim to live for this world only, or for eternity? This is the question of supreme importance, which all who profess to be Christians, and who think seriously, must ask and answer to themselves. There can be no delay here. Time is silently deciding this question for you. Before another day has passed, you will be so much nearer to the kingdom of heaven, or so much farther from it. Another day, another, and another, of this fearful indecision, will be adding to your distance from the path of peace, and rendering your task more difficult if you should afterwards seek to return.

If it be your deliberate desire to live for this world only, all the highest faculties of your nature may then lie dormant, for there is no field of exercise here, to make the cultivation of them worth the pains. If it is your deliberate desire to live for this world only, the improvement of the bodily senses becomes more properly the object of primary interest, in order that you may taste, smell, feel, hear, and see, with more acuteness. A little invention, a little calculation, a little observation of cause and effect, may be necessary, in order that the senses may be. gratified in a higher degree; but beyond this, all would indeed be worse than vanity, that would tend to raise the human mind to a knowledge of its own capabilities, and yet leave it to perish with the frail tenement it inhabits.

I cannot, however, suppose it possible that any daughter of Christian parents, in this enlightened country, would deliberately make so blind, so despicable a choice. And if your aim be to live for eternity; if you would really make this an object, not merely to read or to talk about, but to strive after, as the highest good you are capable of conceiving, then is the great mystery of your being unravelled—then is a field of exercise laid open for the noblest faculties of your soul—then has faith its true foundation, hope its unextinguishable beacon, and charity its sure reward.

I must now take it for granted, that the youthful reader of these pages has reflected seriously upon her position in society as a woman, has acknowledged her inferiority to man, has examined her own nature, and found there a capability of feeling, a quickness of perception, and a facility of adaptation, beyond what he possesses, and which, consequently, fit her for a distinct and separate sphere; and I would also gladly persuade myself, that the same individual, as a Christian woman, has made her decision not to live for herself, so much as for others; but, above all, not to live for this world, so much as for eternity. The question then arises—What means are to be adopted in the pursuit of this most desirable end? Some of my young readers will perhaps be disposed to exclaim, "Why, this is but the old story of giving up the world, and all its pleasures!" But let them not be too hasty in their conclusions. It is not a system of giving up which I am about to recommend to them, so much as one of attaining. My advice is rather to advance than to retreat, yet to be sure that you advance in the right way. Instead, therefore of depreciating the value of their advantages and acquirements, it is my intention to point out, so far as I am able, how all these advantages may be made conducive to the great end I have already supposed them to have in view—that of living for others, rather than for themselves—of living for eternity, rather than for time.

I have already stated, that I suppose myself to be addressing young women who are professedly Christians, and who know that the profession of Christianity as the religion of the Bible, involves responsibility for every talent they possess. By responsibility I mean, that they should consider themselves, during the whole of their lives, as in a condition to say, if called upon to answer, whether they have made use of the best means they were acquainted with, for attaining what they believed to be the most desirable end.

Youth and health are means of the utmost importance in this great work. Youth is the season of impressions, and can never be recalled; health is a blessing of such boundless value, that when lost it may safely be said to be sighed for more than any other, for the sake of the countless advantages it affords. Education is another means, which you are now supposed to be enjoying in its fullest extent; for I have already said that I suppose myself to be addressing young women who are popularly spoken of as having just completed their education. Fresh from the master's hand, you will therefore never possess in greater perfection the entire sum of your scholastic attainments than now. Reading and conversation, it is true, may improve your mind; but of your present possessions, in the way of learning and accomplishments, how many will be lost through indolence or neglect, and how many more will give place to claims of greater urgency, or subjects of more lively interest? The present moment, then, is the time to take into account the right use of all your knowledge and all your accomplishments. What is the precise amount of these, we will not presume to ask; but let it not be forgotten, that your accountability extends to the time, the trouble, and the expense bestowed on your education, as well as to what you may have actually acquired. How many years have you been at school??We will suppose from two to ten, and that from one hundred pounds, to five or more, have been expended upon you during this time; add to this the number of teachers employed in your instruction, the number of books appropriated to your use, the time?to say nothing of the patience?bestowed upon you, the anxiety of parents, who probably spared with difficulty the sum that was necessary for your education, their solicitude, their self-denial, their prayers that this sum might be well applied; reflect upon all these, and you will perceive that a debt has been contracted, which you have to discharge to your parents, your family, and to society?that you have enjoyed a vast amount of advantages, for which you have to account to the great Author of your being. Such, then, is your position in life; a Christian woman, and therefore one whose first duty is to ascertain her proper place—a sensitive and intelligent being, more quick to feel than to understand, and therefore more under the necessity of learning to feel rightly—a responsible being, with numberless talents to be accounted for, and believing that no talent was ever given in vain, but that all, however apparently trifling in themselves, are capable of being so used as to promote the great end of our being, the happiness of our fellow-creatures, and the glory of our Creator.

Let not my young friends, however, suppose that I am about to lay down for them some system of Spartan discipline, some *iron rule*, by which to effect the subjugation of all that is buoyant in health, and delightful in the season of youth. The rule I would propose to them is one by which they may become beloved as well as lovely—the source of happiness to others, as well as happy in themselves. My desire is to assist them to overcome the three great enemies to their temporal and eternal good—their selfishness, indolence, and vanity, and to establish in their stead feelings of benevolence and habits of industry, so blended with Christian meekness, that while affording pleasure to all who live within the sphere of their influence, they shall be unconscious of the charm by which they please.

I have already stated, that women, in their position in life, must be content to be inferior to men; but as their inferiority consists chiefly, in their want of power, this deficiency is abundantly made up to them by their capability of exercising influence; it is made up to them also in other ways, incalculable in their number and extent, but in none so effectually as by that order of Divine Providence which places them, in a moral and religious point of view, on the same level with man; nor can it be a subject of regret to any right-minded woman, that they are not only exempt from the most laborious occupations both of mind and body, but also from the necessity of engaging in those eager pecuniary speculations, and in that fierce conflict of worldly interests, by which men are so deeply occupied as to be in a manner compelled to stifle their best feelings, until they become in reality the characters they at first only assumed. Can it be a subject of regret to any kind and feeling woman, that her sphere of action is one adapted to the exercise of the affections, where she may love, and trust, and hope, and serve, to the utmost of her wishes? Can it be a subject of regret that she is not called upon, so much as man, to calculate, to compete, to struggle, but rather to occupy a sphere in which the elements of discord cannot with propriety be admitted—in which beauty and order are expected to denote her presence, and where the exercise of benevolence is the duty she is most frequently called upon to perform.

Women almost universally consider themselves, and wish to be considered by others, as extremely affectionate; scarcely can a more severe libel be pronounced upon a woman than to say that she is not so. Now the whole law of woman's life is a law of love. I propose, therefore, to treat the subject in this light—to try whether the neglect of their peculiar duties does not imply an absence of love, and whether the principle of love, thoroughly carried out, would not so influence their conduct and feelings as to render them all which their best friends could desire.

Let us, however, clearly understand each other at the outset. To love, is a very different thing from a desire to be beloved. To love, is woman's nature—to be beloved is the consequence of her having properly exercised and controlled that nature. To love, is woman's duty—to be beloved, is her reward.

Does the subject, when considered in this point of view, appear less attractive? "No," you reply, "it constitutes the happiness of every generous soul, to love; and if that be the secret of our duty, the whole life of woman must be a pleasant journey on a path of flowers."

Some writers have asserted, that along with the power to love, we all possess, in an equal degree, the power to hate. I am not prepared to go this length, because I would not acknowledge the principle of hatred in any enlightened mind; yet I do believe, that in proportion to our capability of being attracted by certain persons or things, is our liability to be repelled by others, and that along with such repulsion there is a feeling of dislike, which belongs to women in a higher degree than it does to men, in the same proportion that their perceptions are more acute, and their attention more easily excited by the minuter shades of difference in certain things. Although not willingly recognizing the sensation of hatred, as applied to anything but sin, I am compelled to use the word, in order to render my meaning more obvious; and certainly, when we listen to the unrestrained conversation of the generality of young ladies, we cannot hesitate to suppose that the sensation of hatred towards certain persons or things, does, in reality, form part of the most important business of their lives.

To love and to hate, then, seem to be the two things which it is most natural and most easy for women to do. In these two principles how many of the actions of their lives originate? How important is it, therefore, that they should learn in early life to love and hate aright. Most young women of respectable parentage and education, believe that they love virtue and hate vice. But have they clearly ascertained what virtue and vice are—have they examined the meaning of these two important words by the light of the world, or by the light of divine truth? Have they listened to the plausible reasoning of what is called *society*; where things are often spoken of by false names, and where vulgar vice is distinguished from that which is sanctioned by good breeding? or have they gone directly to the eternal and immutable principles of good and evil, as explained in the Bible, which they profess to believe? have they by this test tried all their favourite habits—their sweet weaknesses—their darling idols? and have they been willing to abide the result of this test—to love whatever approaches that standard of moral excellence, and to renounce whatever is offensive to the pure eye of Omniscience? Now, when we reflect that all this must be done before we can safely give ourselves up either to love or hate, we shall probably cease to think that our great duty is so easily performed. Youth is the season for regulating these emotions as we ought, because it is comparatively easy to govern our affections when first awakened; after they have been allowed for some time to flow in any particular channel, it requires a painful and determined effort to restrain or divert their course; nor does the constitution of the human mind endure this revulsion of feeling unharmed. As the country over whose surface an impetuous river has poured its waters, retains, after those waters are gone, the sterile track they once pursued, marring the picture as with a scar?a seamy track of barrenness and drought; so the course of misplaced affection leaves its indelible trace upon the character, breaking the harmony of what might otherwise have been most attractive in its beauty and repose.   There is, perhaps, no subject on which young women are apt to make so many and such fatal mistakes as in the regulation of their emotions of attraction and repulsion; and chiefly for this reason—because there is a popular notion prevailing amongst them, that it is exceedingly becoming to act from the impulse of the moment, to be, what they call, "the creatures of feeling," or, in other words, to exclude the high attribute of reason from those very emotions which are given them, especially, to serve the most exalted purposes. "It is a cold philosophy," they say, "to calculate before you feel;" and thus they choose to act from impulse rather than from principle.

The unnatural mother does this when she singles out a favourite child as the recipient of all her endearments, leaving the neglected one to pine away its little life. The foolish mother does this, when she withholds, from imagined tenderness, the wholesome discipline which infancy requires—choosing for her unconscious offspring a succession of momentary indulgences which are sure to entail upon them years of suffering in after life. The fickle friend does this, when she conceives a sudden distaste for the companion she has professed to love. The unfaithful wife does this, when she allows her thoughts to wander from her rightful lord. All women have done this, who have committed those frightful crimes which stain the page of history—all have acted from impulse, and by far the greater number have acted under the influence of misplaced affection. It is, indeed, appalling to contemplate the extent of ruin and of wretchedness to which woman may be carried by the force of her own impetuous and unregulated feelings. Her faults are not those of selfish calculation; she makes no stipulation for her own, or others' safety; when once she renounces principle, therefore, and gives herself up to act as the mere creature of impulse, there is no hope for her, except that experience, by its painful chastisements, may bring her back to wisdom and to peace.

Does this seem a hard sentence to pronounce upon those impetuous young creatures who make it their boast that they never stay to think—that they cannot reason—and were only born to feel? Hard as it is, observation proves it true. If we do not acknowledge any regular system of conduct, habit will render that systematical which is our customary choice; and if we choose day by day to act from impulse rather than principle, we yield ourselves to a fatal and delusive system, the worst consequences of which will follow us beyond the grave.

As youth is the season for making this important choice so it is the season for impressions. You will never remember what you acquire in after life, as you will remember what you are acquiring now. The knowledge you now obtain of evil will haunt you through future years, like a dark spectre in your path; while the glimpses of virtue which you now perceive irradiating the circle in which you move, will re-appear before you to the end of life, surrounded by the same bright halo which adorns them now. If you have loved the virtuous and the good—if you have associated yourselves with their pursuits, and made their aims and objects yours in early life—the remembrance of these early friends will form a bright spot in your existence, to recur to as long as that existence lasts.

It is therefore of the highest importance to the right government of your affections, that you should endeavour to form clear notions of good and evil, in order that you may know how to choose the one and refuse the other; not to take things for granted—not to believe that is always best which is most approved by the world, unless you would prefer the approbation of man to that of God; but to be willing to see the truth, whatever it may be, and as such to embrace it.

In the gospel of Christ there are truths so simple and so clear, so perfectly in keeping one with another, that none need be kept in the dark as to the principles on which they ought to act, if they are but willing to submit themselves to this rule.

I speak here of the practical part of the Scriptures only; but in connexion with the vivid and lasting impressions made upon the mind of youth, I would strongly enforce the importance of choosing that season for obtaining an intimate knowledge of the Scriptures altogether. You can scarcely at present be aware of the extreme value of this knowledge; it will serve you in after life as a rich and precious store to draw upon, not only for your own consolation, and the renewal of your own faith, but for the comfort, guidance, and support of all who come within the sphere of your influence, or depend upon you for aid in the great work of preparing for eternity. Without this knowledge, how feeble will be your arguments on the most important of all subjects, how useless your assertions, and how devoid of efficacy your endeavours to disseminate the principles of Divine Truth! How enviable does the possession of this knowledge now appear to many a zealous Christian who has to deplore the consequences of a neglected youth! for I repeat, that in after life it is almost impossible to impress the mind with the same vividness, and consequently to enrich the memory with the same amount of useful knowledge, as when the aspect of the world is new, and the feelings comparatively unoccupied and unimpressed.

The same observations which occur in relation to the reading of the Scriptures at an early period of life, apply, in degree, to the acquisition of all other kinds of knowledge. Never again will the mind be so free from distraction as now; never again will the claims of duty be so few; never again will the memory be so unoccupied. If, therefore, a store of knowledge is not laid up while the mind is in this state, it will be found wanting when most needed; and difficult indeed, is the task, and mortifying the situation of those, whose information has to be sought, in order to supply the demand of every hour. As well might the cultivator of the soil allow his grain to remain in the fields, until hunger reminded him that bread was wanted on his board; as the woman who expects to fill a respectable station in life, go forth into society unprovided with that supply of knowledge and information which she will there find perpetually required. The use of such knowledge is a different question, and remains yet to be discussed; but on the importance of its acquisition in the season of youth, there can be but one opinion amongst experienced and rational beings.

Of all kinds of knowledge, that of our own ignorance, is the first to be acquired. It is an humbling lesson for those to learn, who are built up on the foundation of what is called a good education; yet, such is the fact, that the knowledge which young ladies bring home with them from school, forms but a very small part of that which they will be expected to possess. Indeed, such is the illimitable nature of knowledge, that persons can only be said to know much or little by comparison. It is by comparing ourselves with others, and especially with those who are more advanced in life, that we first learn the important secret of our own deficiencies. And it is good to keep the mind open to this truth, for without having clearly ascertained our own inferiority, we should always be liable to make the most egregious mistakes, not only by telling those around us what they already know, and wearying our acquaintance with the most tedious common-place; but by the worst kind of false assumption—by placing ourselves in exalted positions, and thereby rendering our ignorance more conspicuous.

All this, however, though a fruitful source of folly and ridicule, is of trifling importance compared with the absolute want—the mental poverty—the moral destitution, necessarily occasioned by an absence of true knowledge; we must begin, therefore, by opening our minds to the truth, not by adopting the opinions of this or that set of persons, but by reading the works of the best authors, by keeping the mind unbiassed by the writings or the conversation of persons infected with prejudice, and by endeavouring to view every object in its full extent, its breadth, its reality, and its importance.

It is the grand defect in woman's intellectual condition, that she seldom makes any equivalent effort to do this. She is not only too often occupied with the mere frivolities of life, to estimate the true value of general knowledge; but, she is also too apt to hang her credulity upon her affections, and to take anything for granted which is believed by those whom she loves. It is true, this servility of mind may appear to some like acting out the law of love, which I am so anxious to advocate; but how is it, if their dearest friends are in error, and if they err in such a way as to endanger their temporal and eternal interests? Is it not a higher and nobler effort of love, to see and rectify such error, than to endeavour to imbibe the same, for the sake of being companions in folly, or in sin?

One of the greatest faults in the system of education pursued in the present day, is that of considering youth as the season for reading short and easy books. Although the ablest of female writers—I had almost said the wisest of women—has left on record her testimony against this practice, it continues to be the fashion, to place in the hands of young persons, all kinds of abstracts, summaries, and short means of arriving at facts; as if the only use of knowledge was to be able to repeat by rote a list of the dates of public events.

Now, if ever an entire history or a complete work is worth reading, it must be at an early period of life, when attention and leisure are both at our command. By the early and studious reading of books of this description, those important events which it is of so much consequence to impress upon the mind, become interwoven in the memory, with the spirit and style of the author; so that instead of the youthful reader becoming possessed of nothing more than a mere table of facts, she is in reality associating herself with a being of the highest order of mind, seeing with the eyes of the author, breathing his atmosphere, thinking his thoughts, and imbibing, through a thousand indirect channels, the very essence of his genius.

This is the only kind of reading which is really worthy of the name. Abstracts and compendiums may very properly be glanced over in after life, for the sake of refreshing the memory as to dates and facts; but unless the works of the best authors have been read in this manner in early life, there will always be something vapid in our conversation, contracted in our views, prejudiced in our mode of judging, and vulgar in our habits of thinking and speaking of things in general. In vain may we attempt to hide this great deficiency. Art may in some measure conceal what is wanting; but it cannot bring to light what does not exist. Prudence may seal the lips, and female tact may point out when to speak with safety, and when to withhold a remark; but all those enlightened views, all that bold launching forth into the region of intellect, all the companionship of gifted minds, which intelligent women, even in their inferior capacity, may at least delight in, will be wanting to the happiness of her who chooses to waste the precious hours of her youth in idleness or frivolity.

Nor is it easy for after study to make up the deficiency of what ought to have been acquired in youth. Bare information dragged in to supply the want of the moment, without arrangement, and without previous thought, too often resembles in its crudeness and inappropriate display, a provision of raw fruits, and undressed food, instead of the luxuries of an elegant and well-furnished board.

I have heard it pleaded by young women, that they did 'not care for knowledge'—'did not wish to be clever.' And if such persons would be satisfied to fill the lowest place in society, to creep through the world alone, or to have silly husbands, and idiot sons, we should say that their ambition was equal to their destiny. But when we see the same persons jealous of their rights as intellectual beings, aspiring to be the companions of rational men, and, above all, the early instructors of immortal beings, we blush to contemplate such lamentable destitution of right feeling, and can only forgive their presumption in consideration to their ignorance and folly. I cannot believe of any of the young persons who may read these pages, that they could be guilty of such an act of ingratitude to the great Author of their being, and the Giver of every good and perfect gift they possess, as deliberately to choose to consign to oblivion and neglect the intellectual part of their nature, which may justly be regarded as the highest of these gifts. I would rather suppose them already acquainted with the fact, that those passions, and emotions, to the exercise of which they believe themselves especially called, are many of them such as are common to the inferior orders of animals, while the possession of an understanding capable of unlimited extension, is an attribute of the Divine nature, and one which raises them to a level with the angels.

CHAP. II
ECONOMY OF TIME.

In all our pursuits, but especially in the acquisition of knowledge, it is highly important to habituate ourselves to minute calculations upon the value and progress of time. That writer who could teach us how to estimate this treasure, and how to realize its fleetness, would confer a lasting benefit upon his fellow-creatures. We all know how to talk of time flying fast. It is, in short, the subject of our most familiar proverbs, the burden of the minstrel's song, the theme of the preacher's discourse, the impress we affix to our lightest pleasures, the inscription that remains upon our tombs. Yet how little do we actually realize of the silent and ceaseless progress of time? It is true, that one of the first exclamations which infant lips are taught to utter is the word 'gone;' and the beautiful expression, 'gone for ever,' occurs with frequency in our poetical phraseology. Clean gone for ever, is the still more expressive language of Scripture; and if any combination of words could be made to convey to us clear and striking impressions of this idea, it would be found amongst those of the inspired writers. Yet still we go on from day to day, insensible, and unimpressed by this, the most sublime and appalling reality of our existence.

The fact that no single moment of our lives, whether happy or miserable, whether wasted or well employed, can ever be recalled, is of itself one of the most momentous truths with which we are acquainted—that each hour of our past existence, whether marked by wisdom or by folly, is gone for ever; and that neither ingenuity, nor effort, nor purchase, nor prayer, can call it back. Nay, so far is it removed from the range of possibility, that we should live again for any portion of our past lives, that it was not even amongst the miracles wrought by the Saviour while on earth. Other apparent impossibilities he did accomplish before the eyes of wondering multitudes, breaking the bonds of nature, and even raising the dead to life; yet, we find not amongst these mighty works, that he said to any single day in man's experience, 'Thou shalt dawn again.' No. Even the familiar face of yesterday is turned away from us for ever; and though so closely followed by the remembrance of the past night, as well might we attempt to grasp the stars, as to turn back and enjoy its sweet repose again.

What then is the consequence? Since time, this great ocean of wealth, is ebbing away from us day by day, and hour by hour; since it must inevitably diminish, and since we know the lowest rate at which it must go, though none can tell how soon it may to them be gone for ever, is it not our first duty to make the best possible use of what remains, and to begin in earnest, before another day shall escape from our hold?

We will suppose the case of a man who finds himself the possessor of a vast estate, with the power to cultivate it as he will, and to derive any amount of revenue from it which his ingenuity or labour may obtain for him; yet, with this condition—that an enemy shall be entitled to take away a certain portion of it every day, until the whole is gone. The enemy might, under certain circumstances, with which the owner could not be acquainted, enjoy the liberty of taking the whole at once; but a certain part he *must* take every day. Now, would not the man who held this property on such a tenure, look sharply to his own interest, and endeavour to discover by what means he could turn his estate to the best account, before its extent should be so far diminished as to cripple his means? Reflecting, too, that each day it was becoming less, and that the smaller its extent, the smaller would be the returns he might expect, would he not begin without the loss of a single day, so to improve his land, to till, to sow, and to prepare for getting in his produce, as that he might derive a lasting revenue of profit from the largest portion, before it should have passed out of his own hands?

A very common understanding, and a very trifling amount of knowledge, would prompt the possessor of such an estate to do this; yet, with regard to time, that most valuable of earthly possessions, how few of us act upon this principle! With some, the extent of this estate is narrowing to a very small circle; but with the class of human beings whom I am addressing, there is, in all human probability, a wider field for them to speculate upon. Illness, it is true, may come and snatch away a large portion, and death may be waiting to grasp the whole: how much more important is it then, to begin to cultivate and reap in time!

Perhaps it is the apparent extent of our prospect in early life, which deludes us into the belief that the enemy is actually not taking anything away. Still there are daily and hourly evidences of the lapse of time, which would serve to remind us of the impossibility of calling it back, if we would but regard them in this light. If, for instance, we have committed an egregious folly, if we have acted unjustly, thrown blame upon the innocent, or spoken unkindly to a dear friend—though it was but yesterday, last night, or this morning—not all our tears, though we might weep oceans, could wash away that single act or word; because the moment which bore that stain upon it, would be gone—and gone for ever.

Again, we scarcely become acquainted with life in any of its serious aspects, before death is presented to our notice. And where are they—"the loved, the lost?" Their days have been numbered—all those long days of companionship in which their friends might have loved, and served them better, are gone for ever. 'And why,' we ask, when the blow falls nearest to ourselves—when the delight of our eyes is taken away as with a stroke— 'why do not the sun, and the moon, and the stars, delay their course?—why do the flowers not cease to bloom?—the light and cheerful morning not fail to return? above all, why do those around us continue their accustomed avocations? and why do we join them at last, as if nothing had occurred?' It is because time passes on, and on, and neither life nor death, nor joy, nor sorrow, nor any of the changes in our weal or wo, present the minutest hinderance to his certain progress, or retard for a single moment his triumphant and irresistible career.

Nor is it simply as a whole, that we have to take into account the momentous subject of time. Every year, and month, and day, have their separate amount of responsibility; but especially the season of youth, because the habits we acquire during that period, have an influence upon the whole of our after lives.

The habit of making correct calculations upon how much can be done in any stated portion of time, is the first thing to begin with, for without this, we are very apt to go on with anything that may happen to interest us, to the culpable neglect of more important duties. Thus, though it may be well for a man to pluck the weeds up in his garden for half an hour after breakfast; yet, if his actual business lies in the counting-house, or the exchange, it would be worse than folly for him to remain plucking weeds up for half the day.

In order to make the best use of time, we must lay out beforehand the exact amount proportioned to every occupation in which we expect to engage. Casualties will perpetually occur demanding an additional allowance, and something must consequently be given up in exchange; but still our calculations may generally be made with a degree of certainty, which leaves no excuse for our being habitually at a loss what to do.

There is a class of young persons, and I fear not a very small one, who rise every morning trusting to the day to provide its own occupations and amusements. They descend from their chambers with a listless, dreamy hope that something will occur to interest, or enliven them, never imagining that they themselves are called upon to enliven and interest others. Such individuals being liable to disappointment every day, almost always learn to look upon themselves as unfortunate beings, less privileged than others, and, in short, ill-treated by faith, or rather by Providence, in being placed where they are.

It is this waiting to be interested, or amused, by anything that may chance to happen, which constitutes the great bane of a young woman's life, and while dreaming on in this most unprofitable state, without any definite object of pursuit, their minds become the prey of a host of enemies, whose attacks might have been warded off by a little wholesome and determined occupation. Their feelings, always too busy for their peace, become morbid, restless, and ungovernable, for want of proper exercise; while imagination, allowed to run riot over a boundless field of vague and half-formed observations, leads their affections in her train, to fix upon whatever object caprice or fancy may select.

It is not attributing too much importance to the right economy of time, to say that it might prevent all this. I presume not to lay down rules for the occupation of every hour. Particular duties must always appertain to particular situations; and since the necessary claims upon our attention are as varied as our individual circumstances, that which in one would be a right employment of time, would be a culpable breach of duty in another.

There are, however, a few general rules which cannot be too clearly or too deeply impressed upon the mind—rules which the rich and the poor would be equally benefitted by adopting; which the meanest and the most exalted individual would alike find it safe to act upon; and by which the wisest and best of mankind might increase their means and extend their sphere of usefulness to their fellow-creatures.

The first of these rules is to accustom yourselves every morning to say what you are intending to do; and every night, with equal faithfulness, to say what you have actually done during the day. If you find any material difference between what you have intended, and what you have achieved, try to proportion them better, and the next day, either lay out for yourself, or, what is far better, endeavour to accomplish more. This is the more to be recommended, because we learn, both by experience and observation, that whenever we bring down our good intentions to a lower scale, it is a certain symptom of some failure either in our moral, intellectual, or physical power. Still there is much allowance to be made for the inexperience of youth, in not being able to limit good intentions by the bounds of what is practicable; it is therefore preferable that a little should be taken off, even from what is good in itself, rather than that you should go on miscalculating time, and means, to the end of life.

There are persons, and some considerably advanced in years, who habitually retire to rest every night, surprised and disappointed that the whole of their day's work has not been done. Now, it is evident that such persons must be essentially wrong in one of these two things—either in their calculations upon the value and extent of time, or in their estimate of their own capabilities; and in consequence of these miscalculations, they have probably been making the most serious mistakes all their lives. They have been promising what they could not perform; deceiving and disappointing their friends, and those who were dependent upon them; besides harassing their own spirits, and destroying their own peace, by frightful miscalculations of imperative claims, when there was no residue of time at all proportioned to such requirements.

The next rule I would lay down is, if possible, of more importance than the first. It is, that you should always be able to say what you are doing, and not merely what you are going to do. "I am going to be so busy—I am going to get to my work—I am going to prepare for my journey—I am going to learn Latin—I am going to visit a poor neighbour." These, and ten thousand other 'goings,' with the frequent addition of the word 'just' before them, are words which form a network of delusion, by which hundreds of really well-intentioned young persons are completely entangled. 'I am just going to do this or that good work,' sounds so much like 'I am really doing it,' that the conscience is satisfied for the moment; yet how vast is the difference between these two expressions when habit has fixed them upon the character!

To the same class of persons who habitually say, 'I am going,' rather than 'I am doing,' belong those who seldom know what they really are about; who, coming into a room for a particular purpose, and finding a book there by chance, open it, and sit down to read for half an hour, or an hour, believing all the while that they are going to do the thing they first intended; or who, setting out to walk for the benefit of their health, drop in upon a pleasant acquaintance by the way, still thinking they are going to walk, until the time for doing so has expired, when they return home, with cold feet and aching heads, half fancying that they have really walked, and disappointed that exercise has produced no better effect.

Now, in these two cases, there may be as little harm in reading the book as in calling upon the acquaintance, and nothing wrong in either: but the habit of doing habitually what we had not intended to do, and leaving undone what we had intended, has so injurious an effect in weakening our resolutions, and impairing our capacity for making exact calculations upon time and means, that one might pronounce, without much hesitation, upon a person accustomed to this mode of action, the sentence of utter inability to fill any situation of usefulness or importance amongst mankind.

I am inclined to think we should all be sufficiently astonished, if we would try the experiment through a single day, of passing quickly and promptly from one occupation to another. It is, in fact, these 'goings to do,' which constitute so large an amount of wasted time, for which we are all accountable. Few persons deliberately intend to be idle; few will allow that they have been so from choice; yet how vast a proportion of the human race are living in a state of self-deception, by persuading themselves they are not idle, when they are merely going to act. Promptness in doing whatever it is right to do *now*, is one of the great secrets of living. By this means, we find our capabilities increased to an amazing amount; nor can we ever know what they really are, until this plan of conduct has been folly tried.

Wisely has it been said, by the greatest of moral philosophers, that there is *a time for everything*. Let it be observed, however, that he has not, amongst his royal maxims, spoken of a time for doing nothing; and it is fearful to think how large a portion of the season of youth is spent in this manner.

Nor is it absolute idleness alone which claims our attention. The idleness of self-delusion has already been described. But there is. besides this, a busy idleness, which operates with equal force against the right economy of time. Busy idleness arises chiefly from a restlessness of feeling, which, without any calculation as to the fitness of time or place, or the ultimate utility of what is done, hurries its possessor into a succession of trifling or ill-timed occupations, frequently as annoying to others, as they are unproductive of any beneficial result. Busy idleness is also a disease most difficult to cure, because it satisfies for thee moment that thirst for occupation, with which every human being is more or less affected, and which has been implanted in our nature for the wisest of purposes. It is under the influence of this propensity to busy idleness, that, with multitudes who have no extraordinary capability for receiving pleasure, amusement is made to supply the place of occupation, and childish trifling that of intellectual pursuit.

It may be asked, how does the law of love operate here? I answer; precisely in this way— We are never so capable of being useful to others, as when we have learned to economize our own time; to make exact calculations as to what we are able, or not able, to do in any given period; and so to employ ourselves as to make the trifles of the moment give place to more important avocations. Without having cultivated such habits, our intentions, nay, our promises, must often fall short of what we actually perform; so that in time, and after many painful disappointments, our friends will cease to depend upon our aid, believing, what may all the while be unjust to our feelings, that we have never entertained any earnest desire to promote their interest.

Above all other subjects, however, connected with the consideration of time, the law of love bears most directly upon that of punctuality. No one can fail in this point, without committing an act of injury to another. If the portion of time allotted to us in this life be aptly compared to a valuable estate, of which an enemy robs us by taking away a certain portion every day; surely it is a hard case that a friend must usurp the same power, and take away another portion, contrary to our expectations, and without any previous stipulation that it should be so. Yet, of how much of this precious property do we deprive our friends during the course of a lifetime, by our want of punctuality? and not our friends only, but all those who are in any way connected with, or dependent upon us. Our friends, indeed, might possibly forgive us the injury for the love they bear us; but there are the poor—the hard-working poor, whose time is often their wealth; and strangers, who owe us no kindness, and who consequently are not able to endure this injury without feelings of irritation or resentment.

The evil, too, is one which extends in its consequences, and widens in its influence, beyond all calculation. Yet, for the sake of conveying to the youthful and inexperienced reader, some idea of its mode of operation, we will suppose the case of a man carrying letters or despatches along one of our public roads, and so calculating his time as to appoint to be met at some post on the road every hour, by this means to transmit his despatches by other couriers along branch-roads to distant parts of the country. The person whose business it is to place these despatches in his hand at a certain time and place, is half an hour too late; consequently, all the couriers along the road are delayed in the same proportion, and there is the loss of half an hour occasioned, not only to each of them, but to all who have depended upon their arrival at a certain time. It is true, that few of us are placed in the same relative position as this man, with regard to our fellow-creatures; yet, none of us act alone; and the mistress of a house, who detains a poor workman half an hour by her want of punctuality, may be the means of his receiving reproof, nay, even abuse, from others who have lost their time in consequence of his delay; while others still, and others yet beyond, through the wider range of a more extensive circle, may have been calculating their time and means in dependence upon the punctuality of this poor man.

If on particular occasions which recur every day, we find we are generally half an hour too late, the evil to others is sometimes easily remedied by making our appointment half an hour later, and abiding by it. But such is not the plan of those who are habitually negligent of punctuality. They go on, varying from their time, one day perhaps an hour, another a quarter of an hour, and occasionally perhaps being before it, until the whole machinery of intercourse with their fellow-creatures is deranged—those of their dependents who are inclined to indolence taking advantage of their delay; those who are impatient, fretting themselves into angry passions at this wanton waste of their precious time; and many whose connexion might perhaps have been highly valuable, leaving them altogether, in consequence of being wearied or disgusted with the uncertainty which attended all their proceedings.

It is not, therefore, our own time only that is wasted by our want of punctuality, but hours, and days, and months' and years of the precious property of others, over which we had no right, and which was not intentionally submitted to our thoughtless expenditure.

It is often alleged by young persons as being of no use for them to be punctual, when others are not so, and that they only waste their own time by being ready at the appointed moment. All this may be too true; for parents and seniors in a family often have themselves to blame for the want of punctuality in the junior members. Yet is it of no importance, whether we are the causes or the subjects of injury—whether we practise injustice towards others, or only endure it ourselves? Surely, no generous mind can hesitate a moment which alternative to choose, especially when such choice refers not to any single act, but to a course of conduct pursued through a whole life-time. Of what material consequence will it appear to us on the bed of death, that certain individuals, at different times of our lives, have kept us waiting for a few hours, which might certainly have been better employed? But it will be of immense importance at the close of life, if, by our habitual want of punctuality, we have been the cause of an enormous waste of time, the property of countless individuals, to whom we can make no repayment for any single act of such unlicensed robbery. It is the principle of integrity, then, upon which our punctuality must be founded, and the law of love will render it habitual.

As there are few persons who deliberately intend to be idle; so there are perhaps still fewer who deliberately intend to waste their own time, or that of their friends. It is the lapse of years, the growth of experience, and the establishment of character on some particular basis, which tell the humiliating truth, that time has been culpably and lamentably wasted. There are other delusions, however, besides those already specified, under which this fruitless expenditure is unconsciously carried on; and none is perhaps, as a whole, more destructive to usefulness, or more fatal to domestic peace, than the habit of being always a little too late—too late to come—too late to go—too late to meet at the place of appointment—too late to be useful—too late to do good—too late to repent and seek forgiveness while the gates of mercy are unclosed. All these may be the consequences of setting out in life, without a firm determination never to yield to the dangerous habit of being a little too late.

In this case it is not so much the absolute waste of time, as the waste of feeling, which is to be regretted; for no one can be habitually ever so little too late, without experiencing at times a degree of hurry and distraction of mind, most destructive of domestic comfort, and individual peace.

To be a few minutes too early, may appear to many as inconsistent with the order of the present day, when everything is pushed to extremity, and it may consequently be considered as a useless waste of time; yet I am inclined to think that the moments in which we can say, "I am ready," are amongst some of the most precious of our lives, as affording us opportunity for that calm survey of human affairs, without which we should pass in a state of comparative blindness along the thickly-peopled walks of life. To be ready a little before the time, is like pausing for a moment to see the great machine of human events at work, to mark the action and the play of every part, and to observe the vast amount of feeling which depends upon every turn of the mighty wheel of time.

Who that has stood still, and watched the expression of the human countenance during the last struggles of a too-late preparation for pleasure, for business, or for trial, has not, in a single moment, read more plain truths on that unguarded page than years of its ordinary expression would have unfolded? Besides this, however, the great advantage we derive from being habitually too early, is the power it gives us to husband our forces, to make our calculations upon coming events, to see how to improve upon yesterday, and to resolve to do so; but, above all other means of strengthening our better resolutions, it affords us time for those mental appeals for Divine blessing and support, without which we have no right to expect either safety, assistance, or success. Fortified in this manner, it is less likely that any unexpected event should unsettle the balance of our minds, because we go forth with calmness, prepared either to enjoy with moderation and thankfulness, or to suffer with patience and resignation.

Young persons are often beguiled into the dangerous habit of being a little too late, by the apparent unimportance of each particular transgression of the kind during the season of youth. If, for instance, they are a little too late for breakfast, the matron of the family commences operations without them, and they can easily gain time upon some of the senior members. At the dinner-hour it is the same. They have only to calculate upon a few impatient words, and a few angry looks; and it is not the least unfavourable feature of their case, that to such looks and words they become so accustomed as scarcely to heed them, nor is it often that they bring any more serious consequences upon themselves by their delay, because the young are generally so kindly assisted and cared for by their friends, that by a long, and patient, and often-repeated process of helping, urging, and entreating, they are, for the most part, got ready for every important occasion, or, in other words, are seldom left behind.

It is in more advanced life that the evil begins to tell upon the happiness of all around them; and let it never be forgotten, that the more exalted their situation, the wider their sphere of influence, the more extensive are the evils resulting from any wrong line of conduct they may choose to pursue. The season of early youth is, therefore, the best time for correcting this tendency, before it has begun to bear with any serious effects upon the good, or the happiness of others.

We will suppose the case of a mistress of a family preparing for a journey. Having been a little too late with everything which had to be done, there is a frightful accumulation of demands upon her attention during the last day, but especially the last half-hour before her departure. In this state of hurry and confusion, wrong orders are given, which have to be counteracted; messengers are sent hither and thither, they scarcely know for what, and still less where to find the thing they seek. Servants grow disorderly, children teasing or frightened, the husband is angry, and sharp words pass between him and his wife. Accidents, of course, occur, for which the innocent are blamed. Time—pitiless time rolls on, apparently with accelerating speed. The distant sound of carriage-wheels is heard. At this crisis a string breaks. Why did it never break before? A flash of absolute passion distorts the face of the matron. All dignity is lost. The carriage is at the door—little children stretch forth their arms—there is no time for tenderness. Scarcely a farewell is heard, as the mother rushes past them, leaving behind her, perhaps for months of absence, the remembrance of her angry countenance, her unjust reproaches, and the apparent want of affection with which she could hurry away from the very beings she loved best in the world. The servants in such a family as this, can scarcely be blamed if they rejoice when their mistress is gone; the husband, if he finds abundant consolation in the peace his absent partner has bequeathed him; or the children, if they fail to look with any very eager expectation to the time of their mother's return.

How, then, does the law of love operate here? It operates upon the woman who is seldom too late, so that when a journey is in expectation, all things are arranged in due time, leaving the last day more especially for attention to the claims of affection, and the regulation of household affairs, upon which will depend the comfort of her family during her absence. Rising a little earlier than usual on that morning, she commends them individually and collectively to the care of the Father of all the families of earth; and this very act gives a depth, a tenderness, and a serenity to the feelings of affection with which she meets them, it may be for the last time. Kind words are then spoken, which dwell upon the memory in after years; provision is made for the feeble or the helpless; every little peculiarity of character or constitution is taken into account; last charges—those precious memorials of earthly love—are given, and treasured up. There is time even for private and confidential intercourse between the husband and the wife; there is time for a respectful farewell to every domestic; there is time, too, for an expression of thankfulness for each one of the many kind offices rendered on that sacred day. At last the moment of separation arrives. Silent tears are seen in every eye, but they are not absolutely tears of sorrow; for who can feel sorrow, when the cup of human love is so full of sweetness?

If, during the absence of such a mother, sickness or death should assail any member of her family, how will the remembrance of that day of separation soothe the absent; while the kind words then uttered, the kind thoughts then felt, the kind services then rendered, will recur to remembrance, invested with a power and a beauty, which never would have been fully known, had no such separation taken place.

It is possible the natural affection of the wife and the mother, in both these cases, may have been the same; yet, how different must be the state of their own feelings, and of those of their separate families, one hour after their departure! and not during that hour only, but during weeks, and months, nay, through the whole of their lives! for the specimen we have given, is but one amongst the many painful scenes which must perpetually occur in the experience of those who are habitually too late.

It is true, I have extended the picture a little beyond the season of early youth, but this was absolutely necessary in order to point out the bearing and ultimate tendency of this dangerous habit—a habit, like many of our wrong propensities, so insidious in its nature, as scarcely to tell upon the youthful character; while, like many other plants of evil growth, its seed is sown at that period of life, though we scarcely perceive the real nature of the poisonous tree, until its bitter root has struck too deep to be eradicated. It is, therefore, the more important, in all we purpose, and in all we do, that we should *look to the end*, and not awake when it is too late to find that we have miscalculated either our time, or our means.

CHAP. III.
CLEVERNESS—LEARNING—KNOWLEDGE.

In order to speak with more precision of those attainments which youth is the season for acquiring, I must class them under three different heads—cleverness, learning, and knowledge. By cleverness, I would be understood to mean, dexterity and aptness in doing everything which falls within the sphere of ordinary duty. Cleverness of the hand, is no mean attainment in a woman. It is, in fact, of almost as much value to her, as dexterity to the surgeon; for though he may have knowledge to understand what is best to be done, unless his hand be skilful to do it, his knowledge will avail him but little in any case of emergency, where the life of a fellow-creature is at stake.

The cleverness of the hand, therefore, though almost entirely neglected in modern education, except as relates to practice on the keys of the piano, is a qualification which, while it takes nothing away from the charm of feminine delicacy, imparts the additional charm of perpetual cheerfulness, added to a capability of general usefulness, and a consequent readiness for action whenever occasion may require our services.

To know how to do every thing which can properly come within a woman's sphere of duty, ought to be the ambition of every female mind. For my own part, I do not believe I have ever learned anything, even down to such a trifle as a new stitch, but I have found a use for it, and that in a surprisingly short space of time; for either it has occupied what would otherwise have been idle time, it has used up what would otherwise have been wasted material, or I have taught it to others who were more in need of it than myself. Besides which, there is the grand preventive this dexterity supplies against ever being at a loss what to do—the happiness it affords, both to ourselves and others, to be perpetually employed—the calm it diffuses over a naturally restless temperament; but, above all, the ability this habit affords in cases of sickness, or other emergency, to turn all our means to account in the service of our friends.

This, however, can never be so thoroughly effected, as when the cleverness of the hand is aided by the faculty of invention. And here I would ask—how is it?—how can it be, that the exercise of this faculty forms so trifling a part of female education? Never does a woman enter upon the actual business of life, whatever it may be, but her ingenuity is taxed in some way or other; and she suffers blame, or endures contempt, just so far as she fails in this respect. If, at a critical juncture of time, any accident takes place in household affairs, woman is expected to cover up the defect, or supply the deficiency. If any article of common use is missing when wanted, woman is expected to provide a substitute. If the accustomed supply of comfort or enjoyment fails, it is woman's fault. No matter how great the deficiency of material with which she has to work, domestic comfort, order and respectability rest with her, and she must be accountable for the falling short in any, or all of these. It is true that she is endowed by nature with the faculty of invention, in a higher degree, perhaps, than men, and skilfully and nobly does she sometimes use it; but does not the very fact of this endowment teach us that it has thus been provided by Providence for the part she has to act in life? and ought we not the more sedulously to carry out this merciful design, by a higher cultivation of so useful a faculty? Why, for instance, should we not have premiums on a small scale, or other encouragements, in our public seminaries, for the most ingenious and useful inventions? Why should there not be a little museum attached to every school, in which such specimens of ingenuity could be kept? We all know there are few simple pleasures which surpass those derived from the exercise of the faculty of invention; might it not, therefore, be rendered as profitable, as it is amusing, by filling up some of the idle hours of a school-girl's life, and occupying the time too frequently appropriated to mere gossip on subjects by no means calculated to improve the morals, or enlarge the understanding?

The little girl of four years old, seated on a footstool beside her mother, is less happy in the rosy cheeks and shining curls of her new doll, than in the shawl she has herself invented for it, or the bonnet her sister is making. It is the same throughout the whole season of early youth. What is drawing, that most delightful of all amusements to a child, but the exercise of the faculty of invention? So soon as this exercise is reduced to a science, so soon as "perspective dawns," and the juvenile performer is compelled to copy, the charm of the performance in a great measure ceases. It is true, it will be restored a hundredfold when acquaintance with the rules of art shall enable the young student again to design, and with better effect; but during her infancy, she has far more enjoyment in her own red-brick house, with a volume of green smoke issuing from every chimney; and in her own round-bodied man, whose nose is emulous of a beak, and his eye in the centre of his head, than in the most elaborate and finished drawings which a master could lay before her; not, certainly, because she sees more symmetry or likelihood in these creatures of her own formation, but simply because of the pleasure she enjoyed while inventing them.

It is a subject of delightful reflection, and it ought to be a source of unfailing gratitude, that some of those natural propensities which afford us the greatest pleasure, are, in reality, capable of being made conducive to the greatest good. Thus, when the little quiet girl is so happy and so busy with her pencils, or her scissors, she is indulging that natural propensity of her mind, which is, in after life, to render her still happier, by enabling her to turn to the best account every means of increasing the happiness of those around her, of rendering assistance in any social or domestic calamity that may occur, of supply in every time of household need, and of comfort in every season of distress.

But if the value of invention, and the ready application of existing means, be overlooked under all other circumstances in a sick-room, none can doubt its efficacy. The visitations of sickness, however unlikely, or unlooked for, they may be to the young, are liable to all—the gay and the grave, the rich and the poor, the vigorous and the feeble; and we have only to visit some of those favourite spots of earth which have become the resort of invalids from every land, to see how often the most delicate females are plunged into all the solemn and sacred mysteries of the chamber of sickness and death.

It is under such circumstances that ingenuity, when connected with kindly feeling, and readiness to assist, is of the utmost possible value. There may be the same kind feeling without it; but how is such feeling to operate?—by teasing the invalid perpetually about what he would like, or not like? The querulous and fretful state of mind which suffering so often induces, is ill calculated to brook this minute investigation of its wants and wishes; and such is the capricious nature of a sickly appetite, that every anticipated relish is apt to pall, before the feeble desire can be gratified. We are therefore inflicting positive pain upon the sufferer—mental pain, in addition to that of the body, by compelling him to choose, and then to appear discontented, or ungrateful, in becoming dissatisfied with his own choice.

How thankful, then, ought women to be, that they possess, by nature, the faculty of invention; and how careful ought to be their cultivation of this precious gift, when it can enable them to relieve from pain and annoyance those who already feel that they have enough of both. How happy, in comparison, is that woman, who, by the habitual exercise of her ingenuity, is able so to make the most of the means within her power, as to supply, without its having to be solicited, the very thing which is most needed; and though her endeavours may possibly fail again and again, there will sometimes be a smile of grateful acknowledgement on the lips of the sufferer, that will richly repay her most anxious care; or, if not, she will still be happier, when occupied by a series of inventions for the benefit of one she loves, than those can be who think, and think again, and end by only wishing they could think of any thing that could accommodate, or relieve.

The faculty of invention, however, will fail of more than half its use, if the hand is not early accustomed to obey the head, in all those little niceties of management which female occupations require. There must be a facility in the application and movement of the hand, which can only be acquired in early life; and I would humbly suggest the importance of this in our public seminaries for young ladies, for I confess it has often seemed to me a little hard, that young women of the middle ranks of life, should be dismissed from these establishments, after having spent years with little more exercise of the hand than is required by the music-master; yet are they no sooner plunged into active life, as women—I do not say, as ladies—than the readiest and best, nay, sometimes, even the cheapest, method of doing every thing which a woman can do, is expected of them. In all those cases of failure which must necessarily ensue, parents and brothers are equally dissatisfied; while they themselves, disappointed that their accomplishments are no longer valued as they were at school, and perplexed with the new, and apparently humbling, duties which present themselves, sink into a state of profitless despondency; and all this is owing to the simple fact of their not having been prepared, when young, for what is expected of them in after life.

Far be it from me, however, to advocate the old system of stitching, as the best kind of education for the daughters of England, of whom higher and nobler things are required. But why should we not choose the medium between two extremes? and while we reprobate the elaborate needlework of our grandmothers, why should we not be equally solicitous to avoid the evils arising from an entire disuse of the female hand, until the age of womanhood? Neither would I be supposed to advocate that entire absorption of the female mind in a world of worsted work, which is now so frequently the case immediately on leaving school, and which I am inclined to attribute, in a great measure, to a necessary reaction of the mind, after having been occupied during the whole term of scholastic discipline, in what is so foreign to its nature, that the first days—nay, months, and even years, of liberty, are spent in the busy idleness of assorting different shades of Berlin wool.

These, I must allow, are pleasant amusements in their way, and when the head and the heart are weary, may have their refreshment and their use; but even in these occupations, the beaten track of custom is too much followed. The hand is more exercised than the head. To imitate is more the object than to invent, while, if the same pains were taken to create a pattern as to borrow one, new ideas might be perpetually struck out, and the mind, even in this humble sphere of action, might find as much employment as the hand.

It is sometimes made the subject of regret by learned, well-informed, and highly-gifted women, that the occupations peculiar to our sex are so trifling; or, in other words, that they afford so little exercise for the mind. To say nothing here of the folly and the danger of allowing ourselves to despise such duties as God has set before us, I am disposed to question whether it is not in a great measure our own fault that these duties are invested with so little mind. Invention is surely no mean faculty, and I have shown how it may be exercised, even upon the most trifling affairs of woman's life. Economy is no mean principle, and this may be acted upon in the application of the humblest means to any particular end. Industry is no mean virtue, and we may be practising this, while filling up every spare moment with some occupation of the hand. Cheerfulness is no mean embellishment to the female character; and seldom is cheerfulness preserved, when the hand is allowed to be useless and idle.

I confess there is a listless way of merely "getting through" with female occupations, in which little mind, and still less good feeling, is called into action: but when a lively invention is perpetually at work; when a careful economy is practised for the sake of making the most of all our materials, and sparing our money, it may be for the purpose of assisting the sorrowful or the destitute; where habits of industry are thus engrafted into the character; and where cheerfulness lights up every countenance in a family thus employed; especially where there is any considerable degree of talent or illumination of mind, how many brilliant thoughts may arise out of the simplest subject, and how much rational enjoyment may be derived from the humblest occupations.

I cannot dismiss the subject of cleverness, or dexterity in doing whatever may come within the sphere of female duty, without observing that its importance refers in an especial manner to domestic usefulness. Nor let the young lady, who may read this, too hastily turn away with contempt from so humble a strain of advice. It does not follow, because she knows how to do everything, that she must always do it. But it does follow, that if she wishes to stand at the head of her household, to be respected by her own servants, and to feel herself the mistress of her own affairs, that she must be acquainted with the best method of doing everything upon which domestic comfort depends.

These remarks can of course have no reference to families who occupy a higher rank in society, and whose means enable them to employ a housekeeper as the medium of communication between the mistress and the servants. I speak of those who have to give orders themselves, or who, in cases of illness, receiving company, or other derangements of the usual routine of domestic affairs, have to take an active part in household economy themselves. To such, how unfortunate is it not to have learned, before they attempt to direct others, the best method of applying every means so as to be productive of the greatest comfort, at the least expense. I would of course be understood to mean, with the least possible risk of absolute waste. Your table may be sumptuous or simple, your furniture costly or plain—that will depend upon the rate at which you fix your expenditure, and has nothing to do with the point in question. The absolute waste of material, in whatever is manufactured, prepared, or produced, is an evil of a distinct nature, and can never be allowed to any extent, where it is possible to be avoided, without a deficiency of common sense, or of moral rectitude.

In my observations upon the women of England, I have dwelt so much upon the desirableness of domestic usefulness, that I cannot with propriety enlarge upon it here. Yet, such is my view of this subject, that if I were asked which of the three was most valuable in a woman—cleverness, learning, or knowledge; and supposing all to have an equal accompaniment of good sense, good feeling, and good principle, I believe I should answer in favour of the first, provided the situation of the woman was in the middle rank of life, and she could not enjoy more than one of these valuable recommendations.

Youth is considered to be so exclusively the season for acquiring a skilful touch in the practice of music, that scarcely is the experiment ever tried of acquiring the same dexterity in after life. If then it is the only time for attaining excellence in what is merely an embellishment to the character, of how much importance must this season be for practising the hand in that ready obedience to the head in all affairs of actual usefulness, which justly entitles its possessor to the distinction of cleverness.

In order to convey a more correct idea of my meaning, when I speak of cleverness, I will simply add, that a woman possessed of this qualification is seldom at a loss what to do; seldom gives wrong orders; seldom mistakes the right means of producing the end she desires; seldom spoils, or wastes, or mismanages the work she undertakes; never hurries to and fro in a state of confusion, not knowing what is best to be done first; and never yields to her own feelings, so as to incapacitate her from the service of others, at any critical moment when her assistance may be most needed. Nor are her recommendations only of a negative kind. Her habitual self-possession is a positive good, her coolness, her promptitude, her power to adapt herself to circumstances, all give worth and dignity to her character in the estimation of others; while they afford peace and satisfaction to her own mind.

Learning, Dr. Johnson tells us, is skill in languages or science. With regard to the time spent in the acquisition of languages, I fear I must incur the risk of being thought neither liberal nor enlightened; for I confess, I do not see the value of languages to a woman, except so far as they serve the purpose of conversation with persons of different countries, or acquaintance with the works of authors, whose essential excellencies cannot be translated into our own tongue; and how far these two objects are carried out by the daughters of England, either from necessity or inclination, I must leave to their own consideration.

With regard to the dead languages, the former of these two motives cannot apply. It may, however, be justly considered as a wholesome exercise of the mind, provided there is nothing better to be done, for young women to learn Greek and Latin; but beyond this, I feel perfectly assured, that for any knowledge they will acquire through the medium of the best Greek and Latin authors, our most approved translations would more than answer their purpose. It is true, that a knowledge of these languages gives an insight into the meaning of many important words in our own; yet, an early and extensive reading of our standard books, would unquestionably give the same, along with a greater fund of useful and practical information; and for every purpose of female elocution, I strongly suspect that good Saxon-English would be found as clear, impressive, and convincing, as any which can boast a more classical construction.

There is one motive assigned in the present day, for young ladies learning Greek, but especially Hebrew, which I should be sorry to treat with irreverence or disrespect, because it has weight with some of the most serious and estimable of their sex. I mean the plea of being thus enabled to read the Scriptures in the original. Now, if such young ladies have really nothing better to do, or if from the high order of their natural capabilities they have a chance, even the remotest, of being able to throw some additional light upon our best translations, far be it from me to wish to put the slightest obstacle in their way. Yet, I own it does appear to me a little strange, that after considering the length of time required for attaining a sufficient knowledge of these languages, and the number of learned commentators and divines, who have spent the best part of their valuable lives, in labouring to ascertain the true meaning of the language of the Scriptures, and when the result of those labours is open to the public, it does appear to me a little strange, that any young woman, of moderate abilities, should enter the field with such competitors, in the hope of attaining a nearer approach to the truth than they have done; and I have been led to question, whether it would not be quite as well for such individuals to be content to take the Bible as it is, and to employ the additional time, they would thus become possessed of, in disseminating its truths and acting out its principles, so far as they have already been made clear to the humblest understanding.

These remarks, however, have especial reference to moderate abilities; because there is with some persons a peculiar gift for the acquisition of languages; and believing, as I do, that no gift is bestowed in vain, I would not presume to question the propriety of such young persons spending at least some portion of their lives, in endeavouring to acquire the power of doing for themselves, what has already been done for them.

It is a remarkable phenomenon in our nature, that some of those persons who have the greatest facility in acquiring languages, have the least perception of the genius or spirit of such languages when they are acquired. The knowledge of many languages obtains for its possessor the distinction of being learned; but if she goes no farther, if she never expatiates in the new world of literature, into which her knowledge might have introduced her; she is but like a curious locksmith, who opens the door upon some hidden treasure, and who, instead of examining or appropriating the precious store to which he has obtained access, goes on to another door, and then another, satisfied with merely being master of the keys, and knowing how to unlock at his pleasure.

To women of this class of mind, provided they belong to the middle rank of life, and are not intended either for teachers or translators, of what possible use can be the learning of the dead languages? and to others similarly circumstanced, but without this peculiar talent, there are excellent translations in almost every library, from which they will acquire a greater number of ideas, and become more intimately acquainted with the spirit of the writer, and the customs and the times of which he wrote, than it is probable they ever could have been from their own reading of the same works in the original.

With regard to modern languages, the case is very different. Facilities of communication between one country and another are now so great, that it has become no longer a dream of romance, but a matter of reasonable calculation, with our young women, even in the humble ranks of life, that they should some time or other go abroad. With our modern writers too, it is so much the custom to indulge in the use of at least three languages, while professing to write in one, as to render it almost a necessary part of female education to learn both French and Italian. If these languages have not been sufficiently attended to at school, they may therefore, with the utmost propriety, be added to such studies as it is desirable to continue for some years afterwards; and while their more perfect acquisition is an object of laudable desire, the mind, as it expands in its progress towards maturity, will be better able to appreciate the beauties they unfold.

I have been compelled, during the course of these remarks, to use an expression which requires some explanation. I have said, that a young woman may with propriety learn even the dead languages, provided she has nothing better to do; by which, I would be understood to mean, provided she does not consequently leave undone what would render her more useful or amiable as a woman. The settlement of this question must depend entirely upon the degree of her talent, and the nature of her position in life. If she has no other talent likely to make her so useful as that which is employed in learning Greek, Latin, and Hebrew, this settles the point at once, or if she has no duties so important to her as to ascertain the derivation of words, or to study the peculiarities of heathen writers, then by all means let her be a learned lady, for every study, every occupation of mind, provided it does not include what is evil, must be preferable to absolute idleness.

But may we not turn to the consideration of science as opening a wide field of interesting study, which does more to enlarge the mind, and give right views of common things, than the mere acquisition of language?

"Science!—what have we to do with science?" exclaim half a dozen soft voices at once. Certainly not to give public lectures, nor always to attend them, unless you go, with your understanding prepared by some previous reading, or acquaintance with the subjects, which in then lecture-room are necessarily rather illustrated, than fully explained. Neither is it necessary that you should sacrifice any portion of your feminine delicacy by diving too deep, or approaching too near the professor's chair. A slight knowledge of science in general is all which is here recommended, so far as it may serve to obviate some of those groundless and irrational fears, which arise out of mistaken apprehensions of the phenomena of nature and art; but, above all, to enlarge our views of the great and glorious attributes of the Creator, as exhibited in the most sublime, as well as the most insignificant, works of his creation.

Perhaps one of the lowest advantages, and I am far from thinking it a low one either, which is derived by women from a general knowledge of science, is, that it renders them more companionable to men. If they are solicitous to charm the nobler sex by their appearance, dress, and manners, surely it is of more importance to interest them by their conversation. By the former they may please; by the latter they may influence, and that to the end of their lives. Yet, how is it possible to interest by their conversation, without some understanding of the subjects which chiefly occupy the minds of men? Most kindly, however, has it been accorded by man to his feeble sister, that it should not be necessary for her to *talk much*, even on his favourite topics, in order to obtain his favour. An attentive listener is generally all that he requires; but in order to listen attentively, and with real interest, it is highly important that we should have considerable understanding of the subject discussed; for the interruption of a single foolish or irrelevant question, the evidence of a wandering thought, the constrained attitude of attention, or the rapid response which conveys no proof of having received an idea, are each sufficient to break the charm, and destroy the satisfaction which most men feel in conversing with really intelligent women.

It is also worth some attention to this subject, if we can thereby dispel many of the idle fears which occupy and perplex the female mind. I have known women who were quite as much afraid of a gun when it was not loaded, as when it was; others who thought a steam-engine as likely to explode when it was not working, as when it was; and others still, who avowedly considered thunder more dangerous than lightning. Now, to say nothing of the irritation which fears like these are apt to occasion in minds of a more masculine order, it is surely no insignificant attainment to acquire a habit of feeling at ease, when there is really nothing to be afraid of.

But, far beyond this, the use of science is to teach us not to
□"Wrong thee, mighty Nature!
With whom adversity is but transition;"
and higher still, to teach us how the wisdom and goodness of God pervade all creation. Women are too much accustomed to look at the animal, vegetable, and mineral kingdoms with eyes that may almost literally be said, not to see. An insect is to them a little troublesome thing, which flies or creeps; a flower is a petty ornament, with a sweet perfume; and a mine of coal or copper, something which they read about in their Geography, as belonging to Newcastle, or Wales. I do not say, that their actual knowledge is thus limited; but that they are too much in the habit of regarding these portions of the creation as such, and no more.

Chemistry, too, is apt to be considered by young women as far too elaborate and masculine a study to engage their attention; and thus they are satisfied, not only to go on through life unacquainted with those wonderful combinations and properties, which in some of the most familiar things would throw light upon their real nature, and proper use; but also to remain unenlightened in that noblest school of knowledge, which teaches the sublime truth, that the wonder-working power of God has been employed upon all the familiar, as well as the astonishing objects we perceive; and that the same power continues to be exemplified in their perpetual creation, their order, adaptation, and use.

Chiefly, however, would I recommend to the attention of youth, an intimate acquaintance with the nature and habits of the animal world. Here we may find a source of rational and delightful interest, which can never fail us, so long as a bird is heard to sing upon the trees, or a butterfly is seen to sport among the flowers.

I will not go the length of recommending to my young countrywomen to become collectors, either of animals or of insects; because, as in the case of translations from the best of ancient writers, this has already been done for them, better than they are likely to do it for themselves; and because I am not quite sure, that simply for our own amusement, and without any reference to serving the purpose of science, we have a right to make even a beetle struggle to death upon the point of a pin, or to crowd together boxes full of living creatures, who, in the agony of their pent-up sufferings, devour and destroy one another.

Happily for us, there are ably written books on these subjects, from which we can learn more than from our own observation; and museums accessible to all, where different specimens of insects, and other animals, are so arranged as materially to assist in understanding their nature and classification; and far more congenial it surely must be to the heart and mind of woman, to read all which able and enlightened men have told us of this world of wonder, and then to go forth into the fields, and see the busy and beautiful creatures by which it is inhabited, sporting in the joyous freedom of nature, unharmed, and unsuspicious of harm. Yes, there is an acquaintance with the animal creation, which might be cultivated, so as to do good to the heart, both of the child and the philosopher—an acquaintance which seems to absolve these helpless creatures from the curse of estrangement from their sovereign man—an acquaintance which brings them near to us in all their natural peculiarities, their amazing instincts, and in the voiceless, and otherwise unintelligible secrets of their mysterious existence.

And it is good to be thus acquainted with that portion of creation which acknowledges, in common with ourselves, the great principle of animal life, to know that enjoyment is enjoyment, and that pain is pain, to myriads and myriads of beings, in some respects more beautiful, in others more curious, and in all more innocent, than ourselves. It is good to know, so far as men can know, for what purpose Almighty power has created them. It is good to behold their beauty, to understand their wonderful formation, and to examine the fairy fancy-work of some of their sacred little homes. It is good to be acquainted with the strength of the mother's love, when she stoops her wing to the spoiler, and offers her own life to save her tender brood. It is good to know that the laws of nature, in their filial and parental influences, cannot be violated without sorrow as intense, though not as lasting, as that which tortures the human heart on the separation of parent and child. It is good to know how these creatures, placed by Divine wisdom under the power and dominion of man, are made to suffer or to die when he neglects or abuses them.

The earth and the air, the woods and the streams, the gardens and the fields, tell us of all this. When we sit under the shade of a lofty tree, in the stillness of summer's balmy noon, the note of the woodpigeon salutes us from above. We look up, and the happy couple are nestling on a bough, as closely, side by side, as if the whole world to them was nothing, so long as their faithful love was left. On a lower branch of the same tree, or on a broken rail close by, the little robin sits and sings, looking occasionally askance into the face of that lordly creature whom instinct teaches him to shun. Yet is it less a reproachful, than an inquiring glance, as if he would ask, whether you could really wish to frighten him with all the terrors which agitate his little breast on your approach. And then he sings to you again, a low soft warble; though his voice is never quite so sweet as in the autumn, when other birds are silent, and he still sings on amidst the falling leaves and faded flowers. Next, the butterfly comes wavering into sight, yet hastening on to turn its golden wings once more up to the sunshine. The bee then hurries past, intent upon its labours, and attracted only for a moment by the nosegay in your hand; while the grasshopper, that master of ventriloquism, invites your curiosity—now here, now there, but never to the spot where his real presence is to be found. And all this while, the faithful dog is at your feet. If you rise, at the same moment he rises too; and if you sit down, he also composes himself to rest. Ever ready to go, or stay, he watches your slightest movement; and so closely and mysteriously is his being absorbed in yours, that, although a ramble in the fields affords him a perfect ecstasy of delight, he never allows himself this indulgence, without your countenance and companionship.

But it is impossible so much as to name one in a thousand of the sweet and cheering influences of animal life upon the youthful heart. The very atmosphere we live in teems with it; the woods are vocal—the groves are filled with it; while around our doors, within our homes, and even at our social hearth, the unfailing welcome, the transient glimpses of intelligence, the instinct, the love of these creatures, are interwoven with the vast chain of sympathy, which, through the whole of what may be a wandering and uncertain life, binds us to that spot of earth where we first awoke to a feeling of companionship with this portion of the creatures of our heavenly Father's care.

Nor must we forget the wonderful and mysterious affection which some animals are capable of feeling for man. Often as we may have failed to inspire the love we have sought for among our fellow-creatures, we are all capable of inspiring attachment here; nor does the fact of our being unattractive, or comparatively worthless, amongst mankind, operate in the slightest degree to our disadvantage with this class of beings. Witness the outcast from society—the wanderer on the public roads—the poor and houseless mendicant; he still has his dog—yes, and he bears the cold repulse he meets with when he asks for bread, better than he could bear the desertion of that faithful animal: but he fears it not. The proud may pass him by unheeded, the rich may spurn him from their doors, the vulgar and the unfeeling may make a mockery of his rags and wretchedness; but when the stormy night comes on, and he seeks the almost roofless shed to rest his weary limbs, he is followed even there by one friend, who creeps beside him with a love as watchful and as true as if he shared the silken couch of luxury and ease.

There are little motherless children, too, and others not unacquainted with a feeling of almost orphan solitude, who have felt, at times, how the affection of a dumb animal could supply the disappointed yearnings of a young warm heart. In after life, we may learn to look upon these creatures with respect, because our heavenly Father has thought them worthy of his care; but youth is the season when we love them for their own sakes; and because we then discover that they can be made, by kindness, to love us. In youth alone can we feel to unite them with ourselves in that bond of sympathy, which will never afterwards allow us to treat their sufferings with indifference, or to regard their happiness as beyond the sphere of our duty to promote.

Here, then, the law of love is made to operate through innumerable channels of sweet and natural feeling, extending over a wide field of creation, and reaping its reward of satisfaction wherever a poor animal is rescued from oppression, hunger, or pain.

The study of natural history is, perhaps, the most congenial pursuit to which the mind of youth can be introduced; and it never can begin with this too soon. The history and nature of plants is the next most pleasing study, though far inferior to the first, for this important reason— our acquaintance with animals involves a moral feeling; and not one feeling only, but a vast chain of sympathies and affections, which, if not touched in early life, are seldom afterwards called forth with any degree of earnestness or warmth; and for a woman to be insensible or indifferent to the happiness of the brute creation, is an idea too repulsive to be dwelt upon for a moment.

There is, however, a sickly sensibility indulged in by some young ladies, which I should be the last to recommend. Many, for instance, will nurse and fondle animals, without ever taking the trouble to feed them. Others shrink away with loathing at the sight of pain, which, if they would but exert themselves to remove, might easily be remedied. I remember a young girl with whom I was well acquainted, having watched a cat torment a mouse until she could bear it no longer, when at last, with a feeling of the utmost repugnance to the act, she snatched up the poor lacerated mouse, and killed it in a moment. On seeing her do this, two very delicate and estimable young ladies gave themselves up to shrieks and hysterics, although they had known for the previous half hour that the little helpless animal had been enduring the most cruel torture in the claws of the cat, and they had borne this knowledge with the greatest composure.

It is not, then, a delicate shrinking from the mere sight of pain, which constitutes that kindly feeling towards the animal creation, that forms so estimable a part of the female character; but that expansive sentiment of benevolence towards all the creatures of God's formation, which is founded on the principle of love, and which operates as a principle in prompting us to promote the good of all creatures that have life, and to promote it on the widest possible scale.

But to return to the subject of botany. A woman who does not love flowers, suffers a great want in her supplies of healthy and natural enjoyment. How could the poet Milton, when he pictured woman in her highest state of excellence, have employed our mother Eve, had he made her indifferent to the beauty of the plants of paradise, or negligent of the flowers which bloomed around her? Still, I must acknowledge that there is to many minds, something the reverse of attractive in the first aspect of the study of botany, as it is generally presented to our attention. In this I am supported by one of the most gifted of modern authors, when he speaks of the "ponderous nomenclature" of botany having frightened many a youthful student back from the portals of this study. There are many persons now advanced in life, who deeply regret their want of what is called a taste for botany, when the fault has not been in their natural taste, so much as in the form under which this study was introduced to their notice in youth; and thus they have been shut out through the whole of life, from the pleasure of expatiating in a field, as boundless in its extent, as inexhaustible in its attractions.

These difficulties, however, are not insurmountable to all; and youth is unquestionably the season for forming an intimate acquaintance with this, the loveliest aspect of nature, so that in after life, when duties are more imperative, and occupations more serious, and there is consequently less time for minute investigation, every flower and every plant may be met as a member of a well-known family, and, as such, bear somewhat of the character of a familiar friend.

It is the same with every part of the creation, whether natural history, or botany, or geology, have occupied our attention, or chemistry, or electricity, that great mystery of the visible world, whose all-powerful agency, the most sublime as well as the most insignificant phenomena of nature, are daily, and hourly, tending to develope—an early and intimate acquaintance with each and all of these, must so far enlighten, and enlarge the mind, as to lead our thoughts beyond the narrow limits of material existence, up to that higher region of wonder and of love, where to behold is to admire—to feel is to adore.

From the consideration of the different advantages arising from such studies as it is important should be pursued at an early period of life, we are necessarily led to ask, 'What is the use of Knowledge in general?'

Nothing can well be more vague than the notions popularly entertained of the meaning of knowledge. Dr. Johnson has called it "general illumination of mind." But, if I might be allowed to do so, I should prefer restricting my use of the word knowledge, to that acquaintance with facts, which, in connexion with the proper exercise of a healthy mind, will necessarily lead to general illumination. A knowledge of the world, therefore, as I propose to use the expression, must consequently mean, a knowledge of such facts as the general habits of society develope.

This is universally allowed to be a dangerous knowledge, because it cannot be acquired without the risk of being frequently deceived by the false aspect which society assumes, and the still greater risk of having our moral being too deeply absorbed in the interest and excitement which the study itself affords. No one can obtain a knowledge of the world, by being a mere spectator. It is, therefore, safer and happier to leave this study until the judgment is more matured, and the habits and principles more formed—or rather I should say, to leave it as a study altogether. Time and experience teach us all it is necessary to know on this subject; and even duty urges us forward on the theatre of life, when little enough prepared for the temptations and the conflicts we must there encounter. By absolute necessity, then, we acquire as much knowledge of the world as any rational being needs desire, and that is just sufficient to enable us to judge of the consequences of certain principles, or modes of action, as they operate upon the well-being of individuals, and of society at large. Destitute of this degree of worldly knowledge, we must ever be liable to make the most serious mistakes in applying the principle of benevolence, in forming our estimate of the moral condition of mankind, as well as in regulating our scale of social and relative duty.

A general knowledge of the political and social state of the country in which we live, and indeed of all countries, is of great importance, not only to men, but to women. Nor let my fair readers be startled when I speak of the political state of countries. You have been accustomed to make history your study. An acquaintance with the most important eras in history is considered an essential part of female education. And can it be less essential to know what events are taking place in your own times, than what transpired in past ages? Do not, however, misunderstand me on this important subject. Do not suppose it would add any embellishment to your conversation, for you to discuss what are called politics, simply as such, especially when, as in nine cases out of ten, you do not really understand what you are talking about. Do not take up any question as belonging to *your* side, or *your* party, while ignorant what the principles of that party are. Above all, do not allow yourself to grow warm in your advocacy of any particular candidate for a seat in parliament, because he is a handsome man, or has made a fine speech. All this may supply an opposite party with food for scandal, or for jest; but has nothing at all to do with that patriotic and deep feeling of interest in the happiness and prosperity of her own country, which a benevolent and enlightened woman must naturally entertain.

Destitute as some women are of every spark of this feeling, it is but natural that their conversation should at times be both trifling and vapid; and that when subjects of general importance are discussed, they should be too much occupied with a pattern of worsted work, even to listen.

I one day heard a very accomplished and amiable young lady lamenting that she had nothing to talk about, except a subject which had been playfully forbidden. "Talk about the probability of a war," said I. "Why should I talk about that?" she replied. "It is nothing to me whether there is war or not." Now, this was said in perfect sincerity, and yet the lady was a Christian woman, and one who would have been very sorry to be suspected of not knowing the *dates* of most of the great battles recorded in history. I am perfectly aware that there are intricate questions, brought before our senate, which it may require a masculine order of intellect folly to understand. But there are others which may, and ought to engage the attention of every female mind, such as the extinction of slavery, the abolition of war in general, cruelty to animals, the punishment of death, temperance, and many more, on which, neither to know, nor to feel, is almost equally disgraceful. I must again observe, it is by no means necessary that we should *talk much* on these subjects, even if we do understand them; but to listen attentively, and with real interest when they are discussed by able and liberal-minded men, is an easy and agreeable method of enlarging our stock of valuable knowledge; and, by doing this when we are young, we shall go on with the tide of public events, so as to render ourselves intelligent companions in old age; and when the bloom of youth is gone, and even animal spirits decline, we shall have our conversation left, for the entertainment and the benefit of our friends.

For my own part, I know of no interest more absorbing, than that with which we listen to a venerable narrator of by-gone facts—facts which have transpired under the actual observation of the speaker, in which he took a part, or which stirred the lives, and influenced the conduct, of those by whom he was surrounded. When such a person has been a lover of sterling truth, and a close observer of things as they really were in early youth, his conversation is such as sages, listen to, and historians make the theme of their imperishable pages. Yet, such a companion every woman is capable of becoming; and since old age is not rich in its attractions, is it not well worthy the attention of youth, to endeavour to lay up, as a provision for the future, such sterling materials for rational and lasting interest? It is worthy of observation, however, that such information can never be of half the value when collected in a vague and indefinite form. The lover of sterling truth alone is able to render the relation of facts of any real value. The mere story-teller, who paints the truth in his own colours, may amuse for an evening; but unless we choose truth?absolute truth as our companion in early life, the foundation of our opinions, as well as of our principles, will be ever liable to give way. We must, therefore, cultivate a willingness to see things as they really are. Not as our friends do, or as our enemies do not see them; but simply as they are, and, as such, to speak of them, without the bias of party feeling, or the colouring of our own selfishness. The local customs of the place in which we live, and the habits of thinking of the persons with whom we associate, will naturally, in the course of time, produce considerable effect upon our own views. But in youth, the mind is free to choose, open to conviction, uninfluenced by prejudice, and comparatively unoccupied by previous impressions. It is, therefore, of the utmost importance, in this early stage of life, to cultivate that love of truth which will enable us to see every object as it really is, and to see it clearly; for there are vague impressions, and indefinite perceptions, which create in the mind a succession of shapeless images, as perplexing in their variety, as they are uncertain in their form.

Of persons whose minds are thus occupied, it can scarcely be said that they love the truth, because they seldom endeavour to ascertain what the truth is; and their consequent deviations from the exact line of rectitude in thought and action, brings upon them, not unfrequently, the charge of falsehood, when they have all the while been true to the image floating before them, but which assumed a different character as often as interest or inclination clothed it in fresh colours.

Vague and uncertain habits of thinking and talking in early life, almost necessarily lead to false conclusions; nor is it the least part of the evil, that those who indulge them are extremely difficult to correct when wrong, or rather when not exactly right; because conviction cannot be proved upon uncertainty. All we can say of such persons is, that they are as little wrong, as right. We cannot help them. They are perpetually falling into difficulties, and, so long as they live, will be liable to incur the suspicion of falsehood.

That a little knowledge is a dangerous thing, may be proved by the observation of every day. A little knowledge is generally more talked about than a great deal—more dragged forward into notice, and, in short, more gloried in by its possessor. We will take, as an instance, the subject of phrenology. Dabblers in this study, who like the eclat of pronouncing upon the characters of their neighbours, as discovered through that opaque medium, the skull, are not a little pleased to entertain themselves and others with the phraseology of Gall and Spurzheim; while, with an air of oracular wisdom, they tell how this person is covetous, another prone to kill, a third fond of music, and a fourth in the habit of making comparisons. Now, although a correct knowledge of the exact situation of these different organs in the head, is more difficult to attain than most young persons are aware of; yet, even this part of the study is mere play, when compared with that exercise of mind, which alone would justify any one, even the profoundest philosopher, in pronouncing upon individual character, according to the principles of phrenology. Would any of these fair oracles, for instance, be kind enough to tell us what would be the result, in summing up the elements of human character, where there was an extraordinary development of combativeness, connected with half as much benevolence, nine-tenths of the same amount of hope, one-third of self-esteem, three-fourths of causality, and one-third of constructiveness. And yet, calculations as intricate, as minute, and far more extensive than this, must be entered into, before the science of phrenology, however true, can enable any individual to pronounce upon the character of another.

And thus it is throughout. A little knowledge makes people talk, a little more induces them to think; and women, from the careless and superficial manner in which their studies are frequently carried on, are but too apt to be found amongst the class of talkers. But let us pause a moment, to inquire whether the smallness of their stock of knowledge is really the cause why it is sometimes so unnecessarily brought forward. Is not the evil of a deeper nature? and may it not arise from false notions popularly entertained respecting the real use of knowledge? I will not say there are any women who absolutely *believe* that the use of knowledge is to supply them with something to talk about; but are we not warranted in suspecting that this is the rule, by which the value of knowledge is too frequently estimated?

Now, one simple view of this subject might settle the question at once, as to the desirableness, or even utility, of women bringing forward their knowledge for the purpose of display. It so happens, that few of our sex, under ordinary circumstances, have an opportunity of acquiring as much general knowledge as a man of common attainments, or even as a mere boy. If we mix in country circles, the village schoolmaster has stores of knowledge far beyond our own; and in the society of towns, the man of business, nay, even the mechanic, knows more than we do. The nature of their employments, the associations they form, and the subjects which engage their attention, all tend to give to the minds of men in general, a clearness of understanding on certain points, and an acquaintance with important facts, beyond what is possessed by one woman in a thousand; though, at the same time, women have a vast advantage over them in this respect, that the liveliness and facility of their intellectual powers, enable them to invest with interest many of the inferior, and less important topics of conversation.

General knowledge, however, is not less important to them, than to men, in the effect it produces upon their own minds and feelings. A well-informed woman may generally be known, not so much by what she tells you, as by what she does not tell you; for she is the last to take pleasure in mere gossip, or to make vulgar allusions to the appearance, dress, or personal habits, of her friends and neighbours. Her thoughts are not in these things. The train of her reflections goes not along with the eating, drinking, visiting, or scandal, of the circle in which she moves. She has a world of interest beyond her local associations; and while others are wondering what is the price of her furniture, or where she bought her watch; she, perhaps, is mentally solving that important question, whether civilization ever was extinguished in a Christian country.

Nor is it merely to be able to say, when asked, in what year any particular sovereign reigned—that knowledge is worth acquiring. Its highest use is to be able to assist on all occasions in the establishment of truth, by a clear statement of facts; to say what experience has proved; and to overcome prejudice by just reasoning. It enables us also to take expansive views of every subject upon which our minds can be employed, so as never to argue against general principles, from opposite impressions produced merely upon our own minds. As a farther illustration of this narrow kind of reasoning, we will suppose a case. A well-meaning, but ignorant man, derives a considerable income from a sugar plantation in the West Indies, by which he supports a number of poor relations. He argues thus?"If slavery be abolished, it will injure my profits; and I shall no longer be able to support my relations. It is good that I should exercise my benevolent feelings through this channel; consequently, the slave-trade must also be good. I will, therefore, neither vote for the abolition of slavery, nor give my countenance to those who do." A more truly enlightened man, though no more influenced by kindly feeling, would know, that it must always be right to uphold right principles, and that God may safely be trusted with the consequences to ourselves.   Nor is it from our own personal feelings alone, that we become liable to this perversion of judgment, with regard to things in general. Prejudice has ever been found more infectious than the plague, and scarcely less fatal. We hear our friends speak warmly on subjects we do not understand. They argue vehemently, and our minds, from want of knowledge, are open to receive as truth, the greatest possible absurdities, which, in our turn, we embrace and defend, until they become more dear to us than truth itself. The probable conclusion is, that in the course of time, we prefer to remain in error, rather than be convinced that we have all the while been wrong. Thus, it is often ignorance alone, which lays the foundation of many of those serious mistakes in opinion and conduct, for which we have to bear all the blame, and suffer all the consequences, of moral culpability.

Want of general knowledge is also a very sufficient reason why some persons, when they mix in good society, live in a state of perpetual fear lest their deficiencies should be found out. Their's is not that amiable modesty which arises from a sense of the superiority of others; for to admire our friends, or even our fellow-creatures, is always a pleasurable sensation; while a conviction of our own ignorance of such topics as are generally interesting in good society, carries with it a feeling of disgraceful humiliation, perfectly incompatible with enjoyment. Uneasiness, timidity, and shyness, with an awkward shrinking from every office of responsibility, or post of distinction, are the unavoidable accompaniments of this conviction; and from this cause, how many opportunities of extending our sphere of usefulness are lost! How many opportunities of rational and lawful enjoyment, too, especially if, from a consciousness of our own inferiority, we refuse to associate with persons of better information and more enlightened minds. Our sufferings are then of a twofold nature, arising from a sense of mortification at our loss, and from the fretfulness and irritation of temper which such privations naturally occasion.

It is well, too, if envy does not steal in, to poison the little comfort we might otherwise have left — well if we do not look with evil eye upon the higher attainments of our friends —

well if, while we professedly admire, we do not throw out some hint that may tend to diminish their value in the estimation of others.

Thus, there is no end to that culpable want of knowledge, which must be the consequence of an idle or wasted youth. We may, and we necessarily must, learn much in after years by experience, observation, reading, and conversation. But we are then, perhaps, in middle age, only acquiring a bare knowledge of those facts, which ought in by-gone years to have been forming our judgment, fixing our principles, and supplying our minds with intellectual food.

If there is no calculation to be made of the evils arising from a want of knowledge, as little can we estimate the amount of good, of which knowledge lays the foundation. Perhaps one of its greatest recommendations to a woman, is the tendency it has to diffuse a calm over the ruffled spirit, and to supply subjects of interesting reflection, under circumstances the least favourable to the acquisition of new ideas.

Such is the position in society which many estimable women are called to fill, that unless they have stored their minds with general knowledge during the season of youth, they never have the opportunity of doing so again. How valuable, then, is such a store, to draw upon for thought, when the hand throughout the day is busily employed, and sometimes when the head is also weary. It is then that knowledge not only sweetens labour, but often, when the task is ended, and a few social friends are met together, it comes forth unbidden, in those glimpses of illumination which a well-informed, intelligent woman, is able to strike out of the humblest material. It is then that, without the slightest attempt at display, her memory helps her to throw in those apt allusions, which clothe the most familiar objects in borrowed light, and make us feel, after having enjoyed her society, as if we had been introduced to a new, and more intellectual existence than we had enjoyed before.

It is impossible for an ignorant, and consequently a short-sighted, prejudiced woman, to exercise this influence over us. We soon perceive the bounds of the narrow circle within which she reasons, with self ever in the centre; we detect the opinions of others, in her own; and we feel the vulgarity with which her remarks may turn upon ourselves, the moment we are gone.

How different is the enjoyment, the repose we feel in the society of a well-informed woman, who has acquired in early youth the habit of looking beyond the little affairs of every-day existence—of looking from matter to mind—from action to principle—from time to eternity. The gossip of society—that many-toned organ of discord, seldom reaches her; even slander, which so often slays the innocent, she is in many cases able to disarm. Under all the little crosses and perplexities which necessarily belong to household care, she is able to look calmly at their comparative insignificance, and thus they never can disturb her peace; while in all the pleasures of intellectual and social intercourse, it is her privilege to give as bountifully as she receives.

It must not be supposed that the writer is one who would advocate, as essential to a woman, any very extraordinary degree of intellectual attainment, especially if confined to one particular branch of study. "I should like to excel in something," is a frequent, and, to some extent, a laudable expression; but in what does it originate, and to what does it tend? To be able to do a great many things tolerably well, is of infinitely more value to a woman, than to be able to excel in one. By the former, she may render herself generally useful; by the latter, she may dazzle for an hour. By being apt, and tolerably well skilled in everything, she may fall into any situation in life with dignity and ease—by devoting her time to excellence in one, she may remain incapable of every other.

So far as cleverness, learning, and knowledge are conducive to woman's moral excellence, they are therefore desirable, and no farther. All that would occupy her mind to the exclusion of better things, all that would involve her in the mazes of flattery and admiration, all that would tend to draw away her thoughts from others and fix them on herself, ought to be avoided as an evil to her, however brilliant or attractive it may be in itself.

CHAP. IV.
MUSIC, PAINTING, AND POETRY.

As a picture which presents to the eye of the beholder, those continuous masses of light and shade usually recognized under the characteristic of breadth; though it may be striking, and sometimes even sublime in its effect, yet, without the more delicate touches of art, must ever be defective in the pleasure it affords; so the female character, though invested with high intellectual endowments, must ever fail to charm, without at least a taste for music, painting, or poetry.

The first of these requires no recommendation in the present day. Indeed, the danger is, that the fair picture which woman's character ought to present, should be broken up into that confusion of petty lights and shades, which, in the phraseology of painting, is said to destroy its effect as a whole. May we not carry on the similitude still farther and compare the more important intellectual endowments of human character to the broad lights and massive shadows of a picture; music, to the richness and variety of its colouring; painting, to correctness and beauty of its outline; and poetry, to general harmony of the whole, consisting chiefly in the aerial or atmospheric tints which convey the idea of morning, noon, or evening, a storm, a calm, or any of the seasons of the year; with all the varied associations which belong to each.

I have said that music requires no recommendation in the present day, when to play like a professor ranks amongst the highest attainments of female education. Since, then, music is so universally regarded both by the wise and good, not only as lawful, but desirable, it remains to be considered under what circumstances the practice of it may be expedient or otherwise.

In the first place, 'Have you what is called an ear for music?' If you are not annoyed by discord, nor made to suffer pain by a false note, nor disturbed by errors in time, let no persuasion ever induce you to touch the keys of a piano, or the chords of a harp again.

Perhaps you reply, 'But I am so fond of music.' I question it not: for though difficult to be accounted for, many persons, who have no ear, are fond of music. Yet, why not, under such circumstances, be content to be a listener for the rest of your lives, and thankful that there are others differently constituted, who are able to play for your amusement, and who play with ease in a style superior to what you would have attained by any amount of labour? All have not the same natural gifts. You, in your turn, may excel in something else; but as well might an automaton be made to dance, as a woman destitute of taste for music, be taught to play with any hope of attaining excellence, or even of giving pleasure to her friends. It is possible that by an immense expenditure of time and money, a wooden figure might be so constructed, to dance so as to take the proper steps at the right time; but the grace, the ease, indeed all that gives beauty to the movements of the dancer, must certainly be wanting. It is thus with music. By a fruitless waste of time and application, the hand may acquire the habit of touching the right keys; but all which constitutes the soul of music must be wanting to that performance, where the ear is not naturally attuned to "the concord of sweet sound."

It is a good thing to, be a pleased and attentive listener, even in music. And far happier sometimes is the unpretending girl, who sits apart silently listening to another's voice, than any one of the anxious group of candidates for promotion to the music-stool, whose countenances occasionally display the conflicting emotions of hope and fear, triumph and disappointment.

There are, however, amongst men, and women too, certain individuals whose souls may be said to be imbued with music as an instinct. It forms a part of their existence, and they only live entirely in an atmosphere of sound. To such it would be a cold philosophy to teach the expediency of giving up the cultivation of music altogether, because of the temptations it involves; and yet to such individuals, above all others, music is the most dangerous. To them it may be said, that, like charity, though in a widely different sense, *it covers a multitude of sins*; for such is its influence over them, that while carried away by its allurements, they scarcely see or feel like moral agents, so as to distinguish good from evil; and thus they mistake for an intellectual, nay, even sometimes for a spiritual enjoyment, the indulgence of that passion, which is but too earthly in its associations.

I will not say that music is a species of intoxication, but I do think that an inordinate love of it may be compared to intemperance, in the fact of its inciting the passions of the human mind so much more frequently to evil than to good. We are warranted by the language of Scripture to believe, that music is a powerfully pervading principle in the universe of God. The harmony of the spheres is figuratively set forth under the idea of the *morning stars singing together*, and the Apocalyptic vision abounds with allusions to celestial choirs. Indeed, so perfectly in unison is music with our ideas of intense and elevated enjoyment, that we can scarcely imagine heaven without the hymning of the praises of the Most High by the voices of angels and happy spirits. But let it be remembered, that all this is in connection with a purified state of being. It is where the serpent sin has never entered, or after he has been destroyed. So long as the evil heart is unsubdued—so long as there are desperate passions to awaken—so long as the hand of man is raised against his brother—so long as the cup of riotous indulgence continues to be filled—so long as temptation lurks beneath the rose-leaves of enjoyment, music will remain to be a dangerous instrument in the hands of those who are by nature and by constitution its willing and devoted slaves.

Even to such, however, I would fain believe, that when kept under proper restrictions, and regulated by right principles, music may have its use. There can be no need to advise such persons to cultivate, when young, their talent for music. The danger is, that they will cultivate no other.

Between these individuals, and the persons first described, there is a numerous class of human beings, of whom it may be said, that they possess by nature a *little* taste for music; and to these the cultivation of it may be desirable, or otherwise, according to their situation in life, and the views they entertain of the use of accomplishments in general. If the use of accomplishments be to make a show of them in society, then a *little* skill in music is certainly not worth its cost. But if the object of a daughter is to soothe the weary spirit of a father when he returns home from the office or the counting-house, where he has been toiling for her maintenance; to beguile a mother of her cares; or to charm a suffering sister into forgetfulness of her pain; then a very *little* skill in music may often be made to answer as noble a purpose as a great deal; and never does a daughter appear to more advantage, than when she cheerfully lays aside a fashionable air, and strums over, for more than the hundredth time, some old ditty which her father loves. To her ear it is possible it may be altogether divested of the slightest charm. But of what importance is that? The old man listens until tears are glistening in his eyes, for he sees again the home of his childhood—he hears his father's voice—he feels his mother's welcome—all things familiar to his heart in early youth come back to him with that long-remembered strain; and, happiest thought of all! they are revived by the playful lingers of his own beloved child. The brother too—the prodigal—the alien from the paths of peace. In other lands, that fire-side music haunts his memory. The voice of the stranger has no melody for him. His heart is chilled. He says, "I will arise and go to my father's home," where a welcome, a heart-warm welcome, still awaits him. Yet so wide has been the separation, that a feeling of estrangement still remains, and neither words, nor looks, nor affectionate embraces can make the past come back unshadowed, or dispel the cloud which settles upon every heart. The sister feels this. She knows the power of music, and when the day is closing in, that first strange day of partial reconciliation, she plays a low soft air. Her brother knows it well. It is the evening hymn they used to sing together in childhood, when they had been all day gathering flowers. His manly voice is raised. Once more it mingles with the strain. Once more the parents and the children, the sister and the brother, are united as in days gone by.

It requires no extraordinary skill in execution to render music subservient to the purposes of social and domestic enjoyment; but it does require a willing spirit, and a feeling mind, to make it tell upon the sympathies and affections of our nature.

There is a painful spectacle occasionally exhibited in private life, when a daughter refuses to play for the gratification of her own family, or casts aside with contempt the music they prefer; yet when a stranger joins the circle, and especially when many guests are met, she will sit down to the piano with the most obliging air imaginable, and play with perfect good-will whatever air the company may choose. What must the parents of such a daughter feel, if they recollect the fact, that it was at their expense, their child acquired this pleasing art, by which she appears anxious to charm any one but them? And how does the law of love operate with her? Yet, music is the very art, which by its mastery over the feelings and affections, calls forth more tenderness than any other. Surely, then, the principle of love ought to regulate the exercise of this gift, in proportion to its influence upon the human heart. Surely, it ought not to be cultivated as the medium of display, so much as the means of home enjoyment; not so much as a spell to charm the stranger, or one who has no other link of sympathy with us, as a solace to those we love, and a tribute of gratitude and affection to those who love us.

With regard to the application and use of the art of painting, or perhaps we ought to say drawing, there is a very serious mistake generally prevailing amongst young persons, as well as amongst some who are more advanced in life. Drawing, as well as music, is not only considered as something to entertain company with, but its desirableness as an art is judged of precisely by the estimate which is formed of those pieces of polished pasteboard brought home from school, and exhibited as specimens of genius in the delineation of gothic arches, ruined cottages, and flowers as flat and dry as the paper on which they are painted. The use of drawing, in short, is almost universally judged of amongst young ladies, by what it enables them to produce; and no wonder, when such are the productions, that its value should be held rather cheap.

It has often been said with great truth, that the first step towards excellence in the art of drawing, is to learn to *see*; and certainly, nothing can be more correct than that the quickening of the powers of observation, the habit of regarding, not only the clear outline, but the relative position of objects, with the extension of the sphere of thought which is thus obtained, is of infinitely more value in forwarding the great work of intellectual advancement, than all the actual productions of female artists since the world began. There are many very important reasons why drawing should be especially recommended to the attention of young persons, and I am the more anxious to point them out, because, amongst the higher circles of society, it appears to be sinking into disrepute, in comparison with music. Amongst such persons, it is beginning to be considered as a sort of handicraft, or as something which artists can do better than ladies. In this they are perfectly right; but how then are they to reap the advantage to themselves, which I am about to describe as resulting from an attentive cultivation of the graphic art?

Amongst these advantages, I will begin with the least—It is quiet. It disturbs no one; for however defective the performance may be, it does not necessarily, like music, jar upon the sense. It is true, it may when seen offend the practised eye; but we can always draw in private, and keep our productions to ourselves. In addition to this, it is an employment which beguiles the mind of many cares, because it never can be merely mechanical. The thoughts must go along with it, for the moment the attention wanders, the hand ceases from its operations, owing to the necessity there is that each stroke should be different from any which has previously been made. Under the pressure of anxiety, in seasons of protracted suspense, or when no effort can be made to meet an expected calamity, especially when that calamity is exclusively our own, drawing is of all other occupations the one most calculated to keep the mind from brooding upon self, and to maintain that general cheerfulness which is a part of social and domestic duty.

Drawing, unlike most other arts, may be taken up at any time of life, though certainly with less prospect of success than when it has been pursued in youth. It can also be laid down and resumed, as circumstance or inclination may direct, and that without any serious loss; for while the hand is employed in other occupations, the eye may be learning useful lessons to be worked out on some future day.

But the great, the wonder-working power of the graphic art, is that by which it enables us to behold, as by a new sense of vision, the beauty and the harmony of the creation. Many have this faculty of perception in their nature, who never have been taught, perhaps not allowed, to touch a pencil, and who remain to the end of their lives unacquainted with the rules of painting as an art. To them this faculty affords but glimpses of the ideal, in connection with the real; but to such as have begun to practise the art, by first learning to see, each succeeding day unfolds some new scene in that vast picture, which the ever-varying aspect of nature presents. As the faculty of hearing, in the savage Indian is sharpened to an almost incredible degree of acuteness, simply from the frequent need he has for the use of that particular sense; so the eye of the painter, from the habit of regarding every object with reference to its position and effect, beholds ten thousand points of interest, which the unpractised in this art never perceive. There is not a shadow on the landscape, not a gleam of sunshine in the fields, not a leaf in the forest, nor a flower on the lea, not a sail upon the ocean, nor a cloud in the sky, but they all form parts of that unfading picture, upon which his mind perpetually expatiates without satiety or weariness. It is a frequent complaint with travellers, that they find the scenery around them insipid; but this can never occur to the artist, through whatever country he may roam. A turn in the road, with a bunch of furze on one side, and a stunted oak on the other, is sufficient to arrest his attention, and occupy a page in his sketch-book. A willowy brook in the deep meadows, with cattle grazing on its banks, is the subject of another. The tattered mendicant is a picture, of himself; or the sturdy wagoner with his team, or the solitary orphan sitting in the porch of the village-church. Every group around the door of the inn, every party around the ancient elm in the centre of the hamlet, every beast of burden feeding by the way-side, has to him a beauty and a charm, which his art enables him to revive and perpetuate.   It is the same when he mingles in society. Hundreds and thousands of human beings may pass by the common observer without exciting a single thought or feeling, beyond their relative position with regard to himself. But the painter sees in almost every face a picture. He beholds a grace in almost every attitude, a scene of interest in every group; and, while his eye is caught by the classic beauty of an otherwise insignificant countenance, he arrests it in the position where light and shadow are most harmoniously blended; and, behold! it lives again beneath his touch—another, yet the same.

In every object, however familiar in itself, or unattractive in other points of view, the painter perceives at once what is striking, characteristic, harmonious, or graceful; and thus, while associating in the ordinary affairs of life, he feels himself the inhabitant of a world of beauty, from which others are shut out.

Would that we could dwell with more satisfaction upon this ideal existence, as it affects the morals of the artist's real life! Whatever there may be defective here, however, as regards the true foundation of happiness, is surely not attributable to the art itself; but to the necessity under which too many labour, of courting public favour, and sometimes of sacrificing the dignity of their profession to its pecuniary success.

Nor is it an object of desirable attainment to women in general, that they should study the art of painting to this extent. Amply sufficient for all their purposes, is the habit of drawing from natural objects with correctness and facility. Copying from other drawings, though absolutely necessary to the learner, is but the first step towards those innumerable advantages which arise from an easy and habitual use of the pencil. Yet here how many stop, and think their education in the graphic art complete! They think also, what is most unjust of drawing, that it is only the amusement of an idle hour, incapable of producing any happier result than an exact *fac-simile* of the master's lesson. No wonder, that with such ideas, they should evince so little inclination to continue this pursuit on leaving school. For though it is a common thing to hear young ladies exclaim, how much they should like to sketch from nature, and how much they should like to take likenesses, it is very rarely that we find one really willing to take a hundredth part of the pains which are necessary to the attainment even of mediocrity in either of these departments. That it is in reality easier, and far more pleasant, to sketch from nature, than from another drawing, is allowed by all who have made the experiment on right principles; which, however, few young persons are able to do, because they are so seldom instructed in what, if I might be allowed the expression, I should call the *philosophy* of picture-making, or, in other words, the relation of cause and effect in the grouping and general management of objects, so as to unite a number of parts into a perfect and pleasing whole.

Perspective is the first step in this branch of philosophy, but the nature and effect of light and shade, with the proportions and relations of different objects, and harmony, that grand feature of beauty, must all have become subjects of interest and observation, before we can hope to sketch successfully; and especially, before we can derive that high degree of intellectual enjoyment from the art of painting, which it is calculated to afford. Yet all these, by close and frequent attention, may be learned from nature itself, though an early acquaintance with the rules of art will greatly assist the understanding in this school of philosophy.

Amongst the numerous mistakes made by young people on the subject of drawing, none is a greater hinderance to their efforts, than an idea which generally prevails, that not only drawing itself, but each different branch of the art, requires a natural genius for that particular study. Thus, while one excuses herself from drawing because she has no genius for it; another tells you, that although she can draw landscapes with great facility, she has no genius for heads. Now, if genius be, as Madame de Stael informs us, "enthusiasm operating upon talent," I freely grant that it is essential to success in this, as well as every other art. You must not only learn it, but you must absolutely *love* it, was the frequent expression of a very clever master to his pupil. And it is this very love, which of itself will carry on the young student to any point of excellence, which it is desirable for a woman to attain.

It is true, there are greater difficulties to some than to others; just as the eye is more or less acute in its perceptions, or the communication between that and the hand more or less easy. Yet, with the same amount of genius and a little more patience, with a little more humility too, for that has more to do with success in painting than the inexperienced are aware of, these difficulties may easily be overcome.

I have said that humility is necessary to our success, and it operates precisely in this manner. It always happens that the eye has been in training for observation, long before the hand begins to trace so much as a bare outline of what the eye perceives. Thus, our first attempts at imitation fall so far short, not only of the real, but also of the ideal which the mind retains, that if praise of admiration have had anything to do with inciting us to draw, the mortification which ensues will probably be more than a young artist can endure. She must, therefore, be humble enough to be willing to proceed without praise, sometimes without commendation, and occasionally with a more than comfortable share of ridicule, as the reward of her first endeavours; all which might possibly be borne with equanimity, if she did not herself perceive a fearful want of resemblance to the thing designed.

The practice of drawing the human face and figure, is a sufficient illustration of this fact. For one who succeeds in this branch of drawing, there are twenty who succeed in landscapes; because, those who fail assure you, it is so much more difficult to draw faces and figures. This statement, however, is altogether unsupported by reason, since it requires just the same use of the eye and the hand, and just the same exercise of the mind, to draw one object as another; and provided only the object drawn is stationary, it is quite as easy to trace with accuracy the outline of a head, as of a tree, or a mountain.

There is, however, a wide difference in the result. By a slight deviation from the true outline of a mountain, no great injury to the general effect of a landscape is produced; while the same degree of deviation from the outline of a face, will sometimes entirely destroy, not only the likeness, but the beauty, of the whole. Even a branch of a tree, and sometimes a whole tree, may be omitted in a landscape; but if a nose, or an eye, were found wanting in the drawing of a face, it would be difficult to treat the performance with anything like gravity.

Thus, then, the vanity of the young students is more severely put to the test in delineations of the human form, than it can be in landscape drawing; and thus they are apt to say, they have no genius for heads or figures, because their love of excellence, though sufficient for the purposes of landscape drawing, is not strong enough to support them under the mortification of having produced a badly drawn face, or figure.

It is not the least amongst the advantages of drawing, that it induces a habit of perpetually aiming at ideal excellence; in other words, that it draws the mind away from considering the grosser qualities of matter, to the contemplation of beauty as an abstract idea; that it gives a definiteness to our notions of objects in general, and enables us to describe, with greater accuracy, the character and appearance of everything we see.

Nor ought we by any means to overlook the value of that which the pencil actually produces. Sketches of scenery, however defective as works of art, are amongst the precious memorials of which time, the great destroyer, is unable to deprive us. In them the traveller lives again, through all the joys and sorrows of his distant wanderings. He breathes again the atmosphere of that far world which his eye will never more behold. He treads again the mountain-path where his step was never weary. He sees the sunshine on the snowy peaks which rise no more to him. He hears again the shout of joyous exultation, when it bursts from hearts as young and buoyant as his own; and he remembers, at the same time, how it was with him in those by-gone days, when, for the moment, he was lifted up above the grovelling cares of every-day existence.

But, above all, the art which preserves to us the features of the loved and lost, ought to be cultivated as a means of natural and enduring gratification. It is curious to look back to the portrait of infancy, or even youth, when the same countenance is stamped with the deep traces of experience, when the venerable brow is ploughed with furrows, and the temples are shaded with scattered looks of silvery hair. It is interesting—deeply interesting, to behold the likeness of some distinguished character, with whose mind we have long been acquainted, through the medium of his works; but the beloved countenance, whose every line of beauty was mingled with our young affections, when this can be made to live before us, after death has done his fearful work, and the grave has claimed its own—we may well say, in the language of the poet, of that magic skill which has such power over the past, as to call up buried images, and clothe them again in beauty and in youth,

"Bless'd be the art that can immortalize,
The art that baffles Time's tyrannic claim
To quench it."

Beyond these, however, there are uses in the art of drawing so well worthy the consideration of every young woman of enlightened mind, that we cannot too earnestly recommend this occupation to their attention, even although it should be at some sacrifice of that labyrinthine toil of endless worsted-work, with which, in the case of modern young ladies, both head and hand appear to be so perse- veringly employed. I freely grant the charm there is in weaving together the many tints of *German wool*, but what does this amusement do for the mind, except to keep it quiet, and not always that? Now, the substitute I would propose for this occupation, is equally pleasing in the variety of colours employed, and yet calculated to be highly beneficial in its influence upon the mind, by increasing its store of knowledge, and supplying a perpetual source of rational interest, even at times when the occupation itself cannot well be carried on.

My proposition, then, is this; that, in pursuing the study of botany, instead of the unattractive *hortus siccus*, which pleases no one but the scientific beholder, correct and natural drawings should be made of every specimen, just as it appears when growing, or when freshly gathered. Instead of the colourless, distorted, hot-pressed specimens which the botanist now displays, to the utter contempt of all uninitiated in his lore, we should then have beautiful and imperishable pictures of graceful, delicate, or curious plants, looking just as they did when the mountain-wind blew over them, or when the woodland stream crept in amongst their thousand stems, and kissed the drooping blossoms that hung upon its banks. We might then have them placed before us in all their natural loveliness, either the flower, the branch, or the entire plant, and sometimes, to render the picture more complete, the characteristic scenery by which it is usually surrounded.

But if in botany the practice of this art is so desirable, how much more so does it become in entomology, where the study can scarcely be carried on without a sacrifice of life most revolting to the female mind. What beautiful specimens might we not have of the curious caterpillar, with a branch of the tree on which it feeds; then the larva and its silken bed; and, lastly, the splendid butterfly, whose expanded wings no cruel touch could ruffle; all forming pictures of the most interesting and delightful character, and powerfully contrasted in the associations they would excite, with those regular rows of moths and beetles pricked on paper, which our juvenile collectors now exhibit.

It may be said, that even such specimens of insects could scarcely be obtained without some sacrifice of life or liberty; but we all know that when the eye and the hand are habituated to catch the likeness of any object, it is done with increasing facility each time the experiment is made, until a comparatively slight observation of the general appearance, position, and characteristic features of the living model, is sufficient for the artist in the completion of his likeness.

The same facility of delineation would assist our researches through the whole range of natural history. By such means we should not only be supplied with endless amusement, but might at the same time be adding to our store of useful knowledge. We should not only be making ourselves better acquainted with the poetry of nature, but with its reality too. For what is there either practical, or real, in the specimens of plants and insects as we generally find them. Real, they unquestionably are in one sense, as the mummy is a real man; but who would point to that pitiful vestige of mortality as exhibiting the real characteristics of a human being?

It seems to me a perfectly natural subject of repulsion, when the poet exclaims—

"Nor would I like to spread,
My thin and wither'd face,
The *hortus siccus*, pale and dead,
A mummy of my race."

And few there are who would not prefer to such miserable memorials, as actually more real, a well-painted likeness of a departed friend, with the expression of countenance, the dress, the position, and the circumstances with which the memory of that friend was associated.

Drawing is, unfortunately, one of those accomplishments which are too frequently given up at the time of life when they might be most useful to others, when they might really be turned to good account, in that early expansion and developement of mind, which belong exclusively to woman in her maternal capacity; but as this view of the subject belongs more properly to a later stage of the present work, we will pass on to ask, In what degree of estimation poetry is, and ought to be held, by the daughters of England in the present day?

There have been eras in our history, when poetry assumed a more than reasonable sway over the female mind, when an acquaintance with the Muses was considered essential to a polished education, and when the very affectation of poetic feeling proved how high a value was attached to the reality. It would be useless now to speak of the absurdities into which the young and sensitive were often betrayed by this extreme of public taste. Such times are gone by, and the opposite extreme is now the tendency of popular feeling. It is not to be wondered at that this should be the case with men, because as a nation, our fathers, husbands, sons, and brothers are becoming more and more involved in the necessity of providing for mere animal existence. No wonder, then, that in our teeming cities, poetry should be compelled to hide her diminished head; or, that even, pursuing the man of business home to his suburban villa, she should leave him to his stuffed arm-chair, in the aims, of that heavy, after-dinner sleep, which so frequently succeeds to his short and busy day of unremitting struggle and excitement. Nor is this all. If poetry should seek the quiet fields, as in the days of their pastoral beauty, even from these her green and flowery haunts, she is scared away by the steaming torrent, the reeking chimney, and the fiery locomotive; while on the wide ocean, where her ancient realm was undisputed, her silvery trace upon the bosom of the deep waters is now ploughed up by vulgar paddles; and all the voiceless mystery of "viewless winds," which in the old time held the minds of expectant thousands under their command, is now become a thing of no account—a by-word, or a jest.

I speak not with childish or ignorant repining of these things. We are told by political enconomists that it is good they should be so, and I presume not to dispute the fact. Yet, surely if it be the business of man to give up the strength of his body, the energy of his mind, and the repose of his soul, for his country's prosperity or—his own; it is for woman, who labours under no such pressing necessity, to make a stand against the encroachments of this popular tendency, I had almost said—this national disease.

What is poetry? is a question which has been asked a thousand times, and perhaps never clearly answered. I presume not to suppose my own definition more happy than others; but in a work[1] already before the public, I have been at some pains to place this subject in a point of view at once clear and attractive. My idea of poetry as explained in this work, and it remains to be the same, is, that it is best understood by that chain of association which connects the intellects with the affections; so that whatever is so far removed from vulgarity, as to excite ideas of sublimity, beauty, or tenderness, may be said to be poetical; though the force of such ideas must depend upon the manner in which they are presented to the mind, as well as to the nature of the mind itself. When the character of an individual is deeply imbued with poetic feeling, there is a corresponding disposition to look beyond the dull realities of common life, to the ideal relation of things, as they connect themselves with our passions and feelings, or with the previous impressions we have received of loveliness or grandeur, repose or excitement, harmony or beauty, in the universe around us. This disposition, it must be granted, has been, in some instances, a formidable obstacle to the even tenor of the wise man's walk on earth; but let us not, while solicitous to avoid the abuse of poetic feeling, rush into the opposite excess of neglecting this high and heaven-born principle altogether.   It is the taste of the present times to invest the material with an immeasurable extent of importance beyond the ideal. It is the tendency of modern education to instil into the youthful mind the necessity of knowing, rather than the advantage of feeling. And, to a certain extent, "knowledge is power;" but neither is knowledge all that we live for, nor power all that we enjoy. There are deep mysteries in the book of nature which all can feel, but none will ever understand, until the veil of mortality shall be withdrawn. There are stirrings in the heart of man which constitute the very essence of his being, and which power can neither satisfy nor subdue. Yet this mystery reveals more truly than the clearest proofs, or mightiest deductions of science, that a master-hand has been for ages, and is still at work, above, beneath, and around us; and this moving principle is for ever reminding us, that, in our nature, we inherit the germs of a future existence, over which time has no influence, and the grave no victory.[2]

If, then, for man it be absolutely necessary that he should sacrifice the poetry of his nature for the realities of material and animal existence, for woman there is no excuse—for woman, whose whole life, from the cradle to the grave, is one of feeling, rather than of action; whose highest duty is so often to suffer, and be still; whose deepest enjoyments are all relative; who has nothing, and is nothing, of herself; whose experience, if unparticipated, is a total blank; yet, whose world of interest is wide as the realm of humanity, boundless as the ocean of life, and enduring as eternity! For woman, who, in her inexhaustible sympathies, can live only in the existence of another, and whose very smiles and tears are not exclusively her own—for woman to cast away the love of poetry, is to pervert from their natural course the sweetest and loveliest tendencies of a truly feminine mind, to destroy the brightest charm which can adorn her intellectual character, to blight the fairest rose in her wreath of youthful beauty.

A woman without poetry, is like a landscape without sunshine. We see every object as distinctly as when the sunshine is upon it; but the beauty of the whole is wanting—the atmospheric tints, the harmony of earth and sky, we look for in vain; and we feel that though the actual substance of hill and dale, of wood and water, are the same, the spirituality of the scene is gone.

A woman without poetry! The idea is a paradox; for what single subject has ever been found so fraught with poetical associations, as woman herself? "Woman, with her beauty, and grace, and gentleness, and fulness of feeling, and depth of affection, and her blushes of purity, and the tones and looks which only a mother's heart can inspire."

The little encouragement which poetry meets with in the present day, arises, I imagine, out of its supposed opposition to utility; and, certainly, if to eat and to drink, to dress as well or better than our neighbours, and to amass a fortune in the shortest possible space of time, be the highest aim of our existence, then the less we have to do with poetry the better. But may we not be mistaken in the ideas we habitually attach to the word utility? There is a utility of material, and another of immaterial things. There is a utility in calculating our bodily wants, and our resources, and in regulating our personal efforts in proportion to both; but there is a higher utility in sometimes setting the mind free, like a bird that has been caged, to spread its wings, and soar into the ethereal world. There is a higher utility in sometimes pausing to feel the power which is in the immortal spirit to search out the principle of beauty, whether it bursts upon us with the dawn of rosy morning, or walks at gorgeous noon across the hills and valleys, or lies at evening's dewy close, enshrined within a folded flower.

It is good, and therefore it must be useful, to see and to feel that the all-wise Creator has set the stamp of degradation only upon those *things which perish in the using*; but that all those which enlarge and elevate the soul, all which afford us the highest and purest enjoyment, from the loftiest range of sublimity, to the softest emotions of tenderness and love, are, and must be, immortal. Yes, the mountains may be overthrown, and the heavens themselves may melt away, but all the ideas with which they inspired us—their vastness and their grandeur, will remain. Every flower might fade from the garden of earth, but would beauty, as an essence, therefore cease to exist? Even love might fail us here. Alas! how often does it fail us at our utmost need! But the principle of love is the same; and there is no human heart so callous as not to respond to the language of the poet, when he says—

"They sin who tell us love can die

□□*□*□*

Its holy flame for ever burneth,
From heaven it came, to heaven returneth;
Too oft on earth a troubled guest,
At times deceived, at times opprest,
It here is tried and purified,
And hath in heaven its perfect rest;
It soweth here with toil and care,
But the harvest-time of love is there."

All these ideas are excited, and all these impressions are made upon the mind through the medium of poetry. By poetry, I do not mean that vain babbling in rhyme, which finds no echo, either in the understanding or the heart. By poetry, I mean that ethereal fire, which touched not the lips only, but the soul of Milton, when he sung of

"Man's first disobedience,"

and which has inspired all who ever walked the same enchanted ground, from the father of poetry himself, down to

"The simple bard, rough at the rustic plough."

Thousands have felt this principle of poetry within them, who yet have never learned to lisp in numbers; and perhaps they are the wisest of their class, for they have thus the full enjoyment which poetic feeling affords, without the disappointment which so frequently attends upon the efforts of those who venture to commit themselves in verse.

Men of business, whose hearts and minds are buried in their bales of goods, and who know no relaxation from the office or the counter, except what the daily newspaper affords, are apt to conclude that poetry does nothing for them; because it never keeps their accounts, prepares their dinner, nor takes charge of their domestic affairs. Now, though I should be the last person to recommend poetry as a substitute for household economy, or to put even the brightest emanations of genius in the place of domestic duty, I do not see why the two should not exist together; nor am I quite convinced that, although a vast proportion of mankind have lost their relish for poetry, it would not in reality be better for them to be convinced by their companions of the gentler sex, that poetry, so far from being incompatible with social or domestic comfort, is capable of being associated with every rational and lawful enjoyment.

Yes, it is better for every one to have their minds elevated, rather than degraded—raised up to a participation in thoughts and feelings in which angels might take a part, rather than chained down to the grovelling cares of mere corporeal existence; and never do we feel more happy, than when, in the performance of any necessary avocation, we look beyond the gross material on which we are employed to those relations of thought and feeling, that connect the act of duty which occupies our hands with some being we love, that teach us to realize, while thus engaged, the smile of gratitude which is to constitute our reward, or the real benefit that act will be the means of conferring, even when no gratitude is there.

What man of cultivated mind, who has ever tried the experiment, would choose to live with a woman, whose whole soul was absorbed in the strife, the tumult, the perpetual discord which constant occupation in the midst of material things so inevitably produces; rather than with one whose attention, equally alive to practical duties, had a world of deeper feeling in her "heart of hearts," with which no selfish, worldly, or vulgar thoughts could mingle?

It is not because we love poetry, that we must be always reading, quoting, or composing it. Far otherwise. For that bad taste, which would thus abuse and misapply so sacred a gift, is the very opposite of poetical. The love of poetry, or, in other words, the experience of deep poetic feeling, is rather a principle, which, while it inspires the love of beauty in general, forgets not the beauty of fitness and order; and therefore can never sanction that which is grotesque or out of place. It teaches us, that nothing which offends the feelings of others can be estimable or praiseworthy in ourselves; for it is only in reference to her association with others, that woman can be in herself poetical. She may even nil a book with poetry, and not be poetical in her own character; because she may at the same time be selfish, vain, and worldly-minded.

To have the mind so embued with poetic feeling that it shall operate as a charm upon herself and others, woman must be lifted out of self, she must see in everything material a relation, an essence, and an end, beyond its practical utility. She must regard the little envyings, bickerings, and disputes about common things, only as weeds in the pleasant garden of life, bearing no comparison in importance with the loveliness of its flowers. She must forget even her own personal attractions, in her deep sense of the beauty of the whole created universe, and she must lose the very voice of flattery to herself, in her own intense admiration of what is excellent in others.

This it is to be poetical; and I ask again, whether it is not good, in these practical and busy times, that the Daughters of England should make a fresh effort to retain that high-toned spirituality of character, which has ever been the proudest distinction of their sex, in order that they may possess that influence over the minds of men, which the intellectual and the refined alone are capable of maintaining?

Let them look for a moment at the condition of woman wherever this high tone of character has been wanting, where she has been identified merely with material things, and, as a necessary consequence, regarded as a soulless and degraded being, essential to society only in her ministration to the general good of man. But we close the scene ere it is fully unfolded. The Daughters of England must feel within themselves that a higher and a nobler destiny is theirs.

↑ The Poetry of Life.
↑ The Poetry of Life.

In the cursory survey we have now taken of what may properly be called the intellectual groundwork of the female character, our attention has been directed not only to those scholastic attainments which are generally comprehended in a good education, but to that general knowledge, which can only be acquired by after-study, by observation, by reading, and by association with good society.

All these, however, are but the materials of character, materials altogether useless, and sometimes worse than useless, without the operation of a master-power to select, improve, and turn them to the best account. With men, this power is most frequently self-interest—with women it is that bias of feeling towards what they are most inclined to love, which is generally recognized under the name of taste; and both these principles begin to exercise their influence long before the mind has attained any high degree of intellectual cultivation, and long before we are aware of our own motives. I have called this principle in woman, taste, because so far as it is biassed by the affections, taste involves a moral; and it is a peculiar feature in the female character, that few things are esteemed which do not recommend themselves in some way or other to the affections. Thus, women are often said to be deficient in judgment, simply from this reason, that judgment is the faculty by which we are enabled to decide what is intrinsically best, while taste only influences us so far as to choose what is most agreeable to our own feelings. It is no uncommon thing amongst young women, to hear them say, they like a thing they do not know why?nay, so warm are their expressions, one would be led to suppose their preference arose from absolute love, and yet, "The reason why, they cannot tell."

It is that habitual tendency of feeling or tone of mind, which I have called taste, that decides their choice; and it is thus that our moral worth or dignity depend upon the exercise of good taste, in the selection we make of the intellectual materials we work with in the formation of character, and the general arrangement of the whole, so as to render the trifling subservient to the more important, and each estimable according to the purpose for which it is used.

I am aware that religious principle is the only certain test by which character can be tried; but I am speaking of things as they are, not as they ought to be; and I wish to prove the great importance of taste, by showing that it is a principle busily at work in directing the decisions of the female mind on points supposed to be too trifling for the operation of religious feeling, and often before any definite idea of religion has been formed. It is strictly in subservience to religion, that I would speak of good taste as being of extreme importance to woman; because it serves her purpose in all those little variations of human life, which are too sudden in their occurrence, and too minute in themselves, for the operation of judgment; but which at the same time constitute so large a sum of woman's experience.

It may be said, that the rules of good taste are so arbitrary, that no one can fully understand them. I can only repeat, what I have said on this subject in "The Poetry of Life," and I think the rule is sufficient for women in general. It is, that the majority of opinion amongst those who are best able to judge, may safely be considered as most in accordance with good taste. Thus, when your taste has received from your parents a particular bias, which you are afterwards led to suspect is not a correct one, inquire with all respect, whether, on that particular subject, your parents are the persons best qualified to judge. Or when you find in society that anything is universally approved or condemned, before accommodating your own taste to this exhibition of popular feeling, ask whether the judges who pronounce such sentence, are competent ones, and if there be a higher tribunal at which the question can be tried—or in other words, judges who understand the subject better, let it be referred to them, before you finally make up your mind.

Perhaps it may be objected that this is a tedious process, and that taste is a thing of sudden conclusion. But let it be remembered, I am now speaking of the formation of a good taste, as a part of the character; not of the operation of taste where it has been found. Nor, indeed, is the suddenness with which some young persons decide in matters of taste, any proof of their good sense. So far from this, we often find them, under the influence of better judges, reduced to the mortifying necessity of changing their opinions to the direct opposite of what they have too hastily expressed.

Still, though the process of forming the taste upon right principles, may at first be slow; and though it may some, times appear too tedious for juvenile impetuosity, the exercise of good taste will in time become so easy, and habitual, as to operate almost like an instinct; and, until it is so, the process I have recommended, will have the great advantage of preventing young ladies from being too forward in expressing their sentiments; and what is of far greater importance, they will be cautious in making their selection of what they admire, and what they condemn. Have we not all seen in society, the ridiculous spectacle of a young and forward girl, exhibiting all the extravagance of juvenile importance in her condemnation of a book, which has not happened to please her fancy; when, had she waited a few minutes longer, the conversation would have taken such a turn, as would have convinced her that amongst wise men, and enlightened women, the work was considered justly worthy of high commendation? With what grace could she, then, after having thus committed herself, either defend, or withdraw her own opinions? or with what complacency could she reflect upon the exposure she had made of her bad taste, before persons qualified to judge? Far wiser is the part, perhaps, of her more diffident companion, who having equally failed in discovering the merits of the work in question, goes home and reads it again, with her attention more directed to its beauties; and who, even if she fails at last in deriving that pleasure from the book which she had hoped, has the humility to conclude that the fault is in her own taste, which she then begins to regulate upon a new principle, and with a determination to endeavour to admire what the best judges pronounce to be really excellent. We must not, however, attach too much importance to good taste, nor require it to operate beyond its legitimate sphere. Taste, unquestionably, gives a bias to the character, in its tendency to what is elevated or low, refined or vulgar; but after all, the part of taste is only that of a witness called into a court of justice, to test the value of an article, which has some relation to the great and momentous decision in which the judge, the jury, and the court, are so deeply interested. As taste is that witness, religion is that judge; and it is only as the one is kept subservient to the other, that it can be rendered conducive to our happiness or our good. The province of taste, then, includes all the minute affairs of woman's life?which belongs to all pleasurable feeling,- held in subordination to religious principle?all which belongs to dress, manners, and social habits, so far as they may be said to be ladylike, or otherwise. Should any consideration, relating to one or all of these points, be allowed to interfere in the remotest degree with the requirements of religion, it is a proof whenever they do so, that the standard of excellence is a wrong one; and the individual who commits so fatal an error, would do well to look to the consequences, and remedy the evil before it shall be too late. Religion never yet was injured by permitting good taste to follow in her train; but that lovely handmaid can deserve the name of taste no longer, if she attempts to step before religion, or in any respect to assume her place. Above every other feature which adorns the female character, delicacy stands foremost within the province of good taste. Not that delicacy which is perpetually in quest of something to be ashamed of, which makes a merit of a blush, and simpers at the false construction its own ingenuity has put upon an innocent remark; this spurious kind of delicacy is as far removed from good taste, as from good feeling, and good sense; but that high-minded delicacy which maintains its pure and undeviating walk alike amongst women, as in the society of men; which shrinks from no necessary duty, and can speak when required, with seriousness and kindness of things at which it would be ashamed indeed to smile or to blush—that delicacy which knows how to confer a benefit without wounding the feelings of another, and which understands also how, and when to receive one—that delicacy which can give alms without display, and advice without assumption; and which pains not the most humble or susceptible being in creation. This is the delicacy which forms so important a part of good taste, that where it does not exist as a natural instinct, it is taught as the first principle of good manners, and considered as the universal passport to good society.

Nor can this, the greatest charm of female character, if totally neglected in youth, ever be acquired in after life. When the mind has been accustomed to what is vulgar, or gross, the fine edge of feeling is gone, and nothing can restore it. It is comparatively easy, on first entering upon life, to maintain the page of thought unsullied, by closing it against every improper image; but when once such images are allowed to mingle with the imagination, so as to be constantly revived by memory, and thus to give their tone to the habitual mode of thinking and conversing, the beauty of the female character may indeed be said to be gone, and its glory departed.

But we will no longer contemplate so unlovely—so unnatural a picture. Woman, happily for her, is gifted by nature with a quickness of perception, by which she is able to detect the earliest approach of anything which might tend to destroy that high-toned purity of character, for which, even in the days of chivalry, she was more reverenced and adored, than for her beauty itself. This quickness of perception in minute and delicate points, with the power which woman also possesses of acting upon it instantaneously, has, in familiar phraseology, obtained the name of tact; and when this natural gift is added to good taste, the two combined are of more value to a woman in the social and domestic affairs of every-day life, than the most brilliant intellectual endowments could be without them.

When a woman is possessed of a high degree of tact, she sees, as if by a kind of second-sight, when any little emergency is likely to occur; or when, to use a more familiar expression, things do not seem likely to go right. She is thus aware of any sudden turn in conversation, and prepared for what it may lead to; but, above all, she can penetrate into the state of mind of those with whom she is placed in contact, so as to detect the gathering gloom upon another's brow, before the mental storm shall have reached any formidable height; to know when the tone of voice has altered, when an unwelcome thought has presented itself, and when the pulse of feeling is beating higher or lower in consequence of some apparently trifling circumstance which has just transpired.

In these and innumerable instances of a similar nature, the woman of tact, not only perceives the variations which are constantly taking place in the atmosphere of social life, but she adapts herself to them with a facility which the law of love enables her to carry out, so as to spare her friends the pain and annoyance which so frequently arise out of the mere mismanagement of familiar and apparently unimportant affairs. And how often do these seeming trifles—

"The lightly uttered, careless word"—

the wrong construction put upon a right meaning—the accidental betrayal of what there would have been no duplicity in concealing—how often do these wound us more than direct unkindness. Even the young feel this sometimes too sensitively for their own peace. But while the tears they weep in private, attest the severity of their sorrow, let them not, like the misanthrope, turn back with hatred or contempt upon the world which they suppose to have injured them; but let them rather learn this wholesome lesson, by their own experience, so to meet the peculiarities of those with whom they associate, as to soften down the asperities of temper, to heal the wounds of morbid feeling, and to make the current of life run smoothly, so far as they have power to cast the oil of peace upon its waters.

Such then is the general use of tact. Particular instances of its operation would be too minute, and too familiar, to occupy, with propriety, the pages of a book; for, like many other female excellencies, it is more valued, and better understood, by the loss a character sustains without it, than by any definite form it assumes, even when most influential upon the conversation and conduct. This valueable acquirement, however, can never be attained without the cultivation in early life of habits of close observation It is not upon the notes of a piece of music only, not upon a pattern of fancy-work, nor even upon the pages of an interesting book, that the attention must alone be brought to bear; but upon things in general, so that the faculty of observation shall become so sharpened by constant use, that nothing can escape it.

Far be it from me to recommend that idle and vulgar curiosity, which peeps about without a motive, or, worse than that, with a view to collect materials for scandal. Observation is a faculty which may be kept perpetually at work, without intrusion or offence to others; and at the same time, with infinite benefit to ourselves. Every object in creation, every sound, every sensation, every production either of nature or of art, supplies food for observation, while observation in its turn supplies food for thought. I have been astonished in my association with young ladies, at the very few things they appear to have to think about. Generally speaking, they might be all talked up in the course of a week. And what is the consequence? It is far beyond a jest, for the consequence too frequently is, that they grow weary of themselves, then weary of others, and lastly weary of life—of life, that precious and immortal gift, which they share with angels, and which to them, as to the angelic host, has been bestowed in order that therewith they may glorify the gracious Giver.

Now, this very weariness, which at the same time is the most prevalent disease, and the direct calamity, we find amongst young women; since it not only makes them useless and miserable, but drives them perpetually into excitement as a momentary relief—this weariness arises out of various causes with which young people are not sufficiently made acquainted, and one of the most powerful of which is, a neglect of the habit of observation.

"I have seen nobody, and heard nothing to-day," is the vapid remark of one to whom the glorious heavens, and the fruitful earth, might as well be so much paint and patchwork. "What an uninteresting person!" exclaims another, who has never looked a second time at some fine expressive countenance, where deep feeling tells its own impassioned story. "I wish some one would come and invite us out to tea," says a third, whose household library is stored with books, and whose parents have within themselves a fund of intelligence, which they would be but too happy to communicate, could they find an attentive listener in their child. "But my life is so monotonous," pleads a fourth, "and my range of vision so limited, that I have nothing to observe." With those who live exclusively in towns, I confess this argument might have some weight; and for this reason, I suppose it is, that town-bred young women are often more ignorant than those who spend a portion of their early life in the country—not certainly because there is really less to be observed in towns, but because the mind, in the midst of a multitude of moving images, is comparatively unimpressed by any. I confess, too, there is something in the noise and tumult of a crowded city, which stupifies the mind, and blunts its perception of individual things, until the whole shifting pageant assumes the character of some vast panorama, upon which we look, only with regard to the whole, and forgetful of each individual part.

"It is true, I have taken my accustomed walk in the city," observes a fifth young woman, "but I have found nothing to think about." What! was there nothing to think about in the squalid forms of want and misery which met you at every turn?—nothing in the disappointed look of the patient mendicant as you passed him by?—nothing in the pale and half-clad mother, seated on the step at the rich man's door, folding her infant to her bosom, and shrouding it with the "wings of care?"—was there nothing in all that was doing amongst those busy thousands, for supplying the common wants of man; the droves of weary animals goaded, stupified, or maddened, none of which would ever tread again the greensward on the mountain's side, or slake its thirst beside the woodland brook?—was there nothing in the bold and beautiful charger, the bounding steed, or the sleek and well-fed carriage-horse, contrasted with the galled and lacerated victims of oppression, waiting for their round of agony to come again?—was there nothing in the vastness of man's resources, the variety of his inventions, the power of combined effort, as displayed in that perpetual succession of luxuries both for the body and the mind?—was there nothing in that aspect of order and industry, so important to individual, as well as national prosperity?—was there nothing, in short, in that mighty mass of humanity, or in the millions of pulses beating there, with health or sickness, weal or wo?—was there nothing in all this to think about? Why, one of our late poets was wont to weep as he walked along Fleet-street and the Strand; so intense were his sympathies with that moving host of fellow-beings. And can young and sensitive women be found to pass over the same ground, and say they find nothing to think about? Still less could we expect to meet with a being thus impervious in the country; for there, if human nature pleases not, she may find

"——— books in the running brooks,
Sermons in stones, and good in everything."

Whether it arises from an intellectual, or a moral defect, that this happy experience is so seldom realized, is a question of some importance in the formation of character. If young ladies really do not wish to be close observers, the evil is a moral one, and I cannot but suspect that much truth lies here. They wish, undoubtedly, to enjoy every amusement which can be derived from observation, but they do not wish to observe; because they either have some little pet sorrow which they prefer brooding over to themselves, or some favourite subject of gossip, which they prefer talking over with their friends, or they think it more ladylike not to notice common things, or more interesting to be absorbed, to start when spoken to, and to spend the greatest portion of their time in a state of reverie.

If such be the choice of any fair reader of these pages, I can only warn her that the punishment of her error will eventually come upon her, and that as surely as she neglects in youth to cultivate the expansive and pleasure-giving faculty of observation, so surely will life become wearisome to her in old age, if not before. There are, however, many whose error on this point arises solely out of their ignorance of the innumerable advantages to be derived from a close observation of things in general. Their lives are void of interest, their minds run to waste, they are constantly pining for excitement, without being conscious of any definite cause for what they suffer. They see their more energetic and intelligent companions animated, interested, and amused, with something which they are consequently most anxious to be made acquainted with, supposing it will afford the same pleasure to them; when, to their astonishment, they find it only some object which has for a long time met their daily gaze, without ever having made an impression upon their own minds, or excited a single idea in connexion with it. To such individuals it becomes a duty to point out, as far as we are able, the obstacles which stand in the way of their deriving that instruction and amusement from general and individual observation, which would fill up the void of their existence, and render them at the same time more companionable, and more happy.

There is a word in our language of most inexplicable meaning, which by universal consent has become a sort of test-word amongst young ladies, and by which they try the worth of everything, as regards its claim upon their attention. I mean the word *interesting*. In vain have I endeavoured to attach any definite sense to this expression, as generally used by the class of persons addressed in this work. I can only conjecture that its signification is synonymous with *exciting*, and that it is applicable to all which awakens sentiment, or produces emotion. However this may be, the fact that a person or a thing is considered amongst young ladies as uninteresting, stamps it with irremediable obloquy, so that it is never more to be spoken, or even thought of; while, on the other hand, whatever is pronounced to be interesting, is considered worthy of their utmost attention, even though it should possess no other recommendation; and thus, not only heroes and heroines, but books, letters, conversation, speeches, meetings public and private, friends, and even lovers, are tried by this universal test, and if they fail here, wo betide the luckless candidate for female favour! Of those who have hitherto been slaves to this all-potent word, I would now ask one simple question?Is it not possible to create their own world of interest out of the materials which Providence has placed before them? or must they by necessity follow in the train of those who languish, after the excitement of fictitious sorrow, or who luxuriate in the false sentiment of immoral books, and the flattery of unprincipled men, simply because they find them interesting?   Never has there been a delusion more insidious, or more widely spread, than that which arises out of the arbitrary use of this dangerous and deceitful word, as it obtains amongst young women. Ask one of them why she cannot read a serious book; she answers, "the style is so uninteresting." Ask another why she does not attend a public meeting for the benefit of her fellow-creatures; she answers that "such meetings have lost their interest." Ask a third why she does not make a friend of her sister; she tells you that her sister "does not interest" her. And so on, through the whole range of public and private duty, for there is no call so imperative, and no claim so sacred, as to escape being submitted to this test: and on the other hand, no sentiment that cannot be reconciled, no task that cannot be undertaken, and no companionship that cannot be borne with, under the recommendation of having been introduced in an interesting manner.

Of all the obstacles which stand in the way of that exercise of the faculty of observation, which I would so earnestly recommend, I believe there is none so great as the importance which is attached to the word "interesting," amongst young women. Upon whatever interests them, they are sufficiently ready to employ their powers of observation ; but with regard to what does not, they pass through the pleasant walks of daily life, as if surrounded by the dreary wastes of a desert. Of want of memory, too, they are apt to complain, and from the frequency with which this grievance is spoken of, and the little effort that is made against it, one would rather suppose it an embellishment to the character than otherwise, to be deficient in the power of recollecting. It is a fact, however, which personal experience has not been able to controvert, that whatever we really observe, we are able to remember. Ask one of these fair complainers, for instance, who laments her inability to remember, what coloured dress was worn by some distinguished belle, for what piece of music she herself obtained the most applause, or what subject was chosen by some beau-ideal of a speaker, and it is more than probable her memory will not be found at fault, because these are the things upon which she has employed her observation; and, had the subjects themselves been of a higher order, an equal effort of the same useful faculty, would have impressed them in the same imperishable characters upon her memory.

After considering the subject in this point of view, how important does it appear that we should turn our attention to the power which exists in every human being, and especially during the season of youth, of creating a world of interest for themselves, of deviating so far from the tendency of popular taste, as sometimes to leave the Corsairs of Byron to the isles of Greece, and the Gypsies of Scott to the mountains of his native land; and while they look into the page of actual life, they will find that around them, in their daily walks, beneath the parental roof, or mixing with the fireside circle by the homely hearth, there are often feelings as deep, and hearts as warm, and experience as richly fraught with interest, as ever glowed in verse, or lived in story. There is not, there cannot be any want of interest in the exercise of the sympathies of our nature upon common things, when no novel has ever exhibited scenes of deeper emotion, than observation has revealed to every human being, whose perceptions have been habitually alive to the claims of weak and suffering humanity; nor has fiction ever portrayed such profound wretchedness as we may daily find amongst the poor and the depraved; and not wretchedness alone, for what language of mimic feeling has ever been found to equal the touching pathos of the poor and simple-hearted? Nay, so far does imagination fall short of reality, that the highest encomium we can pass upon a writer of fiction, is, that his expressions are "true to nature."

This is what we may find every day in actual life, if we will but look for it—intensity of feeling under all its different forms; the mother's tender love; the father's high ambition; hope in its early bud, its first blight, and its final extinction; the joy of youth; the helplessness of old age; patience under suffering; disinterested zeal; strong faith, and calm resignation. And shall we say that we feel no interest in realities of which the novel and the drama are but feeble imitations? It is true that heroes and heroines do not strike upon their hearts, or fall prostrate, or tear their hair before us, every day; but I repeat again, that the touching pathos of true feeling, which all may become acquainted with, if they will employ their powers of observation upon human life as it exists around us, has nothing to equal it in poetry or fiction. If, then, we would turn our attention to human life as it is, and employ our powers of observation upon common things, we should find a never-failing source of interest, not only in the sympathies of our common nature, but in all which displays the wisdom and goodness of the Creator; for this ought ever to be our highest and ultimate aim in the exercise of every faculty we possess, to perceive the impress of the finger of God upon all which his will has designed, or his hand has created.

All I have yet said, on this subject, however, has reference only to the benefit, or the enjoyment, of the individual who employs the faculty of observation. The law of love directs us to a happier and holier exercise of this faculty. No one can be truly kind, without having accustomed themselves in early life to habits of close observation. They may be kind in feeling, but never in effect; for kindness is always estimated, not by the good it desires, but by that which it actually produces. A woman who is a close observer, under the influence of the law of love, knows so well what belongs to social and domestic comfort, that she never enters a room occupied by a family whose happiness she has at heart, without seeing in an instant every trifle upon which that comfort depends. If the sun is excluded when it would be more cheerful to let it shine in—if the cloth is not spread at the right time for the accustomed meal—if the fire is low, or the hearth unswept—if the chairs are not standing in the most inviting places, her quick eye detects in an instant what is wanting to complete the general air of comfort and order which it is woman's business to diffuse over her whole household; while, on the other hand, if her attention has never been directed to any of these things, she enters the room without looking around her, and sits down to her own occupations without once perceiving that the servants are behindhand with the breakfast, that the blinds are still down on a dark winter's morning, that a window is still open, that a chair is standing with its back to the fender, that the fire is smoking for want of better arrangement, or that a corner of the hearth-rug is turned up.

Now, provided all other things are equal, which of these two women would be the most agreeable to sit down with? The answer is clear; yet, nothing need be wanting in the last, but the habit of observation, to render her a more inviting companion. It may perhaps be surmised, if not actually said, of the other, that her mind must be filled with trifles, to enable her habitually to see such as are here specified; but it is a fact confirmed by experience, and knowledge of the world, that a quick and close observation of little things, by no means precludes observation of greater; and that the woman who cannot comfortably sit down until all these trifling matters are adjusted, will be more likely than another, whose faculties have not been thus exercised, to perceive, by an instantaneous glance of the eye, the peculiar temper of her husband's mind, as well as to discover the characteristic peculiarities of some interesting guest; while, on the other hand, the woman who never notices these things, will be more likely to lose the point of a clever remark, and to fail to perceive the most interesting features in the society with which she associates. The faculty of observation is the same, whatever object it may be engaged upon ; and that which is minute, may sharpen its powers, and stimulate its exercise, as well as that which is more important.

With regard to kindness, it is impossible so to adapt our expressions of good-will, as to render them acceptable, unless we minutely observe the characters, feelings, and situation of those around us. Inappropriate kindness is not only a waste of good things, it is sometimes an annoyance—nay, even an offence to the sensitive and fastidious, because it proves that the giver of the present, or the actor in the intended benefit has been more solicitous to display his own generosity, than to promote their real good; or he might have seen, that, with their habits, tastes, and peculiarities, such an act must be altogether useless.

A woman wanting the habit of observation, though influenced by the kindest feelings, will be guilty of a vast amount of inconsistencies, which, summed up together by those whom they have offended, will, in time, obtain for her the reputation of being anything but kind in her treatment of others. Such, for instance, as walking away at a brisk pace, intent upon her own business, and leaving behind some delicate and nervous invalid to endure all the mortification of neglect. When told of her omission, she may hasten back, make a thousand apologies, and feel really grieved at her own conduct; but she will not easily convince the invalid that it would not have shown more real kindness to have observed from the first that she was left behind. No; there is no way of being truly kind, without cultivating habits of observation. Nor will such habits come to our aid in after life, if they have been neglected in youth. Willingness to oblige, is not all that is wanted, or this might supply the defect. Where this willingness exists without observation, how often will a well-meaning person start up with a vague consciousness of some omission, look about with awkward curiosity to see what is wanted, blunder upon the right thing at the wrong time, and then sit down again, after having made every one else uncomfortable, and himself ridiculous.

In connection with the habit of observation, how much real kindness may be practised, even by the most insignificant member of a family. I have seen a little child, far too diffident to speak to the stranger-guest, still watch his plate at table with such assiduity, that no wish remained ungratified, simply from having just what the child perceived he most wanted, placed silently beside him.

From this humble sphere of minute observation, men are generally and very properly considered as excluded. But to women they look, and shall they look in vain, for the filling up of this important page of human experience? Each particular item of the account may be regarded as beneath their notice; but well do they know, and deeply do they regret, if the page is left blank, or if the sum-total is not greatly to their advantage.

Observation and attention are so much the same in their results, that I shall not consider them separately, but only add a few remarks on the subject of attention as it applies to reading.

There is no social pleasure, amongst those it has been my lot to experience, which I esteem more highly than that of listening to an interesting book well read; when a fire-side circle, chiefly composed of agreeable and intelligent women, are seated at their work. In the same way as the lonely traveller, after gaining some lofty eminence, on the opening of some lovely valley, or the closing of some sunset scene, longs to see the joy he is then feeling reflected in the face of the being he loves best on earth; so, a great portion of the enjoyment of reading, as experienced by a social disposition, depends upon the same impressions being made upon congenial minds at the same time. I have spoken of an interesting book, *well* read, because I think the art of reading aloud is far too rarely cultivated; and I have often been astonished at the deficiency which exists on this point, after what is called a finished education.

To my own feelings, the easy and judicious reading of a well-written book, on a favourite subject, is even more delightful than music; because it supplies the mind with ideas, at the same time that it gratifies the ear and the taste. Little do they know of this pleasure, who pass in and out of a room unnecessarily, or who whisper about their thimble or their thread, while this music of the mind is thrilling the souls of those who understand it; and little do they know of social enjoyment, who prefer poring over the pages of a book alone, rather than allowing others share their pleasure at the same time. I am aware that many books may be well worth reading alone, which are not calculated for general reading; and I am aware also, that every fire-side circle is not capable of appreciating this gratification; but I speak of those which are; and I think that woman, as peculiarly a social being, should be careful to arrange and adjust such affairs, as to create the greatest amount of social pleasure. Of this, however, hereafter.

It is more to my present purpose, to speak of those habits of inattention to which many young persons unscrupulously yield, whenever a book is read aloud. It may be remarked, as a certain proof of their want of interest, when they rise to leave the room, and request the reader *not* to wait for them; for though politeness may require some concession on their part, it is a far higher compliment to the reader, and indeed to the company in general, to evince an interest so great, that rather than lose any part of the book, they will ask, as a personal favour, that the reading of it may be suspended until their return, provided only their absence is brief. I have often felt with sympathy for the reader on these occasions, the disappointment he must experience when assured by one of his audience, that to her at least his efforts to give pleasure, and excite interest, have been in vain.

Beyond this there is a habit of secret inattention, of musing upon other things whenever a book is read aloud, which grows upon the young, until they lose the power to command their attention, even when they would. This, however, I imagine to arise in great measure out of the want of cultivating the art of reading; for the monotonous tone we so frequently hear, the misplaced emphasis, and, worse than all, the affectation of reading well, when the reader and not the book is too evidently intended to be noticed, are of themselves sufficient to repel attention, and to excite a desire to do anything rather than listen.

Truly has it been said, that "the sport of musing is the waste of life," for though occasional seasons of mental retirement are profitable to all, the habit of endless and aimless reverie, which some young persons indulge in, is as destructive to mental energy, as to practical usefulness! Hour after hour glides on with them unmarked, while thought is just kept alive by a current of undefined images flowing through the mind.—And what remains? "A weary, stale, flat, and unprofitable" existence; as burdensome to themselves, as unproductive of good to others.

As a defence against the encroachments of this insidious enemy, it is good to be in earnest about everything we do—earnest in our studies—earnest in our familiar occupations—earnest in our attachments—but above all, earnest in our duties. There is a listless, dreamy, halfish way of acting, which evades the stigma of direct indolence, but which never really accomplishes one laudable purpose. Enthusiasm is the direct opposite of this; but in the safe medium between this extreme and enthusiasm, is that earnestness which I would recommend to all young persons as a habit. Enthusiasm to the mind of youth, is vastly more taking than sober earnestness; yet, when we look to the end, how often do we find that the one is discouraged by difficulties, and finally diverted from its object, where the other perseveres, and ultimately succeeds!

Habitual earnestness is directly opposed to habitual trifling; and this latter may truly be said to be the bane of woman's life. To be in earnest is to go steadily to work with whatever we undertake; counting the cost, and weighing the difficulty, and still engaging in the task, assured that the end to be attained will repay us for every effort we make. To do one thing and think about another, to begin and not go on, to change our plan so often as to defeat our purpose, or to act without having formed a plan at all, this it is to trifle, and consequently to waste both time and effort.

By cultivating habitual earnestness in youth, we acquire the power of bringing all the faculties of the mind to bear upon any given point, whenever we have a purpose to accomplish. We do not then find, at the time we want to act, that attention has gone astray, that resolution cannot be fixed, that fancy has scattered the materials with which we were to work, that taste refuses her sanction, that inclination rebels, or that industry chooses to be otherwise engaged. No; such is the power of habit, that, when accustomed from early youth to be in earnest in whatever we do, no sooner does an opportunity for making any laudable effort occur, than all these faculties and powers are ready at our call; and with their combined and willing aid, how much may be attained either for ourselves or others!

The great enemy we have to encounter, both in the use of the faculty of observation, and in the cultivation of habits of earnestness, is indolence; an enemy which besets our path from infancy to age, which stands in the way of all our best endeavours, and even when a good resolution has been formed, persuades us to delay the execution of it. Could we prevail upon the young to regard this enemy, as it really is, a greedy monster following upon their steps, and ever grasping out of their possession, their time, their talents, and their strength—instead of a pleasant fire-side companion, to be dallied with in their leisure hours—what a service would be done to the whole human race! for, to those who have been the willing slaves of indolence in youth, it will most assuredly become the tyrant of old age.

The season of youth, then, is the time to oppose this enemy with success; and those who have quickened their powers of observation by constant exercise, and applied themselves with habitual earnestness to unremitting efforts of attention and industry, will be in no danger of finding life, as it advances, either uninteresting or wearisome; or their own portion of experience destitute of utility and enjoyment.

CHAP. VI.
BEAUTY, HEALTH, AND TEMPER.

These are personal qualifications universally considered to be of great importance to the female sex; yet is there something sad in the contemplation of the first of these, so great is the disproportion between the estimation in which it is regarded by young people in general, and its real value in the aggregate of human happiness. Indeed, when we think of its frailty, its superficial character, and the certainty of its final and utter extinction; and connect these considerations with the incalculable amount of ambition, envy, and false applause, which beauty has excited—we should rather be inclined to consider it a bane than a blessing to the human race.

Female beauty has ever been the theme of inspiration with poets, and with heroes, since the world began; and for all the sins and the follies, and they are many, for which beauty has formed the excuse, has not man been the abettor, if not the cause? Of his habitual and systematic treachery to his weak sister on this one point, what page—what book shall contain the record? Would that some pen more potent than ever yet was wielded by a human hand, would transcribe the dark history, and present it to his view; for happy, thrice happy will be that era, if it shall ever come, in the existence of woman, when man shall be true to her real interests, and when he shall esteem it his highest privilege to protect her—not from enchanted castles, from jealous rivals, or from personal foes, but from the more insidious and fatal enemies which lurk within her own heart—from vanity, from envy, and from love of admiration.

To prove that I lay no unfounded charge at the door of man in this respect, let us look into society as it is. The beautiful woman! What court is paid to her! What extravagances are uttered and committed by those who compose her circle of admirers! She opens her lips;—men of high intellectual pretensions are proud to listen. Some trifling or vapid remark is all she utters. They applaud, if she attempts to be judicious; they laugh, if she aims at being gay; or they evince the most profound reverence for her sentiments, if the tone of her expression is grave. Listen to the flattery they offer at the shrine of this idol of an hour. No; it is too gross—too absurd for repetition. One thing, however, makes it serious. Such flattery is frequently at the expense of rivals, and even of friends; so that, while these admirers foster vanity, they are not satisfied without awaking the demon of envy in a soul—an immortal soul, which it ought to have been their generous and noble aim to shield from every taint of evil, and especially from so foul a taint as that of envy.

But let us turn to another scene in the drama of society. The very same men are disclaiming their unsuccessful efforts to obtain the favour of this beauty, and ridiculing the emptiness and the folly of the remarks they so lately applauded. Time passes on. The beauty so worshipped begins to wane. Other stars shine forth in the hemisphere, and younger *belles* assert superior claims to admiration. Who, then, remains of all that prostrate circle? Not one! They are all gone over to the junior claimant, and are laughing with her at the disappointment of the faded beauty.

This is a dark and melancholy picture, but for its truth I appeal to any who have mixed much in general society, who have either been beautiful themselves, or the confidants of beauty, or who have been accustomed to hear the remarks of men on these subjects, when no beauty was present. I might appeal also to the fact, that personal beauty amongst women alone, receives no exaggerated or undue homage. Were there no men in the world, female beauty would be valued as a charm, but by no means as one of the highest order; and happily for women, an idea prevails amongst them, that those who want this charm, have the deficiency made up to them in talent, or in some other way.

Still, there is so natural and irresistible a delight in gazing upon beauty, that I never could understand the philosophy of those moralists who would endeavour to keep from a lovely girl, the knowledge that she was so. Her mirror is more faithful, and unless that be destroyed, the danger is, that she will suspect such moral managers of some sinister design in endeavouring to deceive her on this point, and that, in consequence, she will be put upon thinking still more of the value of a gift, with the possession of which she is not to be trusted. Far wiser is the part of that counsellor of youth, who, convinced that much of the danger attendant upon beauty, as a personal recommendation, arises out of low and ignorant views of the value of beauty itself, thus endeavours to show the folly of attaching importance to that which the touch of disease may at any hour destroy, and which time must inevitably efface.

The more the mind is expanded and enlightened, the more it is filled with a sense of what is admirable in the creation at large ; and the more it is impressed with the true image of moral beauty, the less it will be occupied with the consideration of any personal claim to flattery or applause. There will always be a circle of humble candidates for favour surrounding the unguarded steps of youth, whose influence will be excited on the side of personal beauty, perhaps more than in any other way. Without disrespect to the valuable class of servants, to which I allude, for I am convinced they *know not what they do*, I must express my fears, that they are often busily at work upon the young mind, long before the age of womanhood, instilling into it their own low views of beauty as a personal distinction; and it is against this influence, more especially as it begins the earliest, that I would call up all the power of moral and intellectual expansion, in order to fill the mind as early as possible with elevated thoughts of the creation in general, and of admiration for that part of it which is separate from self.

A being thus enlightened, will perceive that admiration is one of the higher faculties of our nature unknown to the brute creation, and one, the lawful exercise of which, affords us perhaps more enjoyment than any other. Upon the right employment of this faculty depends much of the moral tendency of human character. It is, therefore, of the utmost importance that we should learn in early life to admire only what is truly excellent; and as there is an excellence of beauty, which it is consonant with the higher attributes of our nature that we should admire, it necessarily follows, that to search for beauty as an essence pervading the universe, is an employment not unworthy of an intelligent and immortal being.

Let us then examine, so far as we are able to do so, "the treasures of earth, ocean, and air;" and we shall see that it has pleased the all-wise Creator, to diffuse the principle of beauty over every region of the world. The deep sea, into whose mysterious caves no human eye can penetrate is full of it. The blue ether, and the sailing clouds, sun, moon, and stars, are they not beautiful? and the fruitful garden of the earth, wherever nature smiles?

"How beautiful is all this visible world!"

Not beautiful in its brightness and sublimity alone, but beautiful wherever the steps of Deity have trod—wherever the hand of the divine artificer has been employed, from the golden glory of a sunset cloud, to the gossamer thread on which are strung the pearls of morning dew. Now, let me ask whether a mind, habitually engaged in the contemplation of subjects such as these, would be likely to be diverted from its noble but natural exercise, by vulgar calculations upon the comparative beauty of a face? No. It would be perfectly aware, where such beauty did exist; but it would also be impressed with the important fact, that in relation to the wondrous and magnificent whole, its own share of beauty constituted so small a part, as scarcely to be worthy of a passing thought.

Those who are accustomed to enlightened views on this subject, will know also that there are different kinds of personal beauty, amongst which, that of form and colouring holds a very inferior rank. There is a beauty of expression, for instance, of sweetness, of nobility, of intellectual refinement, of feeling, of animation, of meekness, of resignation, and many other kinds of beauty, which may all be allied to the plainest features, and yet may remain, to give pleasure long after the blooming cheek has faded, and silver grey has mingled with the hair. And how far more powerful in their influence upon others, are some of these kinds of beauty! for, after all, beauty depends more upon the movements of the face, than upon the form of the features, when at rest; and thus, a countenance habitually under the influence of amiable feelings acquires a beauty of the highest order, from the frequency with which such feelings are the originating cause of the movements or expressions which stamp their character upon it.

Who has not waited for the first opening of the lips of a celebrated belle, to see whether her claims would be supported by

"The mind, the music breathing from her face;"

and who has not occasionally turned away repelled by the utter blank, or worse than blank, which the simple movement of the mouth, in speaking, or smiling, has revealed?

The language of poetry describes the loud laugh as indicative of the vulgar mind; and certainly there are expressions, conveyed even through the medium of a smile, which need not Lavater to inform us that refinement of feeling, or elevation of soul, have little to do with the fair countenance on which they are impressed. On the other hand, there are plain women sometimes met with in society, every movement of whose features is instinct with intelligence; who, from the genuine heart-warm smiles which play about the mouth, the sweetly modulated voice, and the lighting up of an eye that looks as if it could "comprehend the universe," becomes perfectly beautiful to those who understand them, and still more so to those who live with them, and love them. Before such pretensions to beauty as these, how soon do the pink and white of a merely pretty face vanish into nothing!

Yet, if the beauty of expression should be less popular amongst women, from the circumstance of its being less admired by men than that of mere form and complexion, they do well in this, as in every other disputed question of ultimate good, to look to the end. Men have been found whose admiration of beauty was so great, that they have actually married for that alone, content, for its sake, to dispense with the presence of mind. And what has been the end to them, or rather to the luckless beings whose misfortune it was to be the objects of their choice?— A neglected and degraded lot, imbittered by the fretfulness of disappointment on the part of their husbands; while, on the other hand, women, whose attractions have been of a more intellectual nature, have maintained their hold upon the affections of their companions, through life, even to the unlovely season of old age.

But, in addition to the insufficiency of mere beauty, there is another cause why men are so frequently disappointed in selecting merely pretty wives. They have a habit of supposing that if a woman is pretty, and not very clever, she must be amiable. Yet, how often do we find that the most wayward temper, the most capricious will, and beyond all calculation the most provoking habits, are connected with a weak and unenlightened mind. And added to all this, there is the false position the young beauty has held in society, the flattery to which she has been exposed, the dominion she has been permitted to assert, the triumph she has been accustomed to feel over others, the strength her inclinations from constant indulgence have attained—all these have to be contended with, in addition to the incapacity of her imbecile and undisciplined mind; and surely of this catalogue of evils, any one might be sufficient to counterbalance the advantages of mere personal beauty in a companion for life—a companion who is to tread with her husband the rough road of experience, and whose influence upon his character and feelings will not end on this side the grave.

Let us, however, not think hardly of the feeble-minded beauty, simply as such. She is as little to be blamed for the natural imbecility of her mental powers, as to be commended for her personal charms. Both are to her the appointments of a wise Providence; but as both combined are the means of exposing her to evils for which she is really to be pitied, so she ought to be kindly protected from the dangers to which she is exposed; and since she possesses not in herself sufficient perception to know, that in consequence of her beauty she is made to occupy a false position in society, from which she will assuredly have to descend, it becomes the duty of all who have her happiness at heart, to warn her, that in her intercourse with the world, she must not look for a sincere and disinterested friend in man.

I am far from asserting that there are not instances of noble and generous-hearted men, who know how to be the friend of woman, and the protector of her true interests; yet, such is the general tone of social intercourse, that these instances are lamentably rare.

The most objectionable part, however, of what I would call the minor morals of social life, as regards the subject of female beauty, has not yet been alluded to. Man is sincere in one sense, in his admiration of real beauty while it lasts; and if when the ruling star begins to wane, he suns himself in the rays of another luminary, he is still faithful to beauty as the object of his worship, though the supposed divinity may be invested in a different shrine. If, then, his professions of admiration were offered only to the really beautiful, scarcely one woman in a hundred would be injured by the personal flattery of man. But, unfortunately, that large proportion of the female sex, who are not exactly pretty, nor altogether plain, are exposed to the same system of flattery, for charms which they really do not possess. I have often wondered whether there ever was a woman so destitute of personal attractions, that no man, at some time or other of her life, had ever told her she was beautiful; and it is a well-known fact, that the more we doubt our possession of any particular attraction, the more agreeable is every assurance from others that such attraction does exist.

Thus there is an endless train of mischief let in upon the minds of the young and inexperienced, by what men are accustomed to regard in the light of harmless pleasantry, or as an almost necessary embellishment to polished manners. It may be said, that the plain woman has her glass, to which she can refer for never-failing truth. It is true, she has; but there is a vast difference between looking for what we do not wish to see, and for what we do. Besides which, when a young plain woman first mixes in society, she sees the high distinction which mere beauty obtains for its possessor, and she finds herself comparatively neglected and forgotten. In her home she is doubtless valued in proportion to her merits; but in company, what avail the kind and generous heart which beats within her bosom, the bright intelligence of her mind, the cordial response she would offer in return for kindness, the gratitude, the generous feeling which animate her soul? Who, in all that busy circle, cares to call forth any of these? Nay, so little do all or any of them avail her in society, that she begins in time to suspect she is personally repulsive; and what woman of sensitive or delicate feelings ever conceived this idea of herself, without experiencing, along with it, a strange sense of loneliness and destitution, as if excluded from the fellowship of social kindness—shut out from the pale of the lovely, and the beloved? If, then, the treacherous voice of man but whispers in her ear, that these hard thoughts about herself have no foundation, who can wonder if she is found too ready to "lay the flattering unction" to her heart? or who can wonder if the equanimity of her mind becomes disturbed by a recurrence of those painful doubts, occasionally to be dispelled by a recurrence of that flattery too?

To young women. thus circumstanced, I would affectionately say—Beware! Beware of the unquiet thoughts, the disappointment, the rivalry, the vain competition, the fruitless decoration, and all that train of evils which ensue from vacillating between the two extremes of flattering hopes, and mortified ambition. Go home, then, and consult your mirror; no falsehood will be there. Go home, and find, as you have often done before, that even without beauty, you can make the fire-side circle happy there; nor deem your lot a hard one. From many dangers attendant upon beauty you are safe, from many sorrows you are exempt; above all, should you become a wife, from that which is, perhaps, the greatest calamity in woman's history, the loss of her husband's love, because the charms for which alone he valued her, have vanished. This never can be your experience, and so far you are blest.

If personal beauty be so great a good as men persuade us it is, how important does it become to know that there is no certain way of preserving this treasure, but by a strict regard to health! We hear of the beauty of extreme delicacy, of the beauty of a slight hectic, and sometimes of the beauty of constitutional debility and languor, but who ever ventured to speak of the beauty of disease? And yet, all these, if not treated judiciously, or checked in time, will infallibly become disease. On the other hand, we hear of vulgar health, of an unladylike bloom, and of too much strength, giving an air of independence unbecoming to the female character. Sincerely wishing that all who hold these sentiments may make the best use of the advantages of illness, when it does fall to their lot, we will pass on to consider the advantages of health as one of the greatest of earthly blessings.

Perfect health was the portion of our first parents while Paradise was yet untrodden, save by the steps of sinless men, and angels. Since that time, it has become rarely the experience of any of the human family to be altogether exempt from disease ; yet, so much are the sufferings of illness mitigated by the skill of modern science, and the comforts of civilized life, that a slight degree of bodily indisposition is looked upon as an evil scarcely worth the pains which any systematic means of remedy would require.

It is only when health is lost, and lost beyond the hope of regaining it, that we become sensible of its real value. It is then we tax the ingenuity of the physician, and the patience of the nurse, to bring us back, if only so near as to stand upon the verge of that region of happiness from which we are expelled. It is then we see the folly of those who play upon the brink of the precipice which separates this beautiful and blessed region from the troubled waters below. It is then we resign our wealth, our friends, our country, and our home, in the hope of purchasing this treasure. It is then we feel that, although, when in the possession of health, we neglected many opportunities of kindness, benevolence, and general usefulness, yet when deprived of this blessing, we would kneel at the footstool of mercy, to ask those opportunities again, in order that we may use them better.

In early youth, however, little of this knowledge can be experimentally acquired. Little does the pampered child of fond and indulgent parents know what illness is to the poor and the destitute; or what it may be to her when her mother's hand is cold and helpless in the tomb, and when her own head is no longer sheltered by a father's roof. Thus we find young girls so often practising a certain kind of recklessness, and contempt of health, nay, even encouraging, I will not say affecting, a degree of delicacy, feebleness, and liability to bodily ailments, which, if they were not accustomed to the kindest attentions, would be the last calamity they would wish to bring upon themselves. How important is it for such individuals to remember, that the constitution of the body, as well as that of the mind, is, in a good degree, of their own forming;

that the season of youth is the time when the seeds of disease are most generally sown; and that no one thus circumstanced, can suffer a loss of health without inflicting the penalty of anxious solicitude, and, frequently, of unremitting personal exertion, upon those by whom she is surrounded, or beloved.

Fanciful and ill-disciplined young women are apt to think it gives them an attractive air, and looks like an absence of selfishness, to be indifferent about the preservation of their health; and thus they indulge the most absurd capriciousness with respect to their diet, sometimes refusing altogether to eat at proper times, and eating most improperly; at others, running about upon wet grass with thin shoes, as if they really wished to take cold, making no difference between their summer and their winter clothing, or casting off a warm dress for an evening party; refusing to take medicine when necessary, or taking it unsanctioned by their parents, or their best advisers; all these they appear to consider as most engaging features in the female character. But there are those who could tell them such conduct is, in reality, the most consummate selfishness, because it inevitably produces the effect of making them the objects of much necessary attention, and of inflicting an endless catalogue of troubles and anxieties upon their friends. How soon does the stern discipline of life inflict its own punishment for this folly! but, unfortunately, not soon enough, in all instances, to stop the progress of the host of maladies which are thus produced.

Let it not for a moment be supposed, that I would recommend to young women over solicitude on the score of health; for, I believe nothing is more likely than this to induce real or fancied indisposition. Neither would I presume to interfere with the proper province of the physician; yet am I strongly disposed to think, that if the rules I am about to lay down were faithfully adhered to, that worthy and important personage would much less frequently be found beside the couch where the bloom of youthful beauty wastes away.

My first rule is, to let one hour every day, generally two, and sometimes three, be spent in taking exercise in the open air, either on horseback, or on foot. Let no weather prevent this; for, with strong boots, waterproof cloak, and umbrella, there are few situations where an hour's walk, at some time or other of the day, may not be accomplished; and when the air is damp, there is sometimes more need for exercise, than when it is dry. I am perfectly aware of the unpleasantness of all this, unless when regarded as a duty; I am aware, too, that where the health is good, it appears, at times, a work of supererogation; but I am aware, also, of the difference there is in the state both of mind and body, between sitting in the house, or by the fire all day, and taking, during some part of it, a brisk and healthy walk.

How often have I seen a restless, weary, discontented being, moving from chair to chair, finding comfort in none, and tired of every employment; with contracted and uneasy brow, complexion dry and grey, and eyes that looked as if their very vision was scorched up. How often have I seen such a being come in from a winter's walk, with the countenance of a perfect Hebe, with the energy of an invigorated mind beaming forth from his eyes as beautiful as clear, and with the benevolence of a young warm heart reflected in the dimpling freshness of a sunny smile. How pleasant is it then to resume the half-finished work—how refreshing the social meal—how inviting the seat beside the glowing hearth—how frank and free the intercourse with those who form the circle there! And if such be the effect of one single walk, how beneficial must be that of habitual exercise, upon the condition both of mind and body!

Were it possible for human calculation to sum up all the evils resulting from want of exercise, the catalogue would be too appalling. All those disorders which in common parlance, and for want of a more definite and scientific name, are called bilious—and, truly, their name is legion—are mainly to be attributed to this cause. All head-aches, want of appetite, pains under the shoulders, side-ache, cold feet, and irregular circulation, provided there is no positive disease, might, in time, be remedied by systematic attention to exercise. Of its effect upon the temper, and the general tone of the mind, we have yet to speak; but certain I am, that no actual calamity inflicted upon woman, ever brought with it more severe or extended sufferings, than those which result from the habitual neglect of exercise.

My next rule is—to retire early to rest. Wherever I meet with a pale, melancholy young woman, highly nervous, easily excited, unequal in her temper; in the early part of the day languid, listless, discontented, and fit for nothing; but when evening comes on, disposed for conversation, brisk and lively; I feel morally certain, that such a one is in the habit of sitting up late—perhaps of making herself extremely interesting to her friends beside the midnight fire; but I know also, that such a one is eminently in danger of having recourse to stimulants to keep up the activity of her mind; and that during more than half her life—during the morning, that most valuable portion of every day—she is of little value to society; and well will it be for her friends and near connexions, if her listlessness and discontent do not render her companionship worse than valueless to them.

My next rule is to eat regularly, so far as it can be done conveniently to others—at regular times, and in regular quantities; and this I believe to be of more consequence than to be very particular about the nature of the food partaken of, provided only it is simple and nutritious. I know that with a sickly appetite, or where the constitution is under the influence of disease, it is impossible to do this; but much may be done while in a state of health, by striving against that capricious abstinence from food, especially in the early part of the day, which by certain individuals is thought rather lady-like and becoming. I doubt not but this may be the case, so far as it is becoming to look pale, and lady-like to be the object of attention—to be pleaded with by kind friends, and pitied by strangers: but the wisdom and the utility of this system is what I am not the less disposed to call in question.

It is a great evil in society, that the necessary act of eating is looked upon too much as a luxury, and an indulgence. If we regarded it more as a simple act, the frequent recurrence of which was rendered necessary by the absolute wants of the body, we should be more disposed to consider the proper regulation of this act, as a duty within our power to neglect or attend to. We should consequently think little of each particular portion of food set before us, and the business of eating would then be despatched as a regular habit, attention to which could afford no very high degree of excitement or felicity, while at the same time it could not be neglected without serious injury.

My next rule is, to dress according to the season ; a rule so simple and so obvious in its relation to health, as to need no comment.

Thus far my remarks have applied only to the subject of health, where it is enjoyed. The loss of health is a theme of far deeper interest, as it separates us from many of the enjoyments of this world, and brings us nearer to the borders of the world which is to come.

It is a remarkable feature in connexion with the constitution constitution of woman, that she is capable of enduring, with patience and fortitude, far beyond that of the stronger sex, almost every degree of bodily suffering. It is true, that she is more accustomed to such suffering than man; it is true also that a slight degree of indisposition makes less difference in her amusements and occupations than in his. Still there is a strength and a beauty in her character, when labouring under bodily affliction, of which the heroism and fiction affords but a feeble imitation. Wherever woman is the most flattered, courted and indulged, she is the least admirable; but in seasons of trial her highest excellences shine forth; and how encouraging is the reflection to the occupant of a sick chamber, that while the busy circles, in which she was wont to move, close up her vacant place, and pursue their cheerful rounds as gaily as when she was there—that while excluded from participation in the merry laugh, the social meeting, and the cordial intercourse of former friends, she is not excluded from more intimate communion with those who still remain; that she can still exercise a moral and religious influence over them, and deepen the impression of her affectionate and earnest counsel, by exhibiting the Christian graces of patience under suffering, and resignation to the will of God.

Yes, there are many enjoyments in the chamber of sickness—enjoyments derived from the absence of temptation, from proofs: of disinterested affection, and from the unspeakable privilege of having the vanity of earthly things, and the realities of the eternal world, brought near, and kept continually in view. How are we then made acquainted with the hollowness of mere profession! How much that appeared to us plausible and attractive when we mingled in society, is now stripped of its false colouring, and rendered repulsive and odious! while, on the other hand, how much that was lightly esteemed by the world in which, we moved, is discovered to be worthy of our admiration and esteem! How much of human love, where we most calculated upon finding it, has escaped from our hold! but then, how much is left to succour and console us, from those upon whose kindness we feel to have but little claim!

Experience is often said to be the only true teacher; but illness often crowds an age of experience into the compass of a few short days. Often while engaged in the active avocations of life, involved in its contending interests, and led captive by its allurements, we wish in vain that a just balance could be maintained between the value of the things of time and of eternity. It is the greatest privilege of illness, that, if rightly regarded, it adjusts this balance, and keeps it true. From the bed of sickness, we look back upon the business, which, a short time ago, absorbed our very being. What is it then? A mere struggle for the food and clothing of a body about to mingle with the dust. We look back at the pleasures we have left. What are they? The sport of truant children, when they should have been learning to be wise and good, We look back upon the objects which engaged our affections. How is it? Have the stars all vanished from our heaven? Have the flowers all faded from our earth? How can it be? Alas! our affections have been misplaced. We have not loved supremely only what was lovely in the sight of God: and merciful, most merciful is the warning voice, not yet too late, to tell us that He who formed the human heart, has an unquestionable right to claim his own.

I am not one of those who would speak of religion as especially calculated for the chamber of sickness, and the bed of death; because I believe it is equally important to choose religion as our portion in illness, as in health—in the bloom of youth, as on the border of the grave. I believe also, that in reality, that being is in as awful a condition, who lives on from day to day in the possession of all temporal blessings, without religion, as he who pines upon a bed of suffering, without it. But if the necessity of religion be the same, its consolations are far more powerfully felt, when deprived by sickness of every other stay; and often do the darkened chamber, and the weary couch, display such evidence of the power and the condescension of Divine love, that even the stranger acknowledges it is better to go to the house of mourning, than of feasting.

It is when the feeble step has trod for the last time upon nature's verdant carpet, when the dim eye has looked its last upon the green earth and sunny sky, when the weary body has almost ached and pined its last, when human skill can do no more, and kindness has offered its last relief—it is then, that we see the perfect adaptation of the promises of the gospel to feeble nature's utmost need; and while we contemplate the depths of the Redeemer's love, and hear in anticipation the welcome of angels to the pardoned sinner, and see upon his faded lips the smile of everlasting peace, we look from that solemn scene once more into the world, and wonder at the madness and the folly of its infatuated slaves.

All these are privileges, if only to feel them as a mere spectator; and never ought such scenes to be avoided on account of the painful sympathy which the sight of human suffering naturally occasions. Young people are apt to think it is not their business to wait upon the sick, that their seniors are better fitted for such service, that they shall make some serious mistake, or create some inconvenience by their want of knowledge; or at all events, they hold themselves excused. Yet is there many a sweet young girl, who, in consequence of family affliction, becomes initiated in these deep mysteries of Christian charity, before her willing step has lost the playful elasticity of childhood; and never did the maturer virtues of the female character appear less lovely from such precocious exercise. I should rather say, there was a tenderness of feeling, and a power of sympathy derived from early acquaintance with human suffering, which remains with woman till the end of life, and constitutes alike the charm of youth, and the attraction of old age.

I have dwelt long upon the privileges of illness, both to the sufferer and her friends, because I believe that all which is noble, and sweet, and patient, and disinterested in woman's nature, is often thus called forth; as well as all that is most encouraging in the exemplification of the Christian character. But I must again advert to

"Woman in our hours of ease;"

and here I am sorry to say, we sometimes find a fretfulness and petulence under the infliction of slight bodily ailments, which are as much at variance with the moral dignity of woman, as opposed to her religious influence. The root of the evil, however, lies not so often in her impatience, as in a deeper secret of her nature. It lies most frequently in what I am compelled to acknowledge as the besetting sin of woman—her desire to be an object of attention. From this desire, how many little coughs, slight headaches, sudden pains, attacks of faintness, and symptoms of feebleness are complained of, which, if alone, or in the company of those whose attentions are not agreeable, would scarcely occupy a thought. Yet it is astonishing how such habits gain ground, and remain with those who have indulged them in youth, long after such complaints have ceased to call forth a single kind attention, or to engage a single patient ear.

Youth is the only time to prevent this habit fixing itself upon the character; and it might be a wholesome truth for all women to bear in mind, that although politeness may sometimes compel their friends to appear to listen, nothing is really so wearisome to others, as frequent and detailed accounts of our own little ailments. It is good, therefore whenever temptations arise to make these trifling grievances the subject of complaint, to think of the poor, and the really afflicted. It is good to visit them also, so far as it may be suitable in their seasons of trial, in order that we may go home, ashamed before our families, and ashamed in the sight of God, that our comparatively slight trials should excite a single murmuring thought.

Besides, if there were no other check upon these habitual complainers, surely the cheerfulness of home might have some effect; for who can be happy seated beside a companion who is always in "excruciating pain," or who fancies herself so? There are, besides, many alleviations to temporary suffering, which it is not only lawful, but expedient to adopt. Many interesting books may be read, many pleasant kinds of work may be done, during a season of slight indisposition; while on the other hand, every little pain is made worse by dwelling upon it, and especially by doing nothing else.

The next consideration which occurs in connexion with these views of health, is that of temper; and few young persons, I believe, are aware how much the one is dependent upon the other. Want of exercise, indigestion, and many other causes originating in the state of the body, have a powerful effect in destroying the sweetness of the temper; while habitual exercise, regular diet, and occasional change of air, are amongst the most certain means of restoring the temper from any temporary derangement.

Still, there are constitutional tendencies of mind, as well as body, which seriously affect the temper, and which remain with us to the end of life, as our blessing, or our bane; just in proportion as they are overruled by our own watchfulness and care, operating in connexion with the work of religion in the heart.

It would require volumes, rather than pages, to give any distinct analysis of temper, so various are the characteristics it assumes, so vast its influence upon social and domestic happiness. We will, therefore, in the present instance, confine our attention to a few important facts, in connexion with this subject, which it is of the utmost consequence that the young should bear in mind.

In the first place, ill-temper should always be regarded as a disease, both in ourselves and others; and as such, instead of either irritating or increasing it, we should rather endeavour to subdue the symptoms of the disease by the most careful and unremitting efforts. A bad temper, although the most pitiable of all infirmities, from the misery it entails upon its possessor, is almost invariably opposed by harshness, severity, or contempt. It is true, that all symptoms of disease exhibited by a bad temper, have a strong tendency to call forth the same in ourselves; but this arises in great measure from not looking at the case as it really is. If a friend or a relative, for instance, is afflicted with the gout, how carefully do we walk past his footstool, how tenderly do we remove everything which can increase his pain, how softly do we touch the affected part. And why should we not exercise the same kind feeling towards a brother or a sister afflicted with a bad temper, which of all human maladies is unquestionably the greatest?

I know it is difficult—nay, almost impossible, to practise this forbearance towards a bad temper, when not allied to a generous heart—when no atonement is afterwards offered for the pain which has been given, and when no evidence exists of the offender being so much as conscious of deserving blame. But when concession is made, when tears of penitence are wept, and when, in moments of returning confidence, that luckless tendency of temper is candidly confessed, and sincerely bewailed; when all the different acts committed under its influence, are acknowledged to have been wrong, how complete ought to be the reconciliation thus begun, and how zealous our endeavours for the future to avert the consequences of this sad calamity! Indeed, if those who are not equally tempted to the sins of temper, and who think and speak harshly of us for such transgressions, could know the agony they entail upon those who commit them—the yearning of an affectionate heart towards a friend thus estranged—the humiliation of a proud spirit after having thus exposed its weakness—the bitter reflection, that not one of all those burning words we uttered can ever be recalled—that they have eaten like a canker into some old attachment, and stamped with ingratitude the aching brow, whose fever is already almost more than it can bear. Oh! could our calm-tempered friends become acquainted with all this—with the tears and the prayers to which the overburdened soul gives vent, when no eye seeth its affliction, surely they would pity our infirmity; and not only pity, but assist.

These, however, are amongst the deep things of human experience, never to be clearly revealed, or fully understood, until that day when the secrets of all hearts shall be laid open. It is perhaps more to our present purpose, to consider what is the effect upon others, of encouraging wrong tempers in ourselves. Young people are apt to think what they do. of little importance, because they are perhaps the youngest in the family, or at least too young to have any influence. They should remember, that no one is too young to be disagreeable, nor too insignificant to annoy. A fretful child may disturb the peace of a whole household, and an ill-tempered young woman carries about with her an atmosphere of repulsion wherever she goes. The moment she enters a room, where a social circle are enjoying themselves, conversation either ceases or drags on heavily, as if a stranger or an enemy were near; and kindly thoughts, which the moment before would have found frank and free expression, are suppressed, from the instinctive feeling that she can take no part in them. Each one of the company, in short, feels the worse for her presence, a sense of contraction seizes every heart, a cloud falls upon every countenance; and so powerful are the sympathies of our nature, and so rapidly does that which is evil extend its contaminating influence, that all this will sometimes be experienced, when not a word has been spoken by the victim of ill-temper.

It is easy to perceive when most young women are out of temper, even without the interchange of words. The pouting lip, the door shut with violence, the thread suddenly snapped, the work twitched aside or thrown down, are indications of the real state of the mind, at least as unwise, as they are unlovely. Others who are not guilty of these absurdities, will render themselves still more annoying, by a captiousness of conduct, most difficult to bear with any moderate degree of patience ; by conversing only upon humiliating or unpleasant subjects, complaining incessantly about grievances which all have equally to bear, prolonging disputes about the merest trifles beyond all bounds of reason and propriety; and by finally concluding with a direct reproach for some offence which had far better have been spoken of candidly at first.

But there would be no end to the task of tracing out the symptoms of this malady. Suffice it that a naturally bad temper, or even a moderate one badly disciplined, is the greatest enemy to the happiness of a family which can be admitted beneath any respectable roof—the greatest hinderance to social intercourse—the most fatal barrier against moral and religious improvement.

Like all other evils incident to man, a bad temper, if long encouraged, and thoroughly rooted in the constitution, becomes in time impossible to be eradicated. In youth it is comparatively easy to stem the rising tide of sullenness, petulance, or passion; but when the tide has been allowed to gain ground so as to break down every barrier, until its desolating waters habitually overflow the soul, no human power can drive them back, or restore the beauty, freshness, and fertility which once existed there.

No longer, then, let inexperienced youth believe this tide of evil can be stayed at will. The maniac may say, "I am now calm, I will injure you no more:" yet, the frenzied fit will come to-morrow, when he will turn again and rend you. In the same way, the victim of ungoverned temper may even beg forgiveness for the past, and promise, with the best intentions, to offend no more ; but how shall a daughter in her mood of kindness heal the wound her temper has inflicted on a mother's heart, or convince her parent it will be the last? How shall the woman, whose temper has made desolate her household hearth, win back the peace and confidence she has destroyed? How shall the wife, though she would give all her bridal jewels for that purpose, restore the links her temper has rudely snapped asunder in the chain of conjugal affection?

No, there are no other means than those adopted and pursued in youth, by which to overcome this foe to temporal and eternal happiness. Nor let the task appear too difficult. There is one curious fact in connection with the subject, which it may be encouraging to my young friends to remember. Strangers never provoke us—at least, not in any degree proportionate to the provocations of our near and familiar connections. They may annoy us by their folly, or stay too long when they call, or call at inconvenient times; but how sweetly do we smile at all their remarks, how patiently do we bear all their allusions, compared with those of our own family circle. The fact is, they have less power over us, and for this reason, because they do not know us so well. Half the provocations we experience from common conversation, and more than half the point of every bitter taunt, arise out of some intended or imagined allusion to what has been known or supposed of us before. If a parent speaks harshly to us in years of maturity, we think he assumes too much the authority which governed our childhood; if a brother would correct our folly, we are piqued and mortified to think how often he must have seen it; if a sister blames us for any trifling error, we know what her condemnation of our whole conduct must be, if all our faults are blamed in the same proportion. Thus it is that our near connections have a hold upon us, which strangers cannot have ; for, besides the cases in which the offence is merely imagined, there are but too many in which past folly or transgression is made the subject of present reproach. And thus the evil grows, as year after year is added to the catalogue of the past, until our nearest connections have need of the utmost forbearance to avoid touching upon any tender or forbidden point.

Now, it is evident that youth must be comparatively exempt from this real or imaginary source of pain; just in proportion as the past is of less importance to them, and as fewer allusions can be made to the follies or the errors of their former lives. Thus the season of youth has greatly the advantage over that of maturer age, in cultivating that evenness of temper which enables its possessor to pass pleasantly along the stream of life, without unnecessarily ruffling its own course, or that of others. The next point we have to take into account in the right government of temper, is the important truth, that habitual cheerfulness is a duty we owe to our friends and to society. We all have our little troubles, if we choose to brood over them, and even youth is not exempt; but the habit is easily acquired of setting them aside for the sake of others, of evincing a willingness to join in general conversation, to smile at what is generally entertaining, and even to seek out subjects for remark which are likely to interest and please. We have no more right to inflict our moodiness upon our friends, than we have to wear in their presence our soiled or cast-off clothes; and, certainly, the latter is the least insulting and disgraceful of the two.   A cheerful temper—not occasionally, but habitually cheerful—is a quality which no wise man would be willing to dispense with in choosing a wife. It is like a good fire in winter, diffusive and genial in its influence, and always approached with a confidence that it will comfort, and do us good. Attention to health is one great means of maintaining this excellence unimpaired, and attention to household affairs is another. The state of body which women call bilious, is most inimical to habitual cheerfulness; and that which girls call having nothing to do, but which I should call idleness, is equally so. In a former part of this chapter, I have strongly recommended exercise as the first rule for preserving health; but there is an exercise in domestic usefulness, which, without superseding that in the open air, is highly beneficial to the health, both of mind and body, inasmuch as it adds to other benefits, the happiest of all sensations, that of having rendered some assistance, or done some good.

How the daughters of England—those who have but few servants, or, perhaps, only one—can sit in their father's homes with folded hands, when any great domestic movement is going on, and not endeavour to assist, is a mystery I have tried in vain to solve; especially when, by so doing, they become habitually listless, weary, and unhappy; and when, on the other hand, the prompt and willing domestic assistant is almost invariably distinguished by the characteristics of energy and cheerfulness. Let me entreat my young readers, if they ever feel a tendency to causeless melancholy, if they are afflicted with cold feet and headache, but, above all, with impatience and irritability, so that they can scarcely make a pleasant reply when spoken to, let me entreat them to make trial of the system I am recommending; not simply to run into the kitchen and trifle with the servants, but to set about doing something that will add to the general comfort of the family, and that will, at the same time, relieve some member of that family of a portion of daily toil.

I fear it is a very unromantic conclusion to come to, but my firm conviction is, that half the miseries of young women, and half their ill-tempers, might be avoided by habits of domestic activity; because (I repeat the fact again) there is no sensation more cheering and delightful, than the conviction of having been useful; and I have gene- rally found young people particularly susceptible of this pleasure.

A willing temper, then, is the great thing to be attained; a temper that does not object, that does not resist, that does not hold itself excused. A temper subdued to an habitual acquiescence with duty, is the only temper worth calling good; and this may be the portion of all who desire so great a blessing, who seek it in youth, and who adopt the only means of making it their own— watchfulness and prayer.

I have said nothing of the operation of love, as it relates to the subject of this chapter ; but it must be understood to be pre-eminently the life-spring of our best endeavours in the regulation both of health and temper, since none can fail in the slightest degree in either of these points, without materially affecting the happiness of others.

CHAP. VII.
SOCIETY, FASHION, AND LOVE OF DISTINCTION.

Society is often to the daughters of a family, what business or a profession is to the sons; at least so far as regards the importance attached to it, and the opportunity it affords of failure or success. Society! what a capacious and dignified idea this word presents to the girl just entering upon womanhood! What a field for action and sensation! What an arena for the display of all her accomplishments! How much that is now done, thought, and uttered, has society fox its object! How much is left undone, for the sake of society! But let us pause a moment, and ask what society is. Is it a community of tried and trusted friends, united together by the ties of perfect love? Listen to the remarks of those, even of your own family, who return from the evening party, or the morning call. Is it a community of beings with whom mind is all in all, and intellectual improvement the purpose for which they meet? Observe the preparations that are made—the dress, the furniture, the food, the expense that is lavished upon these. Is it a community who even love to meet, and who really enjoy the social hours they spend together? Ask them in what mood or temper they enter upon the fatigues of the evening, or how often they wish that some event would occur to render their presence unnecessary.

There is, however, one class of beings, who generally go into society with no want of inclination, but who rather esteem no trouble too great which is the means of bringing them in contact with it, or which enables them to pass with credit the ordeal which society presents. This class of beings consists of young women who have not had experience enough to know what society really is, or what is the place assigned to them by the unanimous opinion of society, in the circles with which they exchange visits. What an event to them is an evening party! One would think each of the young aspirants to distinction expected to be the centre of a circle, so intense is the interest exhibited by every act of preparation. The consequence of all this, is a more than ordinary degree of causeless depression on the following day, or else an equal degree of causeless elevation, arising perhaps out of some foolish attention, or flattering remark, which has been repeated to half the ladies in the room.

Of all the passions which take possession of the female breast, a passion for society is one of the most inimical to domestic enjoyment. Yet, how often does this exist in connection with an amiable exterior! It is not easy to say, whether we ought most to pity or to blame a woman who lives for society—a woman who reserves all her good spirits, all her becoming dresses, her animated looks, her interesting conversation, her bland behaviour, her smiles, her forbearance, her gentleness for society—what imposition does she practise upon those who meet her there! Follow the same individual home, she is impatient, fretful, sullen, weary, oppressed with headache, uninterested in all that passes around her, and dreaming only of the last evening's excitement, or of what may constitute the amusement of the next; while the mortification of her friends at home, is increased by the contrast her behaviour exhibits in the two different situations, and her expenditure upon comparative strangers, of feelings to which they consider themselves as having a natural and inalienable right. As a cure for this passion, I would propose a few remarks, founded both on observation and experience. In the first place, then, we seldom find that society affords us more pleasing or instructive intercourse than awaits us at home; and as to kindly feeling towards ourselves, if not excited in our nearest connections, how can we expect it from those who know us less, without having practised upon them some deception?

In the next place, we ought never to forget our own extreme insignificance in society. Indeed, it may be taken as a rule with young people in ordinary cases, that one-half of of the persons they meet with in society are not aware of their having been present, nor even conscious of the fact of to their existence; that another half of the remaining number have seen them without any favourable impression; that another half of those who still remain, have seen them with rather unfavourable feelings than otherwise; while, of those who remain beyond these, the affectionate feelings, indulgence, and cordial interest, can be as nothing, compared with what they might enjoy at home.

"How can this be?" exclaims the young visitor, "when so many persons look pleased to see me, when so many invitations are sent me, when some persons pay me such flattering compliments, and others appear so decidedly struck with my appearance?" I should be truly sorry to do anything to cool down the natural warmth and confidence of youth; but, in such cases, my rule for judging is a very simple one, depending upon the result of the following inquiries:— What is the proportion of persons you have noticed in the same company? What is the proportion of those by whom you have felt yourself repelled? What is the proportion of those *you* have really admired? and the proportion of those to whom *you* have been attracted by sympathy, or affection? Ask yourselves these questions, and remember, that whatever may be the flattering aspect of society, you nave no right to expect to receive, in admiration, or good-will, more than you give.

There is another class of young women, who appear to think the only reason for their being invited into society, is, that another place may be occupied, another chair filled, and another knife and fork employed; for as to any effort they make in return for the compliment of inviting them, they might, to all intents and purposes, have been at home. Now, where persons cannot, or dare not, converse—or where that which alone deserves the name of conversation is not suited to the habits or the ways of thinking of those who have been at the trouble of inviting guests—I am a great advocate for cheerful, easy, social chat; provided only, it gives place the instant that something better worth listening to is commenced. That all ingenuous, warm-hearted, unaffected young women, can chat, and some of them very pleasantly too, witness their moments of unrestrained confidence in the company of their friends. There is, then, no excuse for those who go into company, and return from it, without having contributed in any way to the enjoyment of the party they had been invited to meet.

All young persons, however insignificant, must occasionally meet the eye of the mistress of the house where they are visiting, and then is the time to say something expressive of interest in her, or her's; such as inquiring for some absent member of the family; or, at any rate, proving in some way or other, that she and her household have interests with which you are not wholly unacquainted.

One of the most genuine, and at the same time one of the most pleasing compliments ever paid, is that of proving to those we visit, or receive as visitors, that we have been previously aware of their existence. There are many delicate ways of doing this; and while it injures no one, it seldom fails to afford a certain degree of gratification. Social chat, is that which sets people at liberty to talk on their favourite subjects, whatever they may be. In society, too, we meet with a large proportion of persons, who want listeners; and the young, who cannot be supposed to have amassed so large a sum of information as others, ought to consider themselves as peculiarly called upon to fill this respectable department in society, remembering at the same time, that the office of a good listener can never be that of a perfectly silent one. There must be occasionally an animated and intelligent response, intervals of attentive and patient hearing, with a succession of questions, earnestly, but modestly put, and arising naturally out of the subject, to render the part of the listener of any value in general conversation. The vapid response effectually repels; the flat and Uninterested expression of countenance soon wearies; and the question not adapted to the subject cuts short the narration.

Let me not, however, be understood to recommend the mere affectation of interest, or attention; though perfectly aware that such affectation is the current coin, by which the good-will of society is generally purchased. My view of the case is this—that the absence of vanity and selfishness in our own feelings, and benevolence towards others, will induce a real interest in everything which concerns them, at least, so far as it may occupy the conversation of an evening; and are we not as much bound in duty to be social, frank, and talkative to little-minded and common-place persons, provided they have been at the pains to invite and to entertain us, as if they were more intellectual, or more distinguished. Besides, how often do we find in conversation with such persons, that they are able to give us much useful information, which individuals of a higher grade of intellect would never have condescended to give; and, after all, there is a vast sum of practical and moral good effected by persons of this description, whose unvarnished details of common things afford us clearer views of right and wrong, than more elaborate statements.

I have said, already, that the indulgence of mere chat should never be carried too far. In the society of intelligent and enlightened men, nothing can be more at variance with good taste, than for women to occupy the attention of the company with their own little affairs; but especially when serious conversation is carried on, no woman of right feeling would wish to interrupt it with that which is less important. Nor ought this humble substitute for conversation, which I have recommended to those who cannot do better, or appreciate what is higher, on any occasion to be considered as the chief end at which to aim in society. Women possess pre-eminently the power of conversing well, if this power is rightly improved and exercised; but as this subject is one which occupies so large a portion of a previous work,[1] I will only add, that my opinion remains the same as therein expressed, that the talent of conversation is one which it is woman's especial duty to cultivate, because the duties of conversation are amongst those for which she is peculiarly responsible.

When we think of what society might be to the young, and to the old, it becomes a painful task to speak to the in- experienced, the trusting, and the ardent, of what it is. When we think of the seasons of mental and spiritual refreshment, which might thus be enjoyed, the interchange of mutual trust and kindness, the awakening of new ideas, the correction of old ones, the sweeping away of prejudice, and the establishment of truth, the general enlargement of thought, the extension of benevolence, and the increase of sympathy, confidence, and good faith, which might thus be Drought about amongst the families of mankind; we long to send forth the young and the joyous spirit, buoyant with the energies of untried life, and warm with the generous flow of unchecked feeling, to exercise each growing faculty, and prove each genuine impulse, upon the fair and flowery field which society throws open, alike for action, for feeling, and for thought.

But, alas! such is society as it now exists, that no mother venturing upon this experiment, would receive back to the peaceful nest the wing so lately fledged unruffled by its flight, the snowy breast unstained, or the beating heart as true as when it first went forth, elated with the glowing hope of finding in society what it never yet was rich enough to yield.

An old and long-established charge is brought against society for its flattery and its falsehood, and we go on from year to year complaining in the same strain; those who have expected most, and have been the most deceived, complaining in the bitterest terms. But, suppose the daughters of England should now determine that they would bring about a reformation in society, how easily would this be done! for, whether they know it or not, they have the social morals of their country in their power. If the excellent, but humble maxim, 'Let each one mend one,' were acted up to in this case, we should have no room left to find fault with others, for all would be too busily and too well occupied in examining their own motives, and regulating their own conduct, to make any calculations upon what might be done or left undone by others. In the first place, each young woman acting upon this rule, would live for home, trusting that society would take care of its own interests. She would, however, enter into it as a social duty, rather than a personal gratification, and she would do this with kind and generous feelings, determined to think the best she could of her fellow-creatures, and where she could not understand their motives, to give them credit for good ones. She would mix with society, not for the purpose of shining before others, but of adding her share to the general enjoyment; she would consider every one whom she met there, as having equal claims upon her attentions; but her sympathies would be especially called forth by the diffident, the unattractive, or the neglected. Above all, she would remember that for the opportunities thus afforded her, of doing or receiving good, she would have to render an account as a Christian, and a woman; that for every wrong feeling not studiously checked, for every falsehood however trifling or calculated to please, for every moral truth kept back or disguised for want of moral courage to divulge it, for every uncharitable insinuation, for every idle or amusing jest at the expense of religious principle, and for every chance omitted of supporting the cause of virtue however unpopular, or discountenancing vice, however well received, her situation was that of a responsible being, of whom an account of all the good capable of being derived from opportunities like these, would be required.   Need we question for a moment whether such are the feelings, and such the resolutions, of those who enter into society in general. We doubt not but some are thus influenced, and that they have their reward; but with others, old associations and old habits are strong, and they think that one can do nothing against the many; and thus they wait, and wish things were otherwise, but never set about the reformation themselves. Yet, surely these are times for renovated effort on the part of women, to whom the interests of society belong; for let men rule, as they unquestionably have a right to do, in the senate, the camp, and the court; it is women whose sentiments and feelings give tone to society, and society which in its turn influences the sentiments and feelings of mankind. Each generation, as it arises, matures, and consolidates into another series of social intercourse, bears the impress which society has stamped upon the last; and so powerful is the influence thus derived, that the laws of a nation would be useless in defence of virtue, if the voice of society was raised against it.

How often has the tender and anxious mother had to deplore this influence upon the minds of her children! Until they mingled with society, they were respectful, attentive, and obedient to her injunctions, confiding implicitly in the rectitude and the reasonableness of her requirements. But society soon taught them that the views of their parents were unenlightened, old-fashioned, or absurd; that even the motives for enforcing them might not be altogether pure; and that none who mixed in good society, ought to submit to regulations so childish and humiliating.

If, then, such be the influence of society, how important is it that so powerful an agent should be engaged on the side of virtue and of truth. And that it already is so in many most important cases, I acknowledge, to the honour of my country, believing that the general tone of society is highly favourable to that high moral standard, for which England is pre-eminent over every nation of the world. I allude particularly to the preservation of the character of woman from the slightest taint. The rules, or rather the opinions of society, as to what is correct or incorrect in female conduct, extending down to the most minute points of behaviour, are sometimes considered to be too strict, and even rebelled against by high-spirited ignorant young women as being too severe. But let no one, in her blindness or temerity, venture upon the slightest transgression of these rules, because in her young wisdom she sees no cause for their existence. Society has good reasons for planting this friendly hedge beside the path of woman, and the day will come when she will be thankful—truly thankful that her own conduct, even in minute and apparently trifling matters, was not left in early life to the decision of her own judgment, or the guidance of her own will.

It ought rather to be the pride of every English woman, that such are the conditions of society in her native land, that whether motherless or undisciplined in her domestic lot, she cannot become a member of good society, or at least retain her place there, without submitting to restrictions; which, while they deprive her of no real gratification, are at once the safeguard of her peace, the support of her moral dignity, and the protection of her influence as a sister, a wife, a mother, and a friend.

Let us then be thankful to society for the good it has done, and is doing, to thousands who have perhaps no watchful eye at home, no warning voice to tell them how far to. go, and when to go no farther. Nor can we for a moment hesitate to yield our assent to these restrictions imposed upon our sex, when we look at the high moral standing of the women of England, and think how much the tone of society has to do with the maintenance of their true interests. Let us not, however, stop here. If there is so much that is good in society, why should there not be more? Why should there still remain the trifling, the slander, the envy, the low suspicion, the falsehood, the flattery, which ruffle and disfigure the surface of society, and render it too much like a treacherous ocean, on which no well-wisher to the young would desire to trust an untried bark.

A feeling of moral dignity taken with us into society, would be a great preservative against much of this; because it would lift us out of the littleness of low observations, and petty cavillings about dress and manners. A spirit of love would do more, extending through all the different channels of forbearance, benevolence, and mutual trust. But a Christian spirit would do still more; because it would embrace the whole law of love, at the same time that it would impress the seal of truth upon all we might venture to say or do. Thus might a great moral reformation be effected, and effected by the young—by young women too, and effected without presumption, and without display; for the humble and unobtrusive working out of these principles, would be as much at variance with ostentation, as they would be favourable to the cultivation of all that is estimable in the female character, both at home and abroad.

One of the greatest drawbacks to the good influence of society, is the almost unrivalled power of fashion upon the female mind. Wherever civilized society exists, fashion exercises her all-pervading influence. All stoop to it, more or less, and appear to esteem it a merit to do so; while a really fashionable woman, though both reprobated and ridiculed, has an influence in society which is little less than absolute. Yet, if we would choose out the most worthless, the most contemptible, and the least efficient of moral agents, it would be the slave of fashion.

Say the best we can of fashion, it is only an imaginary or conventional rule, by which a certain degree of order and uniformity is maintained; while the successive and frequent variations in this rule, are considered to be the means of keeping in constant exercise our arts and manufactures. I am not political economist enough to know whether the same happy results might not be brought about by purer motives, and nobler means; but it has always appeared to me one of the greatest of existing absurdities, that a whole community of people, differing in complexion, form, and feature, as widely as the same species can diner, should not only desire to wear precisely the same kind of dress, but should often labour, strive, and struggle, deceive, envy, and cheat, and spend their own substance, and often more than they can lawfully call their own—to do what? To obtain a dress, which to them is most unbecoming, or an article of furniture wholly unsuited to themselves and their establishment.

My own idea, and I believe it is founded upon a long-cherished, and perhaps too ardent admiration of personal beauty, is, that fashion ought to favour all which is most becoming. It is true, we should at first be greatly at a loss to know what was becoming, because we should have the power and the prejudice of fashion to contend with; but there can be no doubt that individual, as well as public taste, would be improved by such exercise, and that our manufactures would in the end be equally benefited, though for some time it might be difficult to calculate upon the probable demand. Nor can I think that female vanity would be more encouraged than it now is, by thus consulting personal and relative fitness; because the young woman who now goes into company fashionably disfigured, believes herself to be quite as beautiful as if she was really so. Neither can I see that we are not bound to study how to make the best of our appearance, for the sake of our friends, as well as how to make the best of our manners, our furniture, and our food.

Fashion, however, never takes this into account. According to her arbitrary law, the woman of sallow complexion must wear the same colour as the Hebe; the contracted or misshapen forehead must be laid as bare as that which displays the fairest page of beauty; the form with square and awkward shoulders must wear the same costume as that which boasts the contour of the Graces; and, oh! most pitiful of all, old age must be "pranked up" in the light drapery, the flowers, and gauds of youth! In addition to all this, each one, as an indispensable requisite, must possess a waist considerably below the dimensions which are consistent either with symmetry or health.

It will be an auspicious era in the experience of the daughters of England, when they shall be convinced, that the Grecians had a higher standard of taste in female beauty, than that of the shopkeepers and dressmakers of London. They will then be willing to believe, that to be with- in the exact rule of proportion, is as important a deviation from perfect beauty, as to be beyond it; and that nothing which destroys the grace of easy and natural movement, which deprives any bodily function of its necessary exercise, which robs the youthful cheek of its bloom, or, in short, which ungratefully throws back from our possession the invaluable blessing of health, can be consistent with the good taste or right feeling of an amiable, intelligent, or rational woman. These remarks are applicable, in their fullest force, to every deviation which is sanctioned by fashion, from the strict and holy law of modesty and decorum. And of this most injurious tendency of fashion, how insidious is every encroachment, yet how certain its effect upon the female mind! It is no uncommon thing to hear women express the utmost abhorrence of the costume of some old portrait, who, in the course of a few years, perhaps months, are induced by fashion to adopt, with unblushing satisfaction, an equally, or more objectionable dress. The young girl cannot too scrupulously shroud her modest feelings from the unsparing test of fashion. The bloom of modesty is soon rubbed off by vulgar contact; but what is thus lost to the young female can never be restored. And let her look to the risk she incurs. What is it? On the one hand, to be thought a little less fashionable than her friends and neighbours?on the other, to be thought a little more exposed than a delicate woman ought to be. Is there any comparison between the two? Or is there one of the daughters of England, who would not rather be known to choose the former?   If possessed of any genuine feeling on these important points, a young woman will know by a kind of instinct, that a bare shoulder protruding into sight, is neither a delicate nor a lovely object; that a dress, either so made, or so put on, as not to look secure and neat, is, to say the least of it, in bad taste; and that the highest standard at which a rightly-minded woman can aim with regard to dress, is, that it should be becoming, and not conspicuous. In order to secure this last point of excellence, it is unquestionably necessary to conform in some measure to the fashion of the times in which we live, and the circle of society in which we move; yet, surely this may be done to an extent sufficient to avoid the charge of singularity, without the sacrifice either of modesty or good taste.

Whatever may be the beneficial influence of fashion upon the interests of the country at large, its effects upon individual happiness are injurious in proportion to their extent; and in what region of the world, or amongst what grade of humanity, has not this idol of the gilded shrine, this divinity of lace and ribbons, not wielded the sceptre of a sovereign, and asserted her dominion over mankind? All bow before her, though many of her subjects disclaim her title, and profess to despise her authority. Nor is her territory less extensive, because her empire is one of trifles. From the ermine of the monarch, to the sandal of the clown; from the bishop's lawn, to the itinerant's cravat; from the hero's mantle, to the mechanic's apron; it is fashion alone which regulates the form, the quality, and the cost.

Fashion is unjustly spoken of as presiding only in the festive dance, the lighted hall, the crowded court. Would that her influence were confined to these alone! but, alas! we find her in the most sedate assemblies, cooling down each tint of colouring that else might glow too warmly, smoothing off excrescences, and rounding angles to one general uniformity of shape and tone. Her task, however, is but a short one here, and she passes on through all the busy haunts of life, neglecting neither high nor low, nor rich nor poor, until she enters the very sanctuary, and bows before the altar, not only walking with the multitude who keep holy day, but bending in sable sorrow over the last and dearest friend committed to the tomb. Yes, there is something monstrous in the thought, that we cannot weep for the dead, but fashion must disguise our grief; and that we cannot stand before the altar, and pronounce that solemn vow, which the deep heart of woman alone can fully comprehend, but fashion must be especially consulted there.

Yet worse even than all this, is the influence which our love of fashion has upon our servants, and upon the poor. Every Christian woman sees and deplores the evil, and many wholesome restrictions are laid upon poor girls, in their attendance at Sunday-schools, and other establishments for their instruction; but are not the plans most frequently adopted for the correction of this evil, like telling little children at table that good things are not safe for them, yet eating them ourselves, and making much of them too, as if they were the greatest treat.

Christians, I believe, will find they have much to give up yet, before the cause of Christ will prosper as they wish it in our native land. Never will the young servant cease to walk the streets with pride and satisfaction, in the exhibition of her newly purchased and fashionable attire, so long as she sees the young ladies in the family she serves, make it their greatest object to be fashionably dressed. They may say, and with some justice, that she has no right to regulate her conduct by their rule; they may reason with, and even reprove her too; but neither reasoning nor reproof will have the power to correct, so long as example weighs down the opposite scale. The vanity, the weakness of woman is the same in the kitchen as in the drawing-room; and if fashion is omnipotent in one, we can not expect it to be powerless in the other.

The question then has come to this—shall we continue to compete with our servants in dress, now that excess has become an evil; or shall we endeavour, for their sakes well as our own, to compete with them in self-denial, and in courage to do right? How can we pause—how can we hesitate in such a choice? Our decision once made on this important point, we shall soon find that fashion has been with us, as well as with them, a hard mistress. Yes, fashion, has often demanded of us the only sum of money we had been able to lay by for the needy poor; while with them it has wrung the father's scanty pittance from his hand, to supply the daughter with the trappings of her own disgrace. Fashion with us has often set on fire the flame of envy, and imbittered the shafts of ridicule; while with them it has been a fruitful source of deceit, dishonesty, and crime. Fashion with us has often broken old connexions, made us ashamed of valuable friends, and proud of those whose friendship was our bane; while with them it has been the means of introducing the young and the unwary to the companionship of the treacherous and the depraved. I have said, that fashion is a hard mistress: when we contemplate some scenes exhibited, not to the eye of the stranger, but within the circle of private families in this prosperous and enlightened country, we are often led to doubt, whether its boasted happiness is really so universal as patriot poets and patriot orators would teach us to believe. There is a state of things existing behind the scenes in many English homes, an under-current beneath the fair surface of domestic peace, to which belong some of the most pressing anxieties, the darkest forebodings, and the bitterest reflections of which the human mind is capable, and all arising out of the great national evil of competing with our neighbours in the luxuries and elegances of life, so as to be living constantly up to the extent of our pecuniary means, and too frequently beyond them.   It is not likely that young women should understand this evil in its full extent, or be aware of the many sad consequences resulting from it, but they do understand that it is not necessity, nor comfort, nor yet respectability, which makes them press upon their parents the often-repeated demand for money, where there is none to spare. No; it is fashion, the tyrant-mistress upon whose service they have entered, who calls upon them to be dressed in the appointed livery of all her slaves; and thus they wring a father's heart with sorrow, perhaps deprive him of the necessary comforts of old age; or they send away unpaid a poor and honest tradesman, because they cannot, "absolutely cannot," appear in company with an unfashionable dress.

Now, does it never occur to the amiable, and the affectionate, that a particular colour or form of dress is hardly worth a parent's heart-ache? I know it does; and they feel sorry sometimes to be thus the cause of what they would persuade themselves was unnecessary pain. But fashion is a cruel, as well as a hard mistress; and she tells them that, despite the remonstrances of parental love, despite the legal claims of those whose need is greater than their own, despite the stain upon their father's house and name, if found unable to discharge his lawful debts, her rule is absolute, and she must be obeyed. Yes, I know it does come home to the hearts of the feeling and the kind, to make these frequent and these urgent applications, where they know that the pecuniary means of the family are small; and sometimes they do try to go forth into company again, with a dress not cut according to the newest mode. But fashion is revengeful, as she is cruel; and she turns upon them with the ridicule of gayer friends, and asks whether the garb they wear was the costume of the ark; and, instantly, all that is noble, and generous, and disinterested in their nature, sinks, and they become subject, perhaps, to as much real suffering for the time, as if they had destroyed a mother's peace, or involved a father in pecuniary difficulty.

But let them not be discouraged at thus being deprived for an instant of moral dignity, and moral power. The better feelings of their nature will rally, the vitality of higher principles will revive, if they will but make a stand against the enemy; or, rather, if they will but reflect, that fashion, under whose tyranny they are quailing, is, in reality, an enemy, and not a friend. She is an enemy, because she has incited them to much evil, and to no good. She is an enemy, because when they sink into poverty or distress, led on by her instigation, she immediately forsakes, and leaves them to their fate. Fashion never yet was on the side of suffering, of sorrow, or of want. Her favourite subjects are the successful, the arrogant, the vain-glorious; the objects of her contempt are the humble, the afflicted, and the poor.

Let the young, then, bear about with them the remembrance of this fact, that there are strong influences which obtain even in good society, hut which are not really to be weighed in the balance against the minutest fraction of Christian duty; and that fashion, although approved, and even courted by all classes and denominations of mankind, and present, by general invitation, at all places of public resort, even on occasions the most sacred and solemn, so far from having part or lot in any thing pertaining to religion, can only display the symbols of her triumph in the house of prayer, as a badge of human weakness, and a proof that our follies and infirmities are with us even there.

Beyond the love of fashion, which is common to all classes of society, there sometimes exists in the female breast a passion of a deeper and still more dangerous nature, which society has a powerful tendency to call forth; I mean the love of distinction. In man, this passion is ambition. In woman, it is a selfish desire to stand apart from the many; to be something of, and by, herself; to enjoy what she does enjoy, and to appropriate the tribute which society offers her, distinct from the sisterhood to which she belongs. Of such women it may truly be said, "they have their reward."

The first and most frequent aim to which this passion directs itself, is to be the idol of society; which is synonymous with being the butt of ridicule, and the mock of envy, to all who witness her pretensions, especially to all who have failed in the same career. No sooner does a woman begin to feel herself the idol of society, than she finds around her daily path innumerable temptations, of which she had never dreamed before. Her exalted position is maintained, not by the universal suffrage of her friends for at least one half of them would pluck her down if they were able; but by the indefatigable exercise of her ingenuity in the way of evading, stooping, conciliating, and sometimes deceiving; as well as by a continued series of efforts to be cheerful when depressed, witty when absolutely dull, and animated, brilliant, and amusing, when disappointed, weary, or distressed.

When we think that all this must be gone through, evening after evening, in the same company, as well as amongst strangers, and without excitement as well as with, in order to prevent the title of the occupant of that distinguished place from being disputed, we are led to exclaim, that the miner, the convict, and the slave have an easier and a happier lot than her's. Nor is this all. The very eminence on which she stands, renders all her faults and failures so much the more conspicuous; while it enables every stander-by to test the validity of her pretensions, and to triumph over every flaw.

What a situation for a woman!—for a young, affectionate, trusting, and simple-hearted woman! No, never yet was simplicity of heart allied to ambition. And the woman who aspires to be the idol of society, must be satisfied to give up this fair handmaid from her train—this pearl from her coronet—this white rose from her wreath. When a woman's simplicity of heart is gone, she is no longer safe as a friend, faithful as a sister, or tender and true as a wife. But as a mother! nature revolts from the thought, that infant weakness should be cradled in the bosom whose simplicity is gone.

Another form which the love of distinction assumes, is that of singularity. I have already said much on the subject of good taste, to show that it holds an important place amongst the excellencies of woman, so much so, as almost to supply the want of judgment, where that quality is deficient. Nothing, however, can more effectually prove the absence of good taste in women, than to be singular by design. Many are so constituted as to be unavoidably singular; but even this is only reconciled by their friends on the ground that they would lose much in originality and strength of character, by studying to be more like the generality of women.

One of the most wholesome and effectual checks upon this juvenile and ill-judged desire to be singular, might be derived from the fact, that singularity in woman invariably excites remarks, that such remarks almost as invariably degenerate into scandal, and that scandal always destroys good influence. However innocent a woman may be, how much soever she may desire to be useful to others, the fact of her being the subject of scandal effectually destroys her power; for no one likes to be dictated to by a person of whom strange things are spoken; and the agent of Christian benevolence is airways less efficient, for being generally considered odd. Still, if the world would pause here, all might be well. But our oddities, while they provoke the laughter of the gay, seem unaccountably to have the effect of awakening the anger of the grave; so that we not unfrequently find persons more severely reflected upon for comparatively innocent peculiarities, than for acts of real culpability.

A repetition of such reflections and injurious remarks passing through society, upon the principle of a snow-ball over a drifted plain, obtains in time a sort of bad name, or questionable character, for the individual against whom they are directed, which no explanation can do anything to clear away; because founded on facts of so singular a nature, that few people understand how, in the common course of things, they could have happened, and consequently few have charity enough to believe they could originate in anything but evil. It is thus that the character of woman so often suffers unjustly from her oddities. Strangers cannot understand why we acted as we did, enemies suggest a bad motive as the most probable, gossips take up the scandal, and friends in their turn believe it true; while we, surprised and indignant that so innocent a mode of action should bear so injurious a construction, are unable to defend it, simply because it was out of the ordinary pale of human conduct, though prompted by the same motives which influence the rest of mankind.

It may justly be said of the world, that in one sense it is a cruel censor of woman; but in another it is kind. It is, as I have just described, unjustly severe upon individual singularity; but by its harsh and ready censures, how many does it deter from entering upon the same course of folly, so sure to end in wounded feeling, if not in loss of influence and respectability.
Let it then, be kept in mind, that woman, if she would preserve her peace, her safe footing in society, her influence, and her unblemished purity, must avoid remark as an individual, at least in public. The piquant amusements of home, consist much in the display of originality of character, and there it is safe. There her feelings are understood, her motives are trusted to, because they have been long known, and there the brooding wing of parental love is, ever ready to shroud her peculiarities, from too dangerous an exposure. In the world it is not so. Society is very false to us in this respect. For the sake of an evening's, entertainment, singularity is encouraged and drawn out. The mistress of the house, who wishes only to see her party amused, feels no scruple in placing this temptation, before unguarded youth. But let not the ready laugh, the gay response, the flattering attention, for a moment deceive, you as to the real state of the case. It is "seeming all," and those who have been the most amused by your singularities, will not be the last to make them the subject of bitter and injurious remark. If these observations upon society should appear to any, cynical or severe, or calculated to depress the natural ardour of youth, rather than direct it into safer and more wholesome channels; it must be remembered, that my design throughout this work, is to speak of the world as it is, not merely as it ought to be; and though I know there are circles of society, where aims, and motives, and laws of union exist, of a far higher order than to admit of the falsehood or the littleness to which I have alluded; yet such, it must be acknowledged, is the general tone of ordinary visiting or mixing in company, that the follies of

unguarded youth meet with little candour, and still less kind correction, even amongst those who are associated with us as friends. I know that the voice of experience is an unwelcome one, when thus lifted up against that of the world, which speaks so smoothly in its first intercourse with the young and inexperienced; and far more delightful would it be, to send forth the joyous spirit into social life with all its native energies unchecked. There is one grateful and welcome thought, however, which reconciles the task I have imposed upon myself. It is, that none of these energies need therefore be destroyed, or deprived of natural and invigorating exercise. There are home-societies, and little chosen circles of tried and trusted friends; meetings, perhaps, but rarely occurring, or only accidental, amongst those who speak with different voices the warm familiar language of one heart; and here it is that the genuine feelings of unsophisticated nature may safely be poured forth; here it is that youth may live, and breathe, and be itself, alike without affectation, and without reserve; here it is, that the spirit of joy may bound and revel unrestrained, because all around it is the atmosphere of love, and the clear bright radiance of the sunshine of truth.   There is yet another flight of female ambition, another course which the love of distinction is apt to take, more productive of folly, and of disappointment, perhaps, than all the rest. It is the ambition of the female author who writes for fame. Could those young aspirants know how little real dignity there is. connected with the *trade* of authorship, their harps, would be exchanged for distaffs, their rose-tinted paper would be converted into ashes, and their Parnassus would dwindle to a molehill.

Still there is something which the young heart feels in being shut out from intellectual sympathies at home—something in burning and throbbing with unexpressed sensations, until their very weight and intensity become a burden not to be endured; something in the strong impulse of a social temperament, which longs to pour forth its testimony to the force of nature and of truth; something in those mysterious, but deep convictions, which belong to every child of earth, that somewhere on this peopled globe, beneath the glow of sunnier skies; or on the frozen plain, the desert, or the ocean; amidst the bowers- of beauty, or the halls of pride; within the hermit's cave, the woodman's cot, or wandering with the flocks upon the distant hills; there is—there must be, some human or spiritual intelligence, whose imaginations, powers, and feelings, operate in concert with our own. And thus we feel, and thus we write in youth, without any higher motive, because within our homes, tracing our daily walks, or mixing with the circle called society, we find no, chord of sympathy which answers to the natural music of our secret souls.

All this, however, is but juvenile romance. The same want of sympathy which so often inspires the first effort of female authorship, might often find a sweet and abundant interchange of kindness in many a faithful heart beside the homely hearth. And after all, there is more true poetry in the fire-side affections of early life, than in all, those sympathetic associations with unknown and untried developments of mind, which ever have existed either amongst the sons or the daughters of men.

Taking a more sober view of the case, there are, unquestionably, subjects of deep interest with which women have opportunities peculiar to themselves of becoming acquainted, and thus of benefiting their fellow-creatures through the medium of their writings. But, after all, literature is not the natural channel for a woman's feelings; and pity, not envy, ought to be the meed of her who writes for the public. How much of what with other women is reserved for the select and chosen intercourse of affection, with her must be laid bare to the coarse cavillings, and coarser commendations, of amateur or professional critics. How much of what no woman loves to say, except to the listening ear of domestic affection, by her must be told—nay, blazoned to the world. And then, in her seasons of depression, or of wounded feeling, when her spirit yearns to sit in solitude, or even in darkness, so that it may be still; to know and feel that the very essence of that spirit, now embodied in a palpable form, has become an article of sale and bargain, tossed over from the hands of one workman to another, free alike to the touch of the prince and the peasant, and no longer to be reclaimed at will by the original possessor, let the world receive it as it may.

Is such, I ask, an enviable distinction? I will offer no remarks of my own upon the unsatisfactory nature of literary fame. No man, or woman either, could write for the public, and not feel thankful for public approbation; thankful for having chosen a subject generally interesting to mankind, and thankful that their, own sentiments had met with sympathy from those for whose sake they had been expressed. But, on this subject, I will quote the eloquent language of one,[2] who better knew what contradictory elements exist in a young, an ardent, and an affectionate heart, combined with an aspiring and commanding intellect.

"What is fame to woman, but a dazzling degradation. She is exposed to the pitiless gaze of admiration; but little respect, and no love, blends with it. However much as an individual she may have gained in name, in rank, in fortune, she has suffered as a woman. In the history of letters, she may be associated with men, but her own sweet life is lost; and though, in reality, she may flow through the ocean of the world, maintaining an unsullied current, she is nevertheless apparently absorbed, and become one with the elements of tumult and distraction. She is a reed shaken with the wind; a splendid exotic, nurtured for display; an ornament, only to be worn on birth-nights and festivities; the aloe, whose blossom is deemed fabulous, because few can be said to behold it; she is the Hebrew, whose songs are demanded in a 'strange land;' Ruth, standing amid the 'alien corn;' a flower, plunged beneath a petrifying spring; her affections are the dew that society exhales, but gives not back to her in rain; she is a jewelled captive, bright, and desolate, and sad !"

↑ The Women of England.
↑ Miss Jewsbury.

CHAP. VIII.
GRATITUDE AND AFFECTION.

As one who has been conducting an inexperienced traveller through an enemy's country, joyfully enters with him upon the territory of a well-known and familiar friend; so the writer, whose stern duty it has been to disclose the dangers and deceitfulness of the world to the unpractised eye of youth, delights to open to it that page of human life, which develops all that is most congenial to unsophisticated nature. And can anything be more so to woman, than gratitude and affection? How much of her experience—of the deepest well-springs of her feeling—of those joys peculiar to herself, and with which no stranger can intermeddle—are embodied in these two words!

If our sense of obligation in general bears any proportion to our need of kindness, then has woman, above all created beings, the greatest cause for gratitude. The spirit of man, even in early life, bears a widely different impress from that of woman. The high-spirited and reckless boy flings from him half the little grievances which hang about the girl, and check her infant playfulness, sending her home to tell her tale of sorrow, or to weep away her griefs upon her mother's bosom. There is scarcely a more affecting sight presented by the varied scenes of human life, than a motherless or neglected little girl; yet so strong is the feeling her situation inspires, that happily few are thus circumstanced, without some one being found to care for, and protect them. It is true, the lot of woman has trials enough peculiar to itself and the look of premature sedateness and anxiety, which sometimes hangs upon the brow of the little girl, might seem to be the shadowing forth of some vague apprehensions as to the nature of her future destiny. These trials, however, seldom arise out of unkindness or neglect in her childhood. The voice of humanity would be raised against such treatment; for what living creature is so helpless and inoffensive as a little girl? The voice of humanity, therefore, almost universally speaks kindly to her in early life. The father folds her tenderly in his arms, toils for her subsistence and comfort, and watches over her expanding beauty, that he may shield it from all blight. The mother's heart yearns fondly as she, too, watches with more intense anxiety, lest a shadow should fall, or a rude wind should blow, upon her opening flower. Thus, while the sons in a family may, perhaps, call forth more of the pride and the ambition of their parents, the daughters claim almost all the tenderness, and more than an equal portion of watchfulness and care.

And can the object of so much solicitude be otherwise than grateful? Oh, no. It may be more consonant with the nature and with the avocations of man, that he should go forth into the world forgetful of these things; but woman in the quiet brooding of her secret thoughts—can she forget, how, in the days of helpless infancy, she was accustomed toescape from the rude gaze, or harsh rebuke, to find a never-failing refuge on her father's knee; how every wish and want was whispered to her mother's ear, which never turned away; how all things appropriated to her use, were studiously made so safe, so easy, so suited to her taste—her couch of rest, her favourite meal, her fairy-world of toys—all these arranged according to her fancy, or her good; until, all helpless, and feeble, and dependant as she was, no fear could break the charm of her security, nor sorrow, save what originated in her own bosom, could cast a shadow over the fire-side pleasures of her sunny home.

"No; woman is not—cannot be ungrateful," exclaim a thousand sweet voices at once! Gratitude forms a part of her nature, and without it she would be unworthy of a name amongst her sex! I freely grant that gratitude is a part of her nature, because there can be no generous or noble character, where gratitude is wanting. But I am not so sure that it is always directed to proper objects.

Young women are almost always grateful for the notice of ladies of distinction; they are grateful for being taken out in carriages, when they have none at home; they are grateful for presents of ornaments, or articles of fashionable clothing which they cannot afford to buy; they are grateful for being invited out to pleasant parties; and, indeed, for what may they not be said to be grateful—extremely grateful; but especially so, for acts of kindness from strangers, or from persons occupying a higher station than themselves.

There is a familiar saying, that charity begins at home; and if by home is meant the circle immediately surrounding ourselves, surely gratitude ought also most especially to begin at home, and for this simple reason—strangers may know, or imagine us to have great merits; but with our demerits, or perhaps I ought rather to say, with that part of our character which comes under the head of disagreeableness, they must necessarily be unacquainted, because no one chooses to be disagreeable to strangers. Against them, too, we have never offended, either by word or act, so that they can have nothing to forgive. But it is not so at home. All our evil tempers and dispositions have been exhibited there, and consequently the kindness received at home is the more generous. There is no one member of the family circle against whom we have not, at one time or another, offended, and consequently we owe them a double share of gratitude, for having kindly overlooked the past, and for receiving us as cordially to their favour as if we had never cost them an uneasy thought. It is nothing in comparison, to win the good-will of strangers. The bare thought of how soon that good-will might be withdrawn, did they know us better, is sufficient of itself to pain a generous mind. But it is much to continue daily and hourly to receive the kind attentions, the forbearance and the love of those who know our meanest faults, who see us as we really are, who have borne with us in all our different moods for months and years, whom our unkindness could not estrange, whom our indifference could not alienate, whom our unworthiness could not repel—it is, indeed, much to be still followed by their affection, to be protected by their anxious care, and to be supported by their unremitting industry and toil. Yes, and there may come a day when the young in their turn will feel

"How sharper than a serpent's tooth it is
To have a thankless child:"

when they will see the smile of gratitude which ought to be their own, worn only for strangers, they will think then of the days of unmurmuring labour—the nights of untiring watchfulness—the ages of thought and feeling they have lived through, and would willingly experience again—the suffering and the shame they would endure if that were necessary, for the sake of the beloved of their souls; and they will wonder—for to blame, they will scarce know how—why nature should have left the heart of their child so void, that for all they have so lavishly bestowed they should receive nothing in return.

If gratitude were looked upon more than it is, as a distinct duty—a debt to be discharged without involving any other payment, I am inclined to think its claims would be more frequently attended to, than they now are. But few young persons are in the habit of sufficiently separating gratitude from admiration, and thus they hold themselves above being grateful in due proportion, to the aged, the unenlightened, or the insignificant; because they do not often feel disposed to offer to such persons the tribute of their praise. Perhaps they are a little ashamed to have owed anything to so inferior a source; while, on the other hand, they are but too proud to acknowledge that they are deeply indebted to those whom they admire.

Now, it is against such encroachments of vanity and selfishness, that the amiable and the high-principled are perpetually on their guard. That gratitude will not grow up with us without culture, is sufficiently evident from the indifference with which all young children treat the donors of their little gifts; receiving them rather as their right, than as a favour. It is, therefore, an excellent habit, for young people, to bear perpetually in mind a sort of memorial, or catalogue, of the names of those by whom every article of their own personal property was given, so that even the most insignificant individual to whom they have been thus indebted, may not be forgotten.

"I am naturally," says a celebrated German writer, "as little inclined to gratitude as any one; and it would even be easy for the lively sense of a present dissatisfaction to lead me first to forget a benefit, and next to ingratitude. In order to avoid falling into this error, I early accustomed myself to take pleasure in reckoning up all I possessed, and ascertaining by whose means I acquired it. I think on the persons to whom I am indebted for the different articles in my collections; I reflect on the circumstances, chances, and most remote causes, owing to which I have obtained the various things I prize, in order to pay my tribute of gratitude to whomsoever it is owing. All that surrounds me is thus animated in my sight, and becomes connected with affectionate remembrances. It is with still greater pleasure that I dwell on the objects, the possession of which does not fall within the dominion of the senses; such as the sentiments I have imbibed, and the instruction I have received. Thus my present existence is exalted and enriched by the memory of the past; my imagination recalls to my heart the authors of the good I enjoy; a sweet reminiscence attends the recollection, and I am rendered incapable of ingratitude."

How beautiful is the simplicity of this confession, from one whose mind was capacious beyond the ordinary extent of man's understanding, and to whose genius the literary and the distinguished of all nations were proud to offer the tribute of their praise. How completely does this passage prove to us, that he who knew so many of the secrets of human nature, knew also that it is not possible to begin too humbly with the exercise of gratitude. The nurse who bore the burden of our childhood, the old servant fallen into poverty and want, the neighbouring cottager who used to let us share her orchard's scanty produce, the poor relations who took us to their lowly home when rich ones were less kind, the maiden aunt who patiently instructed us in all her curious arts, the bachelor uncle who kindly permitted us to derange the order of his house, above all, the venerable grandfather, and his aged helpmate, who used to tell us of the good old ways, and warn us against breaking down the ancient landmarks—all these are pleasant household memories, which ought to cling about the heart until they grow into our very being, and become identified with the elements of thought, and feeling, which constitute our life. There is in fact a species of cruelty, as well as injustice, in disentangling the memory from these early associations. To have received our very nature, our principles, the bias of our sentiments, all that which is understood by distinctiveness of character, from the hands of these old friends, and not to look back and acknowledge it with thankfulness, though the casual notice of a passing stranger furnishes food for gratitude—the fact is scarcely to be thought of, still less believed; and we look to the daughters of England to show us that they know better how to bestow their gratitude.

When the nature of gratitude is considered in its proper light, as a debt which we have contracted, and which consequently must be discharged, we see at once that the merit or demerit of the individual to whom we owe this debt, has nothing whatever to do with our payment of it. A generous mind would perhaps feel more bound to discharge it to an unworthy object, simply because where respect or love was wanting, grateful feeling would be all that could with propriety be offered. But, as in all such cases, the debt, though just, must still be painful and humiliating, it is of the utmost importance, both to young and old, that they should be careful never to be the willing recipients of obligations from persons whom they neither love nor esteem. The young need great watchfulness in this respect, and sometimes, from their over-willingness to incur obligations, involve themselves in connections and associations highly disadvantageous.

It is an excellent plan for young women, always to put this question to themselves before they accept an offered kindness. "Is the person who offers it, one whom I should like to feel indebted to? or am I prepared to make all the return of gratitude to that person, which would, under similar circumstances, be due to the most praiseworthy and distinguished individual of my acquaintance?" If the answer be in the negative, nothing but a meanness of spirit, of which I cannot believe the daughters of England to be capable, could lead to the acceptance of such an obligation.

In this, therefore, as well as in all other cases, it is of the utmost importance that gratitude should be considered as a distinct feeling, in no way involving any other. It sometimes happens, however, and especially during the present rapid march of intellect, that the junior members of a family are far in advance of their parents in the cultivation of their intellectual powers, and this difference occasionally leads to a want of respect towards the heads of the family, which is alike distressing and disgraceful. On the other hand, there are young women—and happy would it be for our nation, if all the daughters of England were such—who, remembering that their parents, however humble and unenlightened, are their parents still; that by their self-denial, and their toil, and as the highest proof of their regard, they have received the education which makes them so much to differ, make it their constant study to offer to them tokens of respect and regard of such a nature as not to draw forth their intellectual deficiences, but to place them on the higher ground of moral excellence. How beautiful, how touching is the solicitude of such young persons, to guard the venerated brow from shame; and to sacrifice even something of the display of their own endowments, rather than outshine those, who, with all their deficiences, still were the oracles of their infant years; and who unquestionably did more during the season of childhood, towards the formation of their real character, than has since been done by the merely intellectual discipline of schools. Yes, we may owe our grammar, our geography, our music, and our painting, to what are called the instructors of our youth; but the seeds of moral character are sown by those who surround us in infancy; and how much soever we may despise the hand by which that seed is scattered, the bias of our moral being is derived from that agent more than from any other.

How just then, and how true is that development of youthful gratitude which looks back to these early days, and seeks to return into the bosom of parental love, the treasures of that harvest which parental love has sown!

And it is meet that youth should do this—youth, whose very nature it is to be redundant with the rills of life, and fruitful in joy, and redolent in bloom, from the perpetual flowing forth of its own glad waters—youth, which is so rich in all that gladdens, and exhilarates; how can it be penurious and niggardly in giving out? No, nature has been so munificent to youth, it cannot yet have learned the art of grudging; and gratitude, the most liberal, the most blessed of all human feelings, was first required of us as a debt, that we might go on paying according to our measure, through all the different stages of existence; and though we may never have had money or rich gifts, the poorest amongst us has been able to pay in kindness, and sometimes in love.

In the cultivation and exercise of the benevolent feelings of our nature, there is this beautiful feature to be observed in the order of divine providence—that expenditure never exhausts. Thus the indulgence of gratitude, and the bestowment of affection, instead of impoverishing, render more rich the fountain whence both are derived; while, on the other hand, the habit of withholding our generous affections, produces the certain effect of checking their growth, and diminishing the spontaneous effusion of kindness.

The habit of encouraging feelings of gratitude towards our fellow-creatures, of recalling their friendly and benevolent offices towards ourselves, of thinking what would have been our situation without them, and, in short, of reckoning up the items of the great debt we all have incurred, especially in infancy and youth, has a most beneficial effect upon the mind, in the bias it gives towards the feeling and expression of gratitude in general, not only as confined to the intercourse of social life, or the interchange of kindness amongst our fellow-creatures; but with regard to the higher obligations of gratitude, which every child of sin and sorrow must feel, on being admitted to participation in the promises of the gospel, and the glorious hopes which the gospel was sent to inspire.

I have said, that women, above all created beings, have cause for gratitude. Deprived of the benefits of the Christian dispensation, woman has ever been, and will be ever the most abject, and the most degraded of creatures, oppressed in proportion to her weakness, and miserable in proportion to her capability of suffering. Yet, under the Christian dispensation, she who was the first in sin, is raised to an equality with man, and made his fellow-heir in the blessings of eternal life. Nor is this all, A dispensation which had permitted her merely to creep, and grovel through this life, so as to purchase by her patient sufferings a title to the next, would have been unworthy of that law of love by which pardon was offered to a guilty world. In accordance with the ineffable beneficence of this law, woman was therefore raised to a moral, as well as a spiritual equality with man; and from being first his tempter, and then his slave, she has become his helpmate, his counsellor, his friend, the object of his most affectionate solicitude, the sharer of his dignity, and the partaker in his highest enjoyments.

When we compare the situation of woman, too, in our privileged land, with what it is even now in countries where the Christian religion less universally prevails, we cannot help exclaiming, that of all women upon earth, those who live under the salutary influence of British laws and British institutions, have the deepest cause for gratitude. And can the daughters of Britain be regardless of these considerations? Will they not rather study how to pay back to their country, in the cultivation and exercise of their best feelings, the innumerable advantages they are thus deriving. And what is the sacrifice? Oh! blessed dispensation of love—that we are never so happy as when feeling grateful; and never so well employed, as when acting upon this feeling !

While, then, they begin first by retracing all the little rills of kindness by which their cup of benefit has been filled, let them not pause in thought, until they have counted up every item of that vast catalogue of blessings which extend from human instrumentality, to divine; nor let them pause in action, until they have rendered every return which it is possible for a finite being, aided by watchfulness and prayer, to make.

What a subject for contemplation does this view of gratitude afford, to those who say they find nothing to interest them in human life! What a field of exercise for those who complain that they find nothing to do!

Affection, too, is a subject in which the interests of woman are deeply involved, because affection in a peculiar manner constitutes her wealth. Beyond the sphere of her affections, she has nothing, and is nothing. Let her talents be what they may, without affection they can only be compared to a splendid casket, where the gem is wanting. Affection, like gratitude, must begin at home. Let no man choose for the wife of his bosom, a woman whose affections are not warm, and cordial, and ever flowing forth at her own fire-side. Yet there are young women whose behaviour in society, and amongst those whom they call their friends, exhibits every sign of genuine affection, who are yet cold, indifferent, and inconsiderate to their brothers, sisters and parents. These are the women against whom men ought to be especially warned, for sure I am, that such affection ought never to be trusted to, as that which is only called into life by the sunshine of society, or the excitement of transient intercourse with comparative strangers.

Affection also resembles gratitude in this, that the more we bestow, the more we feel, provided only it is bestowed upon safe and suitable objects. It is the lavish and reckless expenditure of this treasure in early life, and simply under the direction of fancy, without regard to natural claims, which so often leaves the heart of its possessor poor, and cold, and joyless.

Here, then, the claims of nature and of home may always be attended to with safety. No young girl can be too affectionate at home, because the demerits of a brother, a sister, or a parent, except in some rare and peculiar instances, constitute no disqualification for being the recipients either of her gratitude or her affection. But her approval and her admiration must still be kept distinct, lest her affection for an unworthy relative should render her insensible to the exact line of demarcation between moral good and evil. Were it not thus wisely and mercifully permitted us to continue to love our nearest connections, even when not deserving of general esteem, where would the prodigal, or the outcast, be able to find a shelter, when the horrors of a wounded conscience might drive them back from the ways of guilt? The mother's heart is subject to a higher, holier law than that which separates her erring child from the fellowship of mankind; the father meets his returning son while yet afar off; and the sister—can she withhold her welcome?—can she neglect the study of all those little arts of love, by which a father's home may be rendered as alluring as the world?

While the young of both sexes are suffering from the consequences of a system of education, under which the cultivation of moral principle bears no proportion to the cultivation of the intellectual powers, it is desirable to offer all the assistance we can in the improvement of that portion of human character which is at once the most important and the most neglected. In order to strengthen the good resolutions of those who are really desirous of paying the attention and the respect to old age which is justly its due, I would suggest to the accomplished young reader, an idea which it is highly probable may never before have crossed her mind, but which I feel assured will stain her cheek with shame, if she has ever allowed herself to treat her parents, or even her grand-parents with contempt, as inferior in the scale of consideration to herself, because of their want of mental cultivation.

Let her remember, then, whatever their deficiency in other points of wisdom may be, that there is one in which they must be her superiors. She may occasionally be obliged to correct their grammatical inaccuracies; she may be able not only to dazzle them with her accomplishments, but even to baffle them in argument; yet there is one fundamental part of true knowledge, in consideration of which, every youthful head must bow to age. Not ten thousand times the sum of money expended on your education would be sufficient to purchase this treasure of human wisdom for you. And there sits the aged woman, with her white locks, and her feeble hands, a by-word, and perhaps a jest, from the very helplessness of worn-out nature; yet, all the while, this humble and neglected being may be rich in the wealth which princes are too poor to buy; for she is rich in experience, and that is where you are poor. The simple being you despise has lived to see the working out of many systems, the end of many beginnings, the detection of much falsehood, the development of much truth; in short, the operation of principles upon the lives and conduct of men; and here, in this most important point of wisdom, you are—you must be her inferior.

The wisdom of experience, independently of every other consideration, presents a strong claim upon the respectful attention of youth, in cases where propriety of conduct is a disputed point between parent and child. Young persons sometimes think their parents too severe in the instructions they would enforce; but let it ever be remembered, that those parents have experience to direct them; and that, while the child is influenced only by inclination, or opinion, founded upon what must at least be a very limited and superficial knowledge of things in general, the opinion of the parent is founded upon facts, which have occurred during a far longer acquaintance with human nature, and with what is called the world.

Let the experience of the aged, then, be weighed against your modern acquirements, and even without the exercise of natural affection, we find that they are richly entitled to your respectful attention. But there is something beyond this consideration in the overflowing of the warm and buoyant feelings of youth, which so naturally and so beautifully supply the requirements of old age, that scarcely can we picture to ourselves a situation more congenial to the daughters of England, than one of those fire-side scenes, where venerated age is treated with the gratitude and affection which ought ever to be considered as its due.

It sometimes happens that the cares and the anxieties of parental love have a second time to be endured by those who have had to mourn the loss of their immediate offspring. Perhaps a family of orphan sons and daughters have become their charge, at a time of life when they had but little strength of body, or buoyancy of spirit, to encounter the turbulance of childhood, and the waywardness of youth, How admirably, then, are the character and constitution of woman adapted to the part which it becomes her duty and her privilege to act. Even the kindest amongst boys would scarcely know how to accommodate himself to the peculiarities of old age. But woman has an intuitive perception of these things; and the little playful girl can be gentle and still, the moment she sees that her restlessness, or loud mirth, would offend.

And what woman, I would ask, was ever less estimable for this early exercise of self-discipline? None can begin too soon. The labour of love is never difficult, except to those who have put off compliance with this sacred duty until too late in life; or who, while the affections of the heart were young and warm, have centered them in self, and lived for self alone. The social scenes upon which imagination loves to dwell, are those where self has never found a place amongst the household gods. They are those where the daughters of a family, from the oldest to the very infant, are all too happy in the exercise of their affections, to think of self. Theirs is a relative existence, and their enjoyments consist more in giving than receiving. Affections thus cherished in the cordial intercourse of home, may early be sent forth on errands of kindness to all who are fortunate enough to come within the sphere of their operations; and happy is the man who chooses from such a family the companion of his earthly lot!

CHAP. IX.
FRIENDSHIP AND FLIRTATION.

 How much of what is most lovely, and most valuable to us in the course of our earthly experience, arises out of the poverty and the feebleness of our nature. Friendship would never have existed, but for the absolute want of the human heart, from its utter inability to perform the functions of life without a participator in its joys, a recipient of its secrets, and a soother of its sorrows.

Youth is the season when we most feel this want; later in life, we learn as it were to stand alone. Interests and claims, which have little to do with the affections, press upon us on every hand, and hem us into a narrow and accustomed path, from which there is little temptation to deviate. But in youth we seem to walk at large, with no boundary to our horizon; and the fear and uncertainty which necessarily attend our movements, render a companion, with whom we may consult, deliberate, and sympathize, absolutely necessary to our cheerfulness and support.

It is a subject of surprise to many, that the young so seldom enter into close and intimate friendship with the members of their own family. Were this more frequently the case, how much more candour and simplicity of heart would mingle with the intercourse of friends! To the members of our own family, we must of necessity appear as we really are. No false or flattering aspect can deceive those whose eyes are constantly upon our conduct ; and we are consequently less tempted to put forward our best feelings before them, in the hope of concealing our worst. In such intimacies the nearest friends have the least suspicion of each other's truth. After-circumstances can bring forth no unexpected development of character on either side; nor can there be the wounded feeling, which falsehood, however unpremeditated or unconsciously practised, never fails to produce. Again, there would be the strength of natural ties to mingle with this bond the recollections of childhood, the oft-repeated forgiveness, the gratitude to which allusion has already been made—all these would blend together in a union the most sacred, and the most secure, which perhaps is ever found on earth.

Nor do I scruple to call this union the most secure, because it is the only intimacy in which everything can with propriety be told. There are private histories belonging to every family, which, though they operate powerfully upon individual happiness, ought never to be named beyond the home-circle; and there are points of difference in character, and mutual misapprehensions, with instances of wounded feeling, and subjects of reproof and correction, which never can be so freely touched upon, even in the most perfect union of conjugal affection. On this subject, however, I have already spoken so fully in another work,[1] that little room is left for farther notice here: I will, therefore, only allude to some of the causes which I believe most frequently operate against young persons choosing their confidants at home, and especially for the communication of their religious feelings, or impressions.

It is a melancholy thought, that the want of consistency in the private and domestic habits of religious professors, may possibly be the means of inducing young persons to seek their spiritual advisers amongst those with whom they are less intimately acquainted, and of whom they have consequently formed a higher estimate; while, on the other hand, a diffidence of themselves, perhaps a misgiving, both as to their past and future conduct, renders them unwilling to communicate fully and freely with those who daily watch their steps, lest the suspicion of hypocrisy should fall upon them for having given utterance to sentiments and emotions, so much at variance with the general course of their lives.

That these hinderances to home-confidence should sometimes exist, where the parties are perfectly sincere in their good intentions, I am quite prepared to believe; but there are other cases, and perhaps more frequent ones, in which the sincerity is less perfect, where the dread of being committed to any particular line of conduct consistent with the sentiments or emotions expressed, operates against their being so much as spoken of to any who compose the family circle.

It would be taking a dark view of human nature, indeed, to suppose that those who know us best are less disposed than strangers to attach themselves to us; yet, I would ask the young aspirant to intimacy with a new acquaintance, whether she is entering upon that intimacy with a sincere and candid wish to be to that friend exactly what she is at home? If not, she is, to all intents and purposes, a deceiver. And there is much deceit in all our early friendships, though I am far from supposing it to be all intentional. Indeed, I am convinced it is not, because this heart-searching process is what few young persons submit to, before commencing an intimacy.

In friendship, as well as in all other reciprocal engagements, it is highly important to limit our expectations of benefit according to the exact measure of our deserts; and by this means we may avoid many of those bitter disappointments, for which the world is so unjustly and unsparingly blamed. The world is bad enough; but let us be honest, and take our share of condemnation, for making at least one item of the world such as it is; and by thus acquiring the habit of strict and candid self-examination in early life, we see that we have little right to charge the world with falsehood, when our first engagement, beyond the circle of our own family, has been entered into by a system of deceit.

There is, too, a rashness and impetuosity in the formation of early friendships, which of themselves are sufficient to render such intimacies uncertain, and of short duration. Few characters can be considered as really formed, under the age of twenty-one, or twenty-five; yet friendships sometimes begin at a much earlier date. It is not in nature, then, that the friend we loved at sixteen, should be the same to us at twenty-six; or that the features of our own character should have undergone no change during that period. Yet it must not be called falsehood, or fickleness either, which causes such friendships to fail. It is consistent with the laws of reason, and of nature, that they should do so; for had the same individuals who thus deplore each other's falsehood, met for the first time at the age of twenty-six, they would probably each have been the very last which the other would have chosen as a friend.

Again, there must be an equality in friendship, to render it either lasting or desirable-an equality not only in rank and station, but, as far as may be, in intellectual advantages. However warm may be the attachment of two friends of different rank in society, they must occasionally be involved in dilemmas, from which it is impossible to escape without wounded feeling, either on one side or both. Each of these friends, it must be remembered, will have her relatives and connections, through whom her pride will be perpetually subject to imaginary insult, and her susceptibility to real pain. Those who are inferior in mind are, however, much more objectionable as friends, than those who are inferior only in worldly circumstances; because they must always be incapable of judging of persons more highly gifted than themselves, and thus they will bestow their praise and their blame with equal injustice. The ignorant, too, are always prejudiced; and, therefore, in the choice of friends whose minds are unenlightened, the young must necessarily incur the risk of imbibing opinions formed upon false conclusions, which in all probability will exercise a powerful influence upon the whole of their subsequent lives.

Young people are too apt to think the only use of talent is to interest in conversation; if, then, they find themselves interested without it, they are satisfied to dispense with this quality in a friend. But how empty—how unprofitable must become that intimacy where mind is not taken into account—how worthless, how unsatisfactory in every case of trial, the society of that friend who cannot advise, as well as pity.

Were it not for equality being requisite to the mutual participation of the pleasures of friendship, I should strongly recommend all young persons to seek a friend amongst those who are older, and more experienced than themselves. In this case, however, too much must not be expected in return, for it is scarcely possible that the confiding intimacy of a young girl should always be interesting, or even acceptable to a woman more advanced in life; unless, indeed, the kindness of relationship should render the office of the elder confidant a welcome duty.

Regardless of these wholesome rules, it is more than probable that the greater part of my young readers will go on forming intimacies according to circumstances, or individual fancy, and with little reference to future consequences. In time, however, some of these intimacies will become irksome, while others will die away. It will then become a serious question, 'Whom shall I endeavour to retain as friends?' Try, then, to ascertain, in this stage of your short experience, whose society has had the happiest effect upon your own character; and let not this great question remain unsettled, until you have ascertained, with regard to each one of the individuals who have composed your circle of nominal friends, whether they have generally left you better or worse for a day spent in their company—more willing to submit to the requirements of religious duty, or more disposed to consider those requirements unreasonable and severe.

The pleasure or amusement immediately derived from the society of an individual, is a dangerous and deceitful test by which to try the value of their friendship; but the direct influence of their society upon our own state of mind, not while they are with us, but after the charm of their society is withdrawn, is a means of judging, which no rational and responsible being ought to neglect. If, for instance, in the circle of our favourite associates, there is one who habitually awakens the laughter of merriment, and charms into magic fleetness the hours you pass together; yet if the same individual leaves you flat, and dull, and indisposed for the useful and less pleasing occupations of life; beware of making her your friend. But if there be another who, possibly less amusing at the time you converse together, yet leaves you raised above the common level of experience, by the support of true and lofty principles; disposed to reject what is false or mean, and to lay hold on what is good; lifted out of the slavery of what is worldly or trifling, and made stronger in every generous purpose, and every laudable endeavour; let the friendship of that individual be bound around your heart, and cherished to the end of life, as one of the richest blessings permitted us to enjoy on earth.

By this rule, those who are candidates for our friendship, may safely be tried; but there is yet a closer test, which must be applied to friendship itself. If the friend you have chosen, never attempts to correct your faults, or make you better than you are, she is not worthy of the name; nor ought she to be fully confided in, whatever may be the extent of her kindness to you, or the degree of her admiration of your character.

Having well chosen your friend, the next thing is, to trust her, and to show that you do so. Mutual trust is the strongest cement of all earthly attachments. We are so conscious of weakness ourselves, that we need this support from others; and no compliment paid to the ear of vanity was ever yet so powerful in its influence, as even the simplest proof of being trusted. The one may excite a momentary thrill of pleasure, the other serves, for many an after day, to nourish the life-springs of a warm and generous heart.

It is needless to say how effectually a suspicious, or a jealous temper, destroys this truth. If we really loved our friends as we ought, and as we probably profess to love them, we should be less watchful of their conduct towards ourselves, than of ours to them ; nor should we grudge them the intimacy of other friends, when conducive to their enjoyment, if our own attachment was based upon pure and disinterested affection. Friendship, which is narrowed up between two individuals, and confined to that number alone, is calculated only for the intercourse of married life, and seldom has been maintained with any degree of lasting benefit or satisfaction, even by the most romantic and affectionate of women. True friendship is of a more liberal and expansive nature, and seldom flourishes so well as when extended through a circle. A circle of young female friends, who love and trust each other, who mutually agree to support the weak in their little community, to confirm the irresolute, to reclaim the erring, to soothe the irritable, and to solace the distressed; what a realization does this picture present of the brightest dreams of imagination, when we think what woman might be in this world to her own sex, and to the community at large!

And is this, then, too much to expect from the daughters of England—that woman should be true to woman? In the circle of her private friends, as well as from her own heart, she learns what constitutes the happiness and the misery of woman, what is her weakness and what her need, what her bane and what her blessing. She learns to comprehend the deep mystery of that electric chain of feeling which ever vibrates through the heart of woman, and which many with all his philosophy, can never understand. She learns that every touch of that chain is like the thrilling of a nerve; and she thus acquires a power peculiar to herself, of distinguishing exactly between the links which thrill with pleasure, and those which only thrill with pain.

Thus, while her sympathy and her tenderness for a chosen few is strengthened by the bond of friendship into which she has entered, though her confidence is still confined to them, a measure of the same sympathy and tenderness is extended to the whole sisterhood of her sex, until, in reality, she becomes what woman ever must be—in her noblest, purest, holiest character—the friend of woman.

What should we think of a community of slaves, who betrayed each other's interests 1 of a little band of shipwrecked mariners upon a friendless shore, who were false to each other? of the inhabitants of a defenceless nation, who would not unite together in earnestness and good faith against a common enemy? We are accustomed to hear of the meanness of the powerful, when they forsake the weak; but there is a meanness of a lower grade—when the weak forsake each other.

No party, however, can be weak, which has truth for its element, and love for its bond of union. Women are only weak in their vanity, their selfishness, their falsehood to each other. In their integrity, their faithfulness, their devoted affection, they rise to an almost superhuman eminence; because they are strong in the elements of immaterial being, and powerful in the nature which is capable, when regenerated, of being shared with angels.

From the nature of true friendship, we turn to the consideration of what are its requirements. These, also, are mutual. If we expect to receive, we must be studious to give. An interchange of kind offices and evident proofs of affection are essential to the vitality of friendship; avoiding, however, the slightest approach to anything like a debtor and creditor account of the number of presents given or received, or even of the number of letters exchanged.

It seems a strange anomaly in friendship, that young persons, however ardently attached, should so seldom write, except when a letter is considered to be due by a certain length of time having elapsed since the last was received. It often happens, that one friend is particularly engaged, while the other has an abundance of unoccupied time; but a letter is still required by the idle party, or the love which she thinks so glowing and so tender, finds no channel of expression to her friend. Perhaps a friend is ill; and then is the time, above all others, when real love would dictate a succession of kind letters, such as would not tax the afflicted, or the feeble one, with the effort of making any return. There is, in fact, a mystery about the letter-writing of young women, which I have never been able fully to understand. It occupies their time; it used to drain their purses, or the purses of their friends; it calls forth more complaining than almost any thing else they have to do; the letters they receive are seldom fraught with much interest; and yet they plunge into this reciprocity of annoyance, as if the chief business of life was to be writing or receiving letters.

Still I am far from supposing that this means of interchanging sentiment and thought, might not be rendered highly beneficial to the youthful mind; because I believe writing is of great importance as a branch of education. Without this habit, few persons, and especially women, think definitely. The accustomed occupation of their minds is that of musing; and they are, consequently, seldom able to disentangle a single clear idea from the current of vague thoughts, which they suffer perpetually to flow, and which affords them a constant, but, at the same time, a profitless amusement, in the variety of ideas it presents, alike without form, and void. But, in order to write with any degree of perspicuity, we are, to a certain extent, compelled to think; and, consequently, the habit of writing letters, if the subject-matter be well chosen, might be rendered highly advantageous to young women, who, on the termination of their scholastic exercises, require, more than at any other time of life, some frequently recurring mental occupation, to render their education complete.

The art of writing a really good letter ranks unquestionably amongst the most valuable accomplishments of woman, and next to that of conversing well. In both cases, the first thing to be avoided, is common-place; because, whatever partakes of the nature of common place, is not only vulgar, but ineffective. I know not how I can better define this term, so frequently used, and so little understood, than by saying that common-place consists chiefly in speaking of things by their little qualities, rather than their great ones. Thus it is common-place to speak of religious persons as using cant, to speak of distinguished characters as being well or ill-dressed, and to speak of the works of Shakspeare as being peculiar in their style. It is also common-place to use those expressions of kindness, or sympathy, which custom has led us to expect as a matter of course. And we never feel this more, than in cases of affliction or death; because there is a kind of set phraseology made use of on such occasions, which those who really feel would often be glad to vary, if they only knew how. It is common-place to speak of some fact as recently discovered, to those who have long known it. But above all that is genuine in common-place, the kind of flattery generally adopted by men, when they mean to address themselves pleasantly to women, deserves the credit of pre-eminence. Indeed, so deficient, for the most part, is this flattery, in point, originality, and adaptation, that I have known sensible women, who felt more really flattered by the most humiliating truths, even plainly spoken; because such treatment implied a confidence in their strength of mind and good sense, in being able to bear it.

Common-place letters are such as, but for the direction, would have done as well for any other individual as the one to whom they are addressed. In description especially, it is desirable to avoid common-place. A correspondent making a tour of the Lakes, tells you that on such a day she set off to the summit of Helvellyn. That the first part of the ascent was steep and difficult, the latter more easy; that the view from the summit was magnificent, extending over so many lakes, and so many other mountains; and there ends the story; and well for you, if it does end there. But such writers unfortunately often go on through a whole catalogue of beauties and sublimities, no single one of which they set before you in such a manner as to render it one whit more attractive, or indeed more peculiar in any of its features, than the king's highway.

In the vain hope of avoiding common-place, some young writers have recourse to extravagant expressions when describing little things; a mode of writing, which, besides being the medium of falsehood, leaves them in the uncomfortable predicament of having no language adequate to what is great.

It is difficult to say what is the direct opposite of common-place, without giving lengthened quotations from the best style of epistolary correspondence, with which the literature of our country during the last century abounds. There is a quality both in writing and conversation, to which I can give no other name than *freshness*, which is not only opposite in its nature and effect to common-place, but on which I believe depends more than half the pleasure and amusement we derive from the intercourse of mind with mind. Few persons possess this charm; because few are humble enough to suppose that it would be any advantage to them; and those who do, are always in danger of losing it by writing too much. The letters of a woman of moderate abilities, and limited sphere of observation, may possess this great beauty; while those of a more highly gifted, or accomplished writer, may want it; because it must ever depend upon a capability of receiving vivid impressions, combined with a certain degree of simplicity of heart. The first consideration in commencing a letter should be, "What is my object in writing it?" If simply for the relief of your own mind you take up the pen, remember that such a communication can only be justified by pressing and peculiar circumstances, and that it ought only to be addressed to the nearest and dearest of your friends, whose love for you is of such a nature as to pardon so selfish an act. A higher object in writing, is to give pleasure, or afford benefit, to an absent friend; it is therefore necessary to place yourself in idea in her circumstances, and consider what she would most wish to know. If her affection for you be such, and such I am aware affection often is, that she has no desire beyond that of receiving intelligence concerning yourself, let your descriptions of your state and circumstances be clear and fresh; so that she may see you as you really are, and, as it were, live with you through the enjoyments or the trials of every day. How strong and lively may be the impressions thus conveyed?how deep the interest they excite, provided only the writer will condescend to be sufficiently simple?sufficiently sincere.   It is, however, only under peculiar circumstances, such as change of scene and situation, that young persons can have much of this kind to communicate. What then are they to say? Shall the minute details of family affairs be raked up, to fill their letters? This is at least a dangerous alternative, more especially as it too frequently induces a habit of exaggeration, in order to make what is called "a good story" out of a mere trifle; and thus, that worst kind of falsehood, which is partly true, becomes perpetuated through the medium of pen and paper.

To avoid this danger on the one hand, and the weariness of writing without anything to say, on the other, would it not be practicable for young women to agree, for their own improvement and that of their friends, to correspond on some given subject, and if unequal to the task of treating it in a style of an essay, they might at least relate to each other some important or amusing facts, which they had met with in the course of their reading, and by relating them in their own language, and then comparing them with that of the author, they would be learning valuable lessons in the art of composition? for of all kinds of style, that of easy narrative is the most useful.

The study of nature in this department of mental improvement, might be made to afford a never-failing source of interest, both for individual thought and familiar communication. The peculiarities of plants and animals, and even the different traits of human character developed by people of different countries and grades of society, might all contribute to the same object, so as in time to displace from the page of female correspondence, the trifling, the common-place, or the more mischievous gossip, which that page too generally unfolds.

In speaking of a mutual interchange of tokens of affection being essential to the vitality of friendship, I am far from including under this head, those expressions of endearment which are sometimes used by young women, so indiscriminately, as entirely to lose their individual force and value. Indeed, I am not quite sure that terms of endearment made use of as a matter of course, are desirable under any circumstances; because there will be occasions, even with the most warmly attached, when the tones of the voice, and the expression of the countenance, indicate anything but love; and having heard these tender epithets still made use of on such occasions, it is scarcely possible to retain our value for them when applied with real tenderness and respect. It also frequently happens, where these epithets are commonly used, that the very individual who has just been speaking to us injuriously of another, turns to the injured party with the same expression of endearment so frequently applied to ourselves, and which we consequently become extremely willing to dispense with for the future.

It is the peculiar nature of friendship, that it will not be mocked. All manner of weakness, and a fearful sum of follies and transgressions, it is willing to bear with; but faithfulness is a requisite without which it is impossible it should continue to exist. It is not necessary, in order to be faithful to our friends, that we should be always praising them, nor yet that we should praise them more than they deserve. So far from this, we do them real injury by too much praise, because it always occasions disappointment in those who cultivate their acquaintance upon the strength of our evidence in their favour. Nor is it necessary, when we hear their characters discussed in company, to defend them against every charge; at least to deny their having those faults which are conspicuous to every eye. But one thing is necessary on such occasions—that a friend should be ever prompt and anxious to bring forward the evidence which remains on the side of virtue, so far as it may be done with prudence and delicacy.

The indulgence of caprice is another evil prevalent amongst the young, with which friendship disdains that her claims should be put in competition. Capricious persons are those who frequently choose to act under a momentary impulse, in a manner opposed to the general and acknowledged rule of their conduct and feelings. Thus the social companion of yesterday, may choose to be a stranger today. She may have no unkindness in her heart towards you, yet it may suit her mood to meet as if you had never met before. She may have no desire to give you pain, yet her looks may be as forbidding, and her manners as repulsive, as if she had never loved you. She may be habitually cheerful, yet her humour may be to hang her head, and lower her brow, and hardly articulate an answer when you speak to her.

It is scarcely necessary to say, that few things are more ruinous to friendship, and to domestic and social happiness in general, than caprice ; because its very nature is to render every one uncertain, and to chill, to wound, or to irritate all with whom it comes in contact; while friendship requires that you should always be the same, and nothing can be more painful to the feelings of a friend, than to find that caprice, or the indulgence of your own humour, is a matter of more importance to you than her happiness. Such wounds, however, are happily not incurable. Friendship, thus repulsed, is soon withdrawn; and the capricious woman has the satisfaction of finding herself left at last to the enjoyment of her different moods alone. There is, in short, something in the very nature of caprice so selfish and ungenerous, so opposed to all the requirements of affection, that in no connection in life, except where the tie is indissoluble, can it long be endured.

But while we are justified in acting upon the repulsion which caprice so naturally excites, there are other trials which, if true, friendship must submit to endure; because they necessarily spring out of the nature of the human heart, and, instead of being checked by the influence of society, they are fostered by it, and subsist upon the very elements of which it is composed. One of these evils is a spurious kind of social intercourse, falsely denominated friendship, which, unfortunately, sometimes links itself with the true. I say falsely, for that friendship is not worthy of the name, which is founded upon tale-bearing and detraction. Yet, how much of the intimacy of young women consists in the magnifying and telling of little troubles, particularly of a domestic nature, and most commonly injurious to some member of the household to which they belong.

Let the young be especially warned against this most insidious and most dangerous temptation; and let them be assured, that there are few causes of more bitter repentance in after life, than the reflection that they have thus wantonly made themselves enemies to those of their own house. There is one fact which ought of itself to deter them from the indulgence of this habit. It is, that friendship based on such a foundation, is never lasting. No; friendship must have love, not hate, for its element. If the intimacy of youth consists in evil speaking, and injurious thoughts, it soon becomes assimilated with the poisonous aliment on which it feeds. The friend becomes an enemy; and what is the consequence? The shafts of slander are turned against yourself, and the dark secrets you have revealed, go forth to the world as swift witnesses against you, as well as against those to whom duty and natural affection should have kept you true.

Besides which, there are few cases of human conduct where inexperienced youth can be a correct or sufficient judge. It may appear to you at the time you speak of family grievances, that a parent has been too severe, that a sister has been selfish, or that a brother has been unjust. But you are not even capable of judging of yourself, as regards the impression produced by your own behaviour upon others; how then can you pronounce upon the motives of others in their behaviour to you? more especially how are you to lift the veil of experience, and penetrate the deep mysteries of parental love? yet, how otherwise are you to understand

"The secrets of the folded heart
That seemed to thee so stern?"

There are hordes of human beings, once partakers with us in the privileges and enjoyments of our native land, now branded with infamy, and toiling in chains upon a distant shore, who have to regret, when too late, some guilty theft committed in early youth upon the property of a confiding and indulgent master. And the voice of our country cries out against them for the injury and ingratitude, as well as for the injustice, of what they have done. And is it possible that within the fair and polished circles of the same favoured land, where woman blooms and smiles, and youth is radiant with joy, and happy in the security of domestic peace— is it possible that woman can so far forget her heart-warm affection, her truth, her devotedness of soul, as, while hex hands are pure from the contamination of so foul a crime as theft, to permit her tongue to be the instrument of injury more deep than robbery—more bitter than the loss of wealth.

We will not—we cannot believe it ; because the time is coming when the daughters of England, admonished of their duties on every hand, will learn to look, not to the mere gratification of an idle moment, in what they say, and what they do, but to the eternal principles of right and wrong; and to the great balance in which human actions are weighed, in reference not only to time, but to eternity.

It is good for many reasons that youth should early acquire a habit of checking its own impulses, and never is this more important than when under temptation to speak injuriously of others. A few years more of experience, a few more instances of personal trial, a little more self-knowledge, and a little more observation of others, will in all probability open your understandings to an entirely altered view of human nature, of the motives which influence the conduct of mankind, as well as of the claims of affection when combined with those of duty. You will then see, how unjust have been your first conclusions, how your thoughts have wronged those whom you were unable to understand; and happy will it be for you when making this discovery, to reflect that you have scrupulously kept your erroneous views and injurious suspicions confined to the knowledge of your own heart.

Friendship, if true, has much to bear from the idle and mischievous gossip of society. Indeed, gossip may justly be considered as having destroyed more youthful attachments, than selfishness, falsehood, or vanity; though all these three have done their part in the work of destruction. It is easy to say, 'I care not for such and such injurious reports.' 'The opinion of the world is of no consequence to me,' and it is undoubtedly the part of wisdom not to allow such causes to operate against our peace of mind. Unfortunately, however, for us, the world is made up of our friends, as well as of those who are strangers to us; and in this world it is the malignant office of gossip to set afloat rumours of what is evil, rather than statements of what is good. Were such rumours welcomed only by the credulity of strangers, they would certainly be of little consequence to us; but, alas, for the faithfulness of affection; our friends, though at first surprised at last believe them; and then comes the trial of friendship, for to be injuriously and unjustly thought of by those who ought to know us better, and simply because common report has circulated some charge against us, is that, which, perhaps more than anything else, destroys our confidence in the profession, the language, the very name of friendship.

The character of woman in every situation in life, has ever been found most admirable, when most severely tried; and I know that her friendship is equal to remaining unshaken by difficulties and dangers, which might well be supposed to move a firmer nature than her's. But I speak of the little trials of minute and every-day experience, for it is against these that woman seldom brings her highest principles and best feelings to bear. It is in the sunshine of society that friendship most frequently withers, because the "love that tempests never shook" may expire under the deadly breathing-upon of common slander.

On the first view of this subject, it seems impossible to believe that mere gossip, which we unanimously agree to regard as being in so many instances false, should operate with such potency in dissolving the tenderest ties of early life. Yet I appeal to experience, and observation too, when I ask, whether the ranks of society are not thronged with individuals closely assimilated in their habits and ways of thinking, mutually in want of the consolations of friendship, and adapted to promote each other's happiness, of whom it may be said with melancholy truth,

"Alas! they had been friends in youth,
But whispering tongues can poison truth."

What then is the part which friendship ought to act in a case where rumour is strong against a friend? The part of true friendship is always a straightforward and decided one. First ask whether the charge brought against your friend be wholly at variance with the principles you know to regulate her conduct in general, wholly at variance with the sentiments uniformly expressed in her confidential intercourse with you, and wholly at variance with the tenor of her previous life. If such be the case, reject it with a noble indignation: for even if in one instance your friend has actually departed from the general principles of her conduct, her habitual sentiments, and her accustomed mode of action—and if in the end you find that the world has all the while been right, while you have been mistaken—it is better a thousand times to have felt this generous, though misplaced confidence, than to have been hastily drawn in to entertain an injurious suspicion of a friend.

Still, where the evidence is strong against a friend, where it increases and becomes confirmed, it would be blindness and folly to continue to disregard it. But before you yield even to such accumulating evidence, more especially before you act upon it, or suffer one syllable to pass your lips in support of the charge, or even of other charges of a similar nature to that openly alleged, fail not, as you value everything that is just and equitable in the conduct of one human being towards another—fail not to appeal directly to the injured party, so as to allow her an opportunity of exculpating, or at least of excusing, herself.

If this had but been done in one instance out of a thousand, where slander has scattered her poison upon the foundation of human love, what a different position would woman now maintain in the scale of moral excellence. How much of real good the hand of friendship might by this means have drawn out from seeming evil; how many a wounded bosom the balm of friendship might have healed; how many of those who are now lonely and unloved might have been linked together in the endearing fellowship of mutual affection!

People talk as if the worst thing that could happen to us, was to be deceived; they dare not be generous, they dare not trust, because they should thereby incur the risk of being deceived. That this theory may very properly be acted upon in business, I am quite disposed to allow; but if in friendship there is no other alternative than to listen to injurious rumour, to lean to the side of suspicion, and to believe the first report against a friend; let me rather be deceived a thousand times, for then I shall at least enjoy the consciousness of having known what it was to trust, as well as love.

Friendship has many trials. Though vanity and selfishness are at the root of many of these, they are for the most part too minute, and apparently too trifling, for description. Perhaps the greatest of these arises out of the undue value attached by women to the general attentions of men. For the assistance, the protection, and the disinterested kindness of the other sex, all women ought to be deeply grateful; but for those common attentions which good breeding dictates, without reference to the individual on whom they are bestowed, I own I cannot see why they should ever be so much the subject of envy amongst women, as to cast a shade upon their intercourse with each other.

This part of my subject necessarily leads me to the consideration of what, for want of a more serious name, I am under the necessity of calling flirtation; by which I would be understood to mean, all that part of the behaviour of women, which in the art of pleasing, has reference only to men. It is easy to understand whether a woman is guilty of flirtation or not, by putting her conduct to this simple test—whether, in mixed society, she is the same to women as to men.

Although nothing could be more revolting to the feelings of a true-hearted woman, than needlessly to make a public exposure of the weaknesses and follies of her own sex, yet something of this is not only justifiable, but necessary in the present case, in order to contrast the conduct of those who are truly admirable, with that which is only adopted for the purpose of courting admiration. Nor would I speak uncharitably, when I confess, that, like others, I have often seen a drooping countenance suddenly grow animated, an oppressive headache suddenly removed, and many other symptoms of an improved state of health and spirits as suddenly exhibited, when the society of ladies has become varied by that of the nobler sex; and never does female friendship receive a deeper insult, than when its claims are thus superseded by those, perhaps, of a mere stranger.

Though the practice of flirtation, or the habit of making use of certain arts of pleasing in the society of men, which are not used in that of women, is a thing of such frequent occurrence, that few can be said to be wholly exempt from it; yet we rarely find a woman so lost to all sense of delicacy, as to make an open profession of flirtation. Indeed, I am convinced, that some do actually practise it unconsciously to themselves, and for this reason I am the more anxious to furnish them with a few hints, by which they may be better able to detect the follies of their own conduct.

In the first place, then, allow me to ask, why it is necessary, or even desirable, for young women to do more to please men than women? Their best friends, as friends only, will ever be found amongst their own sex. There is but one relation in life in which any of the men whom they meet with in mixed society can be anything to them; and surely they can have no thought of marrying half those whom they take more pains to please, than they take in their intercourse with their own sex. What then, can be the state of mind of her who exercises all her powers of fascination upon beings in whom she can have no deep, or real interest? She must have some strong motive, or why this total change in her behaviour, so that her female friends can scarcely recognize in her the same individual, who, an hour before, was moping, fretful, listless, and weary of herself, and them? She must have some strong motive, and it can be no other than one of these two— either to gain the admiration, or the affection, of all those whom she favours with the full exhibition of her accomplishments in the art of pleasing. If her motive be simply to gain their admiration, it is a blind and foolish mistake into which her vanity has betrayed her, to suppose that admiration is to be purchased by display, or to imagine that the open and undisguised claims she makes upon it, are not more calculated to disgust than attract.

But there remains the second, and stronger motive; and this would seem, at first sight, to demand more delicacy of treatment, since it is generally considered an amiable propensity in woman's nature to desire to be beloved. Let her, however, be honest, sincere, and honourable, in the means she adopts for the gratification of this desire. Let her require nothing for which she is not prepared to make an adequate return. The kindness, the generosity, the integrity of her character demand this. If, therefore, her desire be to obtain the love of all those with whom she engages in the business of flirtation, she is either on the one hand involved in a very serious and alarming outlay of affection; or, on the other, in a system of selfishness and meanness, for which every honest-hearted woman ought to blush. I have used the words selfishness and meanness, because the art of flirtation deserves to be described by no better; because it is selfish to endeavour to obtain that for which we know that a return will be expected, which we are not the least prepared to make; because it is mean to use, in obtaining it, a degree of art, which makes us appear better, or more admirable, than we really are.

Is it not good, then, for woman to bear about with her, even in early life, the conviction that her only business with men in society, is to learn of them, and not to captivate, or dazzle them; for there is a boldness—an indelicacy, in this exercise of her influence, as much at variance with good taste, as with right principle, and real feeling. Is it not good, also, to bear about with her the remembrance, that no woman ought to be so brilliant or so agreeable in mixed society, as in her own domestic circle. There is no harm in pleasing, it is at once her privilege, and her power; but let her influence through the exercise of this means be what it may, there will come in after life sore trials, under which she will need it all; and poor indeed is that woman, who, when affection wanes, and disappointment chills the glow of youthful ardour, feels that she has expended all her powers of pleasing in public, or upon comparative strangers.

I have said, that all women plead not guilty to the charge of flirtation in themselves; yet, all are ready to detect and despise it in their friends. All can detect in others, when the bland and beaming smile is put on for the occasion; when expressive looks are interchanged; when glittering curls are studiously displayed; when songs are impressively sung; when flowers which have been presented, are preserved and worn; when unnecessary attentions are artfully called forth; but, above all, for it is best to cut short this catalogue of folly, when conversation is so ingeniously turned as to induce, and almost compel some personal allusion, in which a compliment must almost unavoidably be couched.

And in all this system of absurdity, containing items of folly too numerous for tongue or pen to tell, from the glance of a beautiful eye, to the expression of a mutual sentiment; from the gathering of a favourite flower, to the awakening of a dormant passion; from the pastime of an idle moment, to the occupation of years; in all this, it is deeply to be regretted, that the influence of man is such, as to excite, rather than to repress—to encourage this worse than folly, rather than to warn and to correct. Indeed, whatever may be the excellencies of man in every other walk of life, it is a subject of something more than regret, that these excellencies are so little called forth in his intercourse with woman in mixed society. As a father, a husband, a brother, and a friend, his character assumes a totally different aspect. And why, I would ask of him, if his eye should ever deign to glance over these pages,—why is he not the friend of woman in society, as well as in the more intimate relations of social and domestic life?

Time was, when warriors and heroes deemed it not incompatible with glory or renown, to make the cause of helpless woman their's. Nay, such was the respect in which her claims were held, that the banner could not wave in battle, nor the laurel-wreath in peace, so proudly as when lances were broken, and lays were sung, in defence of her fair fame. On what did that fame then rest?—on what must it rest for ever? On her moral purity—on her exemption from mean and grovelling thoughts, and on her aspirations after what is noble, and refined, and true. And is woman less deserving now, than she was a thousand years ago, of the kindness, the protection, the honourable and fair dealing, of man? So far from this, she has made rapid progress in the work of moral renovation, having gained in real worth, more than she has lost in romantic feeling. But one hinderance to her improvement still remains—one barrier against her progress in the path of wisdom and of truth. It is the influence of man, in his intercourse with her in general society.

Perhaps he is not aware how powerful and extensive this influence is, or he would surely sometimes endeavour to turn it to better account. I wish not to describe it in too flattering a manner, by telling how many a young heart is made to throb for the first time with vanity, and idle thoughts, and foolish calculations, in consequence of his flattery and attentions; but it is most important he should know, that while women naturally and necessarily look to the stronger sex to give character and decision to their own sentiments; it is in the common intercourse of society, that such sentiments are implanted, fostered, and matured.

To speak of the popular style of conversation used by gentlemen when making themselves agreeable to young ladies, as trifling, is the best thing we can say of it. Its worst characteristic is its falsehood, while its worst tendency is to call forth selfishness, and to foster that littleness of mind, for which man is avowedly the despiser of woman. If intellectual conversation occupies the company, how often does he turn to whisper nonsense to woman; if he sees her envious of the beauty of her friend, how often does he tell her that her own charms are unrivalled; if he discovers that she is foolishly elated with the triumph of having gained his attentions, how studiously does he feed her folly, waiting only for the next meeting with a boon companion, to treat the whole with that ridicule which it deserves—deserves, but not from him.

It may be—I would fain believe it is, his wish that woman should be simple-hearted, intelligent, generous, frank, and true; but how is his influence in society exercised to make her any one of these? Woman is blamed, and justly so, for idle thoughts, and trifling conversation; but, I appeal to experience, and ask, whether, when a young girl first goes into society, her most trifling conversation is not that which she shares with men? It is true that woman has the power to repel by a look, a word, or even a tone of her voice, the approach of falsehood or folly; and admirable are the instances we sometimes find of woman thus surrounded as it were by an atmosphere of moral purity, through which no vulgar touch can penetrate. But all are not thus happily sustained, and it seems hard that the weaker sex should not only have to contend with the weakness of their own hearts; but that they should find in this conflict, so much of the influence of man on the side of evil.

In speaking of friendship, I have said nothing of that which might be supposed to exist between the two sexes; because I believe, that, in early youth, but little good can accrue to either party from making the experiment; and chiefly for reasons already stated, that man, in his intercourse with woman, seldom studies her improvement; and that woman, in her's with man, is too much addicted to flirtation. The opinion of the world, also, is opposed to this kind of intimacy; and it is seldom safe, and never wise, to do what society unanimously condemns. Besides which, it is exceedingly difficult for a young and inexperienced girl to know when a man is really her friend, and when he is only endeavouring to gain her favour; the most serious mistakes are, therefore, always liable to be made, which can only be effectually guarded against, by avoiding such intimacies altogether.

Again, it is no uncommon thing for men to betray young women into little deviations from the strict rule of propriety, for their own sakes, or in connection with them; which deviations they would be the first to condemn, if they were in favour of another. Be assured, however, that the man who does this—who, for his own gratification betrays you into so much as the shadow of an error—who even willingly allows you to be placed in an exposed, a questionable, or even an undignified situation—in short, who subjects you, for his own sake, to the slightest breath of censure, or even of ridicule, is not your real friend, nor worthy so much as to be called your acquaintance.

Fain would we hope and trust, that men who would do this, are exceptions to a general rule; and, honourable it is to the sex, that there are those, who, without any personal interest of their own being involved, are truly solicitous to raise the moral and intellectual standard of excellence amongst women; men who speak the truth, and nothing but the truth, even to the trusting and too credulous; who never, for the gratification of an idle moment, stoop to lead the unwise still farther into folly, the weak into difficulty, or the helpless into distress; men who are not satisfied merely to protect the feeble portion of the community, but who seek to promote the safety and the happiness of woman, by placing her on the sure foundation of sound principle; men who are ready to convince her, if she would but listen to their faithful teaching, that she possesses no beauty so attractive as her simplicity of heart, no charm so lasting as her deep and true affection, and no influence so powerful as her integrity and truth.

I cannot leave the subject of the general behaviour of women to the other sex, without adverting to a popular tendency amongst the young and inexperienced, to attach undue importance to the casual notice of distinguished men; such as popular speakers, eloquent ministers of religion, or any who hold conspicuous situations in society. The most objectionable feature which this tendency assumes, is an extravagant and enthusiastic attachment to ministers of religion. I am aware there is much in the character and office of a faithful minister, justly calculated to call forth the respectful admiration both of young and old; that there is also much in his pastoral care of the individual members of his flock equally calculated to awaken feelings of deep and strong attachment; and when such feelings are tempered with reverence, and kept under the proper restraint of prudence and good taste, it is unquestionably right that they should be cherished. My remarks can have no reference to young women whose conduct is thus regulated; but there are others, chiefly of enthusiastic temperament, who, under the impression that it is right to love and admire to the utmost of their power, whoever is worthy of admiration, give way to a style of expression, when speaking of their favourite ministers, and a mode of behaviour towards them, which is not only peculiarly adapted to expose them, as religious professors, to the ridicule of the world; but which, of itself, too plainly betrays their want of reverence and right feeling on the subject of religion in general.

But the duties of friendship remain yet to be considered in their highest and most important character. We have never been intimately associated with any one, even in early youth, without having received from them some bias of feeling, either towards good or evil; and the more our affections were engaged in this intimacy, the more decided this bias has been. What, then, has been the nature of our influence upon them?—upon all to whose bosom-confidence we have been admitted? Is this solemn query to be reserved for the hour of death? or is it not the wiser part of youth to begin with its practical application, while the character is yet fresh and pliant, and before the traces of our influence, if wrong, shall have become too deep to be eradicted?

If your friend is farther advanced in religious experience than yourself, be willing, then, to learn from her example; but be watchful, also, to point out with meekness and gentleness, her slightest deviations from the line of conduct which a Christian professor ought to pursue; and by this means you may not only materially promote her highest interests, but you may also assist in promoting the interests of religion itself, by preserving it from the calumny and disrespect for which such deviations so naturally give occasion.

If your friend is less advanced than yourself in religious experience, or if, as is most probable, you are both in a backward and defective state, suffer not your mind on any account to become regardless of the important fact, that in proportion to the degree of confidence you have enjoyed with that friend, and in proportion with the hold you have obtained of her affections, is the responsibility you incur with regard to her moral and spiritual advancement. It is fruitless to say, "I see her faults, I mourn over her deviations, but I dare not point them out, lest I wound her feelings, or offend her pride." I know the task is difficult, perhaps the most so of any we ever undertake. But our want of disinterested lore, and of real earnestness in the cause of Christ, render it more difficult than it would otherwise be.

We might in this, as in many other instances, derive encouragement from what is accomplished by women in the way of supporting public institutions, and promoting public good. Look at some of the most delicate and sensitive females—how they penetrate the abodes of strangers—how they persevere through dangers and difficulties, repelled by no contumely, and deterred by no hardship, simply because they know that the work in which they labour, is the cause of Christ. And shall we find less disinterested zeal, less ardour, less patience, less self-denial, in bosom-friends who share each other's confidence and love?

I am the more anxious to impress these observations upon the young reader, because the present is peculiarly a time for laudable and extraordinary exertions for the public good; and because I am convinced, that benevolent, and highly salutary, as these exertions are, they will never so fully answer the noble end desired, as when supported by the same principles faithfully acted upon in the intimate relations of private life.

↑ The Women of England.

CHAP. X.
LOVE AND COURTSHIP.

Love is a subject which has ever been open to discussion, amongst persons of all classes, and of every variety of mind and character; yet, after all, there are few subjects which present greater difficulties, especially to a female writer. How to compress a subject which has filled so many volumes, into the space of one chapter, is also another difficulty; but I will begin by dismissing a large portion of what is commonly called by that name, as wholly unworthy of my attention; I mean that which originates in mere fancy, without reference to the moral excellence of the object; and if my young readers imagine, that out of the remaining part they shall be able to elicit much amusement, I fear they will be disappointed; for I am one of those who think that the most serious act of a woman's whole life is to love.

What, then, I would ask, is love, that it should be the cause of some of the deepest realities in our experience, and of so much of our merriment and folly?

The reason why so many persons act foolishly, and consequently lay themselves open to ridicule, under the influence of love, I believe to originate in the grand popular mistake of dismissing this subject from our serious reading and conversation, and leaving it to the unceremonious treatment of light novels, and low jests; by which unnatural system of philosophy, that which is in reality the essence of woman's being, and the highest and holiest amongst her capabilities, bestowed for the purpose of teaching us of how much our nature is capable for the good of others, has become a thing of sly purpose, and frivolous calculation.

The very expression—"falling in love," has done an incalculable amount of mischief, by conveying an idea that it is a thing which cannot be resisted, and which must be given way to, either with or without reason. Persons are said to have fallen in love, precisely as they would be said to have fallen into a fever or an ague-fit; and the worst of this mode of expression is, that amongst young people, it has led to a general yielding up of the heart to the first impression, as if it possessed of itself no power of resistance.

It is from general notions such as these, that the idea, and the name of love, have become vulgarized and degraded: and in connection with this degradation, a flood of evil has poured in upon that Eden of woman's life, where the virtues of her domestic character are exercised.

What, then, I would ask again, is love in its highest, holiest character? It is woman's all— her wealth, her power, her very being. Man, let him love as he may, has ever an existence distinct from that of his affections. He has his worldly interests, his public character, his ambition, his competition with other men—but woman centres all in that one feeling, and

"In that *she* lives, or else *she* has no life."

In woman's love is mingled the trusting dependence of a child, for she ever looks up to man as her protector, and her guide; the frankness, the social feeling, and the tenderness of a sister—for is not man her friend? the solicitude, the anxiety, the careful watching of the mother—for would she not suffer to preserve him from harm? Such is love in a noble mind, and especially in its first commencement, when it is almost invariably elevated, and pure, trusting, and disinterested. Indeed, the woman who could mingle low views and selfish calculations with her first attachment, would scarcely be worthy of the name.

So far from this being the case with women in general, I believe, if we could look into the heart of a young girl, when she first begins to love, we should find the nearest resemblance to what poetry has described, as the state of our first parents when in Paradise, which this life ever presents. All is then coloured with an atmosphere of beauty, and light; or if a passing cloud sails across the azure sky, reflecting a transitory shadow on the scene below, it is but to be swept away by the next balmy gale, which leaves the picture more lovely for this momentary interruption of its stillness and repose.

But that which constitutes the essential charm of a first attachment, is its perfect disinterestedness. She who entertains this sentiment in its profoundest character, lives no longer for herself. In all her aspirations, her hopes, her energies, in all her noble daring, her confidence, her enthusiasm, her fortitude, her own existence is absorbed by the interests of another. For herself, and in her own character alone, she is at the same time retiring, meek, and humble, content to be neglected by the whole world—despised, forgotten, or contemned; so that to one being only she may still be all in all.

And is this a love to be lightly spoken of, or harshly dealt with? Oh no; but it has many a rough blast to encounter yet, and many an insidious enemy to cope with, before it can be stamped with the seal of faithfulness; and until then, who can distinguish the ideal from the true?

I am inclined to think it is from the very purity and disinterestedness of her own motives, that woman, in cases of strong attachment, is sometimes tempted to transgress the laws of etiquette, by which her conduct, even in affairs of the heart, is so wisely restricted. But let not the young enthusiast believe herself justified in doing this, whatever may be the nature of her own sentiments. The restrictions of society may probably appear to her both harsh, and uncalled for; but, I must repeat—society has good reasons for the rules it lays down for the regulation of female conduct, and she ought never to forget that points of etiquette ought scrupulously to be observed by those who have principle, for the sake of those who have not. Besides which, men who know the world so much better than women, are close observers on these points, and nothing can lessen their confidence in you more effectually, than to find you unscrupulous, or lax, even in your behaviour to them individually. If, therefore, your lover perceives that you are regardless of the injunctions of your parents or guardians even for his sake, though possibly he may feel gratified at the moment, yet his opinion of your principles will eventually be lowered, while his trust in your faithfulness will be lessened in the same degree.

In speaking of the entireness, the depth, and the disinterestedness of woman's love, I would not for a moment be supposed to class under the same head, that precocious tendency to fall in love, which some young ladies encourage under the idea of its being an amiable weakness. Never is the character of woman more despicable, than when she stoops to plead her weakness as a merit. Yet some complain that they are naturally so grateful, it is impossible for them to resist the influence of kindness; and thus they fall in love, perhaps with a worthless man—perhaps with two men at once; simply because they have been kindly treated, and their hearts are not capable of resisting kindness. Would that such puerile suppliants for the charity they ill deserve, could be made to understand how many a correct and prudent woman would have gone inconceivably farther than them, in gratitude, and generous feeling, had not right principle been made the stay of her conduct, and the arbitrer of all her actions. Love which arises out of mere weakness, is as easily fixed upon one object as another; and consequently is at all times transferable: that which is governed by principle, how much has it to suffer, yet how nobly does it survive all trial!

I have said, that woman's love, at least all which deserves that name, is almost universally exalted and noble in its commencement ; but that still it wants its highest attribute, until its faithfulness has been established by temptation and trial. Let no woman, therefore, boast of her constancy, until she has been put to the test. In speaking of faithfulness, I am far from supposing it to denote merely the tenacity of adhering to an engagement. It is easy to be true to an engagement, while false to the individual with whom it is contracted. My meaning refers to faithfulness of heart, and this has many trials in the common intercourse of society, in the flattery and attentions of men, and in the fickleness of female fancy.

To have loved faithfully, then, is to have loved with singleness of heart, and sameness of purpose, through all the temptations which society presents, and under all the assaults of vanity, both from within and without. It is so pleasant to be admired, and so soothing to be loved, that the grand trial of female constancy is, not to add one more conquest to her triumph?, where it is evidently in her power to do so; and, therefore, her only protection is to restrain the first wandering thought which might even lead her fancy astray. The ideas which commonly float through the mind of woman, are so rapid, and so indistinctly defined, that when the door is opened to such thoughts, they pour in like a torrent. Then first will arise some new perception of deficiency in the object of her love, or some additional impression of his unkindness or neglect, with comparisons between him and other men, and regret that he has not some quality which they possess, sadness under a conviction of her future destiny, pining for sympathy under that sadness, and, lastly, the commencement of some other intimacy, which at first she has no idea of converting into love.

Such is the manner in which, in thousands of instances, the faithfulness of woman's love has been destroyed, and destroyed far more effectually than if assailed by an open, and, apparently, more formidable foe. And what a wreck has followed! for when woman loses her integrity, and her self-respect, she is indeed pitiable and degraded. While her faithfulness remains unshaken, it is true she may, and probably will, have much to suffer; but let her portion in this life be what it may, she will walk through the world with a firm and upright step; for even when solitary, she is not degraded. It may be called a cold philosophy to speak of such consolation being available under the suffering which arises from unkindness and desertion, but who would not rather be the one to bear injury, than the one to inflict it; and the very act of bearing it meekly and reverently, as from the hand of God, has a purifying and solemnizing effect upon the soul, which the faithless and the fickle never can experience.

 (As friendship is the basis of all true love, it is equally—nay, more important that the latter should be submitted to the same test in relation to its ultimate aim, which ought supremely to be, the moral and spiritual good of its object. Indeed, without this principle at heart, no love is worthy of the name; because, as its influence upon human nature is decidedly the most powerful of any, its responsibilities are in the same proportion serious and imperative. What, then, shall we think of the woman who evinces a nervous timidity, about the personal safety of her lover, without any corresponding anxiety about the safety of his soul?)

But there is another delusion equally fatal with this, and still more frequently prevailing amongst well-meaning young women; I mean, that of listening to the addresses of a gay man, and making it the condition of her marrying him, that he shall become religious. Some even undertake to convert men of this description, without professing any personal interest in the result; and surely, of all the mockeries by which religion is insulted in this world, these are amongst the greatest. They are such, however, as invariably bring their own punishment; and, therefore, a little observation upon the working of this fallacious system upon others, will probably be of more service to the young, than any observations I can offer. I cannot, however, refrain from the remark, that religion being a matter of personal interest, if a man will not submit himself to its influence for his own sake, it is not likely he will do so for the sake of another; and the probability is, that, while endeavouring to convert him, the woman, being the weaker party, will be drawn over to his views and principles; or if hers should be too firm for this, that he will act the hypocrite in order to deceive.her, and thus add a new crime to the sum of guilt already contracted.

With a gay man, therefore, a serious woman can have nothing to do, but to contemplate his character as she would that of some being of a different order or species from her own. Even after such a man has undergone a moral and spiritual change, there will remain something in his tone of mind and feeling, from which a delicate and sensitive woman will naturally and unavoidably shrink. He will feel this himself; and while the humility and self-abasement which this conviction occasions, will constitute a strong claim upon her sympathy and tenderness, they will both be deeply sensible that, in his heart of hearts, there is a remembrance, a shadow, a stain, which a pure-minded woman must ever feel and sorrow for.

'But how are we to know a man's real character?' is the common question of young women. Alas! there is much willing deception on this point. Yet, I must confess, that men are seldom thoroughly known, except under their own roof, or amongst their own companions. With respect to their moral conduct, however, if they have a low standard of excellence with regard to the female sex in general, it is an almost infallible sign that their education, or their habits, have been such as to render them undesirable companions in the most intimate and indissoluble of all connections. Good men are accustomed to regard women as equal with themselves in their moral and religious character, and therefore they seldom speak of them with disrespect; but bad men having no such scale of calculation, use a very different kind of phraseology, when women, as a class, are the subject of conversation.

Again, the world is apt to speak of men as being good, because they are merely moral. But it would be a safe rule for all Christian women to reflect, that such are the temptations to man in his intercourse with the world, that nothing less than the safeguard of religion can render his conduct uniformly moral.

With regard to the social and domestic qualities of a lover, these must also be tried at home. If disrespectful to his mother, and inconsiderate or ungentle in his manners to his sisters, or even if accustomed to speak of them in a coarse, unfeeling, or indifferent manner, whatever may be his intellectual recommendations, as a husband he ought not to be trusted. On the other hand, it may be set down as an almost certain rule, that the man who is respectful and affectionate to his mother and his sisters, will be so to his wife.

Having thus described in general terms the manner in which women ought to love, the next inquiry is, under what circumstances this feeling may be properly indulged. The first restriction to a woman of delicacy, of course, will be never to entertain this sentiment towards one by whom it has not been sought and solicited. Unfortunately, however, there are but too many instances in which attentions, so pointed as not to be capable of being misunderstood, have wantonly been made the means of awakening something more than a preference; while he who had thus obtained this meanest of all triumphs, could smile at the consequences, and exult in his own freedom from any direct committal.

How the peace of mind of the young and the trusting is to be secured against such treatment, it is difficult to say; unless they would adopt the advice of the more experienced, and think less of the attentions of men in general, and more of their own immediate and practical duties, which, after all, are the best preservatives, not only against indolence, melancholy, and romance; but against the almost invariable accompaniment of these evils—a tendency to sentimental attachments. I am aware that I, incur the risk of being considered amongst young ladies as too homely in my notions, even for an admonitress, when I so often recommend good old-fashioned household duties; yet, I believe them nevertheless to be a wholesome medicine both to body and mind, and in no case more useful than in those of sentimentality.

In the bestowment of the affections, few women are tempted to make choice of men of weak capacity. Still there is sometimes a plausible manner, a gentlemanly address, or a handsome exterior, which serves for a while to bewilder the judgment, so as to conceal from detection the emptiness within. It is the constitutional want of woman's nature to have some superior being to look up to; and how shall a man of weak capacity supply this want? He may possibly please for an hour, or a day, but it is a fearful thought to have to dwell with such a one for life.

The most important inquiry, however, to be made in the commencement of an attachment, for it may be too late to make it afterwards, is, whether the object of it inspires with a greater love of all that is truly excellent—in short, whether his society and conversation have a direct tendency to make religion appear more lovely, and more desirable. If not, he can be no safe companion for the intimacy of married life; for you must have already discovered, that your own position as a Christian, requires support rather than opposition. It is the more important, therefore, that this inquiry should be most satisfactorily answered in an early stage of the attachment; because it is the peculiar nature of love to invest with ideal excellence the object of its choice, so that after it has once obtained possession of the heart, there ceases too generally to be a correct perception of good and evil, where the interests of love are concerned.

In addition to this tendency, it is deeply to be regretted, that so few opportunities are afforded to women in the present state of society, of becoming acquainted with the natural dispositions and general habits of those to whom they intrust their happiness, until the position of both is fixed, and fixed for life. The short acquaintance which takes place under ordinary circumstances, between two individuals about to be thus united, for better for worse, until death do them part, is anything but a mutual development of real character. The very name of courtship is a repulsive one; because it implies merely a solicitude to obtain favour, but has no reference to deserving it. When a man is said to be paying his court to an individual of higher rank or authority, he is universally understood to be using flattery and attention, if not artifice, to purchase what his merits alone would not be sufficient to command. I do not say that a similar line of conduct is designedly pursued by the lover, because I believe that in many cases he would be glad to have his character more clearly understood than it is. Yet, here we see, most especially, the evil consequences resulting from that system of intercourse, which prevails between the two sexes in general society. By the time a young woman is old enough to enter into a serious engagement, she has generally become so accustomed to receive the flattery and the homage of men, that she would feel it an insult to be treated with perfect honesty and candour; while, on the other hand, her lover redoubles his assiduity to convince her, that if not actually a goddess, she is at least the most charming of her sex. Need we be surprised if there should often be a fearful awaking from this state of delusion?

I must, however, in justice repeat, that the delusion is not all intentional on either part, for a successful suit, naturally places a man in so agreeable a position, that his temper and disposition, at such times, appear to the best possible advantage; while on the other hand, it would be strange indeed, if a woman so courted, and apparently admired, could not maintain her sweetest deportment, and wear her blandest smiles, through that short period which some unjustly call the happiest of her life, simply because it is the one in which she is the most flattered, and the most deceived.

It is a very erroneous notion, entertained by some young persons, that to make early pretensions to womanhood, is an embellishment to their character, or a means of increasing their happiness. Nothing in reality can be more entirely a mistake. One of the greatest charms which a girl can possess, is that of being contented to be a girl, and nothing more. Her natural ease of manner, her simplicity of heart, her frankness,her guileless and confiding truth, are all opposed to the premature assumption of womanhood. Even her joyous playfulness, so admirably adapted to promote the health both of mind and body,—oh! why does she hasten to lay all this aside for the mock dignity of an artificial and would-be woman? Believe me, the latter loses much of the innocent enjoyment of her early years, while she gains in nothing, except a greater necessity for care and caution.

Were it possible to induce the daughters of England to view this subject in its true light, and to endeavour to prolong rather than curtail the season of their simplicity and buoyancy of heart; how much would be avoided of that absurd miscalculation about the desirableness of contracting matrimonial alliances, which plunges hundreds and thousands into the responsible situation of wives and mothers, before they have well learned to be rational women.

A cheerful, active, healthy, and sound-minded girl, is ever the first to glow with the genuine impulse of what is noble and generous in feeling, thought, and action; and at the same time she is the last to be imposed upon by what is artificial, false, or merely superficial; for there seems to be a power in unsophisticated nature, to repel as if by instinct the mean stratagems of art. The vain, the sentimental, would-be woman, sickly for want of natural exercise, and disappointed in her precocious attempts at dignity and distinction, is the last to yield herself to any genuine impulse; because she must inquire whether it is lady-like and becoming; but, alas for her peace of mind! she is the first to listen to the voice of flattery, and to sink into all the absurdities of an early, a misplaced, or an imaginary attachment.

It is not indeed in the nature of things, that a young girl should know how to bestow her affections aright. She has not had experience enough in the ways of the world, or penetrated sufficiently through the smiling surface of society, to know that some who are the most attractive in their address and manners, are the least calculated for fireside companions. They know, if they would but believe what their more experienced relatives tell them, that the happiness of marriage must depend upon suitability of character; yet, even of this they are incompetent to judge, and consequently they are betrayed into mistakes sometimes the most fatal to their true interests, both here and hereafter.

How much wiser then is the part of her, who puts off these considerations altogether, until a period of greater maturity of judgment, when much that once looked dazzling and attractive shall have lost its false splendour; and when many qualifications of heart and mind, to which she once attached but little value, shall have obtained their due share of importance in her calculations. Her heart will then be less subject to the dictates of capricious fancy; and, looking at human life, and society, and mankind as they really are; looking at herself, too, with a clearer vision, and a more decided estimate of truth, she will be able to form a correct opinion on that point of paramount importance—suitability of character and habits.

Influenced by a just regard to this consideration, a sensible woman will easily see that the man of her choice must be as much as possible in her own sphere of life. Deficient in education, he would be a rude and coarse companion for a refined woman; and with much higher attainments than her own, he would be liable to regard her with disrespect, if not with contempt.

By a fatal misapprehension of what constitutes real happiness, it is often spoken of as a good and great thing, when a woman raises herself to a higher sphere in society by marriage. Could such individuals tell the story of their after lives, it would often be a history of humiliation and sorrow, for which no external advantages had been able to compensate. There are, however, admirable instances of women, thus exalted, who have maintained their own dignity, and the respect of all their connections; so much more important is moral worth than intellectual cultivation, to a woman. In these cases, however, the chief merit of the wife has been, that she never *sought* her elevation.

Having chosen your lover for his suitability, it is of the utmost consequence, that you should guard against that natural propensity of the youthful mind, to invest him with every ideal excellence. Endeavour to be satisfied with him as he is, rather than imagine him what he never can be. It will save you a world of disappointment in after life. Nor, indeed, does this extravagant investiture of the fancy belong, as is sometimes supposed, to that meek* and true, and abiding attachment which it is woman's highest virtue and noblest distinction to feel. I strongly suspect it is vanity, and not affection, which leads a young woman to believe her lover perfect ; because it enhances her triumph to be the choice of such a man. The part of a true-hearted woman, is to be satisfied with her lover, such as he is, and to consider him, with all his faults, as sufficiently exalted, and sufficiently perfect for her. No after-development of character can shake the faith of such a woman, no ridicule or exposure can weaken her tenderness for a single moment; while, on the other hand, she who has blindly believed her lover to be without a fault, must ever be in get of awaking to the conviction that her love exists no longer.

Though truth should be engraven upon every thought, and word, and act, which occurs in your intercourse with the man of your choice, there is implanted in the nature of woman, a shrinking delicacy, which ought ever to prompt her to keep back some of her affection for the time when she becomes a wife. No woman ever gained, but many, very many have been losers, by displaying all at first. Let sufficient of your love be told, to prevent suspicion, or distrust; and the self-complacency of man will be sure to supply the rest. Suffer it not, then, to be unfolded to its full extent. In the trials of married life, you will have ample need for an additional supply. You will want it for sickness, for sorrow, for all the different exigencies of real experience; but, above all, you will want it to re-awaken the tenderness of your husband, when worldly cares and pecuniary disappointments have too much absorbed his better feelings; and what surprise so agreeable to him, as to discover, in his farther progress through the wilderness of life, so sweet, so deep a fountain, as woman's perfect love?

This prudent and desirable restraint of female delicacy during the period of courtship, will prevent those dangerous demands being made upon mere affection to supply interest, for an occasion, which after all, and particularly to men of business, is apt to be rather a tedious one. Let your amusements, then, even during that period, be of an intellectual nature, that your lover may never even for a single moment have occasion to feel that your society grows vapid, or palls upon his taste. It is better a thousand times, that reading or conversation, or the company of others, should be forced upon him, so that he should regret having had so little of yours, than that the idea should once glance across his mind, that he had had too much, or that the time spent with you had not passed so pleasantly as he had expected.

It is a fact too little taken into account by young women, that until actually married, their relative and home-duties are the same after an engagement has been contracted, as before. When a daughter begins to neglect a father or a brother, for the sake of her lover, it is a bad omen for his happiness. Her attentions in this case are dictated by impulse, not duty; and the same misapprehension of what is just, and right, will in future be equally likely to divert them again from their proper object. It is good even to let your lover see, that such is your estimate of duty, that you can afford even to lose his society for a few minutes, rather than neglect the claims of your family.

I have now imagined a young woman brought into the most serious position she has yet occupied; and if her mind is rightly influenced, she will feel it to be one of deep and solemn consideration. If, during the lapse of her previous existence, she has lived for herself alone, now is the time when her regrets are about to begin; if, as I have so earnestly recommended, she has studiously cultivated habits of duty, and thoughts of affectionate and grateful regard towards her home-connections, now is the the when she will fully enter upon the advantages of having regulated her conduct by the law of love. Already she will have begun to contemplate the character of man in a new light. Admitted to his confidence, she will find him at the same time more admirable, and more requiring as regards herself, than she found him in society; and while her esteem increases with the development of his real merits, she will feel her affection equal to every demand, for she will be rich in that abundance which the heart alone can supply, whose warmest emotions have been called forth and cherished in the genial and healthy atmosphere of domestic life. One word before this chapter closes, to those who have arrived at years of womanhood without having known what it was to engage the attentions of a lover; and of such I must observe, that by some unaccountable law of nature, they often appear to be the most admirable of their sex. Indeed, while a sparkling countenance, an easy manner, and?to say the least of it?a *willingness* to be admired, attract a crowd of lovers; it not unfrequently happens, that retiring merit, and unostentatious talent, scarcely secure the homage of one. And yet, on looking around upon society, one sees so many of the vain, the illiterate, and the utterly useless, chosen and solicited as wives, that we are almost tempted to consider those who are not thus favoured as in reality the most honourably distinguished amongst their sex.   Still, I imagine there are few, if any, who never have had a suitable or unsuitable offer, at some time in their lives; and wise indeed by comparison, are those, who rather than accept the latter, are content to enjoy the pleasures, and endure the sorrows of life, alone. Compare their lot for an instant with that of women who have married from unworthy motives. How incomparably more dignified, more happy, and more desirable in every way, does it appear! It is true there are times in their experience when they will have to bear what woman bears so hardly—the consciousness of being alone ; but they escape an evil far more insupportable—that of being a slighted or an unloved wife.

If my remarks throughout this work have appeared to refer directly to a moral training for the married state, it has not been from any want of interest in those of whom I purpose to speak more fully hereafter, who never enter upon this condition, but simply because I believe the moral training which prepares a woman for one sphere of duty, is equally productive of benefit if she fills another; and I rest this belief upon my conviction, that all the loveliest and most estimable propensities of woman's nature, were bestowed upon her for early and continued exercise in a strictly relative capacity; and that, whether married or single, she will equally find the law of Christian love the only certain rule by which to regulate her conduct, so as to render her either happy herself, or the promoter of happiness in others.

CHAP. XI.
SELFISHNESS, VANITY, ARTIFICE, AND INTEGRITY.

It is my intention to occupy the present chapter with farther observations upon the three great enemies to woman's advancement in moral excellence—selfishness, vanity and artifice, as opposed to her disinterestedness, simplicity of heart, and integrity.

It seems to be a strange anomaly in her nature, that in connection with all which woman is capable of doing and suffering for the good of others, there should lurk about her heart a peculiar kind of selfishness, which the strong discipline of personal trial, and often of severe affliction, is frequently required to subdue. It is justly remarked of woman, that in cases of afflictive dispensation, the qualities of her heart and mind generally appear to the greatest advantage, and none of them more so, than her devotedness; by which I would be understood to mean, the power she sometimes evinces of throwing every consideration of self into the balance as nothing, when weighed against the interest or the happiness of those she loves. Supported under some of the most trying vicissitudes of life by this spirit of devotedness, her capabilities of acting and enduring have sometimes appeared almost superhuman; so much so, that when we contemplate woman in this point of view, we almost fail to recognize, as a being of the same species, the idle flutterer of the ball-room, or the listless murmurer beside the parental hearth.

It is a fearful thing to await the coming of "the dark days of sorrow," before the evil spirit of selfishness, shall be exorcised. Let us inquire, then, what aspect this enemy assumes in early life, in order that it may be the more easily detected, and expelled from its favourite citadel, the human heart.

Selfishness has other features besides greediness. It is a very mistaken notion, that because persons give freely, they cannot be selfish; for there is a luxury in giving, which sentimental epicures will sometimes not deny themselves, even for the sake of principle. Thus, some young people are liberal in making presents with their parents' hard-earned money, and even when the same money would be more properly and more justly applied in paying their lawful debts. Such is the mere generosity of impulse, which deserves no better name than self-gratification. Indeed, all acting from mere impulse, may be classed under the head of selfishness; because it has no object beyond the relief or satisfaction of the actor, without reference to its influence or operation upon others.

The aspect which female selfishness most frequently assumes in early life, may best be described as a kind of absorption in self, or a habit of making self at once the centre and limit of every consideration, which habit is far from being incompatible with liberality in giving. Everything, in this case, which forms the subject of conversation or thought, has reference to self; and separate from self, there are few which possess the slightest interest.

"I wish it was always winter," said a young lady very coolly to me, "the glare of the sunshine is so painful to my sight." I reminded her of the poor of our own species, and the animals of the creation in general; but she persisted in wishing it was always winter: and yet this young lady was generous in giving, but, like too many others, she was accustomed to look upon the whole universe only as it bore some relation or reference to herself. Nor does it follow either that such persons should entertain for themselves an inordinate admiration. To hear them talk, one would sometimes be led to suppose that self was the very being with whom, of all others, they were most dissatisfied; yet, all the while, they are too busy finding fault with self, to have time to approve or admire what they might otherwise behold in others.   How different is this state of mind and feeling from that which acknowledges the rule of Christian love! In accordance with this rule, it is highly important to begin early to think much of others, and to think of them kindly. We are all, when young, and especially those who believe themselves gifted with more than ordinary talent, tempted to think it both amusing and clever to find out the faults of others; and amongst the busy, the meddling, and the maliciously disposed, this habit does often unquestionably afford a more than lawful degree of amusement; while to her by whom it is indulged, it invariably proves in the end most destructive to genuine cheerfulness, good humour, and peace of mind; because its own nature being offensive, it raises up against her a host of enemies, by whom all that is wrong in her character is magnified, and all that is good is evil spoken of. At the same time she will also find, that this seeming cleverness is shared with the most vulgar-minded persons of both sexes, and of every grade in society, because none are so low as to be incapable of seeing the faults of their neighbours.

Could such young satirists be convinced how much real enjoyment they sacrifice for the sake of awakening a momentary interest in their conversation, they would surely pause before the habit should have become so far confirmed as to have repelled their nearest friends, and set them apart from all the social sympathies and sweet charities of life; for such is inevitably the consequence of persevering indulgence in this habit, but especially with such as possess no real talent for amusing satire, and who, in their futile attempts to attain the unenviable distinction of being satirical, ascend no farther than to acquire a habit of speaking spitefully. It is almost needless to say, that such women are seldom loved, and seldom sought, in cases where a sympathizing friend or kind assistant is required. When such individuals are overtaken by affliction, they then feel how different a thing it is to have wounded and repelled, from what it is to have soothed and conciliated. Happy for them if they begin to feel this before it is too late!

But if, in connection with their affliction, the minds of such individuals should become subject to impressions of a religious nature, and, as is natural in such cases, they should seek the society of religious people, how deeply will they then deplore that their unfortunate habit of thinking and speaking evil of others should have opened their eyes to a thousand little discrepancies of character, and fancied absurdities of conduct, in those it has become most important to their happiness that they should confide in! How do the ridiculous, the inconsistent, the vulgar, then start up to view, with a prominence that throws every other quality into shade; so that even while they listen to a religious discourse, their thoughts are entirely diverted by some peculiarity in the manner in which it is delivered.

And all this chain of sad consequences may arise out of the simple habit of trying to be striking and amusing in company, so that self may, by that means, be made an object of greater importance. In comparison with such behaviour, how beautiful is that of the simple-hearted young woman, who can be so absorbed in the conversation of others, as to forget that she has taken no part in it herself; but more especially admirable is the conduct of her, who looks only, or chiefly, for what is to be loved and commended in others; and who, though not insensible to the darker side of human nature, draws over it the veil of charity, because she considers all her fellow-creatures as heirs to the same sufferings and infirmities which she endures, yet as children of the same heavenly Father, and subject with herself to the same dispensation of mercy and forgiveness.

The habit of thinking perpetually of self is always accompanied by its just and necessary punishment—a more than ordinary share of wounded feeling. The reason is a very obvious one; that persons whose thoughts are usually thus engaged, are apt to suppose themselves the subject of general observation, and scarcely can a whisper be heard in the same room, but they immediately settle it in their own minds that they are the subject of injurious remark. They are also keenly alive to every slight; such as not being known or noticed when they are met, not being invited to visit their friends, and a thousand other acts of omission, which an unselfish disposition would kindly attribute to some other cause than intentional disrespect.

It is the result of selfishness, too, when we are so unreasonable as to expect that everybody should love us; or when we are piqued and irritated when convinced that some, upon whom we have but little claim, do not. Surely, so unfair a demand upon the good- will of society might be cured by asking, Do we love everybody, do justice to everybody, and deserve to be loved by everybody? For, until this is the case, what title have we to universal affection? It might also tend, in some degree, to equalize the balance of requirement in favour of self, if we would recollect that the faults we most dislike in others, may, all the while be less offensive to us, than ours are to them; and that not only for all the actual faults, but even for the objectionable peculiarities, which society puts up with in us, we owe a repayment, which can only be made in kindness and forbearance to others.

In the manners and appearance of persons accustomed to dwell much upon the slights they are subject to, and the injuries they receive from others, there is a restless uneasiness, and a tendency to groundless suspicion, as much at variance with peace of mind, as with that charity which "thinketh no evil." Compare with such a state of mind and feeling the sunny calm which lives, even in the countenance of her, whose soul is at peace with all the human race; who finds in all, even the most humble, something either to admire, or love; and who esteems whatever kindness she receives from others, as more than her own merits would have entitled her to expect; and we see at once the advantage she enjoys over those with whom self is the subject of paramount interest.

Another fatal enemy to woman's peace, as well as to her moral and spiritual advancement, is her tendency to a peculiar kind of petty artifice, as directly opposed, in its nature, to simplicity of heart, as to integrity. Artifice may possibly be considered too severe a name for what is scarcely more than a species of acting; or, perhaps, it may, with still greater propriety, be called, practising upon others, for the purpose of gratifying selfishness, and feeding vanity.

Affectation is the first symptom of this tendency. There are many kinds of affectation, differing in their moral nature according to the seriousness and importance of what is affected. Affectation of ignorance is, perhaps, the most absurd of all. Yet how often do we find a young pretender to gentility affecting not to know anything which is vulgar or mean: and, amongst this class, taking especial pains to place many things with which every rational being ought to be acquainted.

The affectation of sensibility is, perhaps, the most common of all; because that peculiar faculty of the female mind, bestowed for the purpose of rendering her more efficient as a minister of comfort and consolation, is looked upon rather as a matter of taste, than as a principle; just as if fine feelings were only given to women to look pretty with. Women who are vain of their sensibility, and wish to have it indulged, generally choose weak and flattering friends, to whom they constantly complain of what they suffer from excess of feeling.

It is, indeed, a lamentable fact, and most probably the consequence of some mismanagement in early youth, that the sensitiveness of some women is such as to render them altogether useless, and sometimes worse than useless, in any case of suffering or alarm. If such individuals sincerely regret this disqualification, they are truly deserving of our pity; but if they make a parade of it, no language can be strong enough for their condemnation.

Allusion has already been made to that affectation of modesty which consists in simpering and blushing about what a truly delicate mind would neither have perceived nor understood, nor would have been in the slightest degree amused by if it had.

Affectation of humility is often betrayed by a proneness in persons to accuse themselves of some darling fault; while they repel with indignation the suspicion that they possess any other.

That kind of affectation which relates especially to manner, consists chiefly in assuming a particular expression of countenance, or mode of behaviour, which is not supported by a corresponding state of feeling. Thus an affectation of attention, when the thoughts are wandering, instead of that quiet and fixed look which indicates real interest, produces a certain degree of uneasiness of countenance arising out of the restraint imposed upon nature, which effectually destroys the power of beauty; while those futile attempts at being brilliant, which consist only in flashes of the eye, smiles that have neither appropriateness nor meaning, and an expression of face changing suddenly from grave to gay—from despair to rapture—are sufficient indications of a state of mind almost too degraded and deplorable for ridicule.

Affectation of manner, however, is not unfrequently the result of excessive timidity; and then indeed it claims our tenderest compassion, and our kindest sympathy. I have known little girls, when harshly treated in childhood, acquire a constrained and affected manner, from the constant state of unnatural apprehension in which they lived. This kind of affectation is apt to become in after years a fixed habit, and has subjected many a well-meaning person to unmerited ridicule, and sometimes to contempt. Indeed, affectation of manner ought always to be guarded against, because of the unfavourable impression it is calculated to make upon others; and especially upon those who know of no higher qualities in connection with this peculiarity of manner, and upon whom it is consequently the only impression ever made, and the only standard by which the unfortunate subject of affectation is judged of for life. How much of the influence of good example, and the effect of benevolent effort, is frustrated by this seemingly insignificant cause, may be judged of by the familiar conversation which takes place in society, and particularly amongst the young, when they discuss the merits or demerits of persons from whose influence or authority they would gladly discover a plea for escaping.

Besides the timidity which belongs to constitutional fear, and which so frequently produces affectation of manner, there is a timidity of a widely different kind, about which many serious mistakes are made. I mean the timidity of the vain. Excessive vanity, excites a nervous trembling apprehension in the young candidate for public favour, which is often most erroneously supposed to arise from a low estimate of self. Nor is it impossible that it should arise from this cause, and be the consequence of vanity still; for, if I may use the expression, there is a vanity above par, and another vanity below it—there is a vanity which looks eagerly for homage, believing it to be a right; there is another which scarcely ventures into the field of competition, convinced of its inadequacy to succeed, but which nevertheless, retires with a feeling of sullenness and depression, not much allied to genuine humility. It is that state of vacillation between the excessive pleasure which admiration would afford if obtained, and the excessive pain which anything approaching to ridicule or contempt would occasion, that often imparts to the manners of the young, a blushing nervous kind of hesitation and backwardness, miscalled timidity. The timidity of modest feeling escapes from notice, and is happy; that of vanity escapes, and is piqued and miserable. She who suffers from the timidity of vanity, shrinks from society higher than herself, not so much from fear, as from jealousy of being outshone. The simple-hearted woman, desirous of improvement, esteems it a privilege to go into the company of her superiors, for the sake of what she may learn from those who are better informed, or more estimable, than herself.

In contemplating the nature and effects of artifice, or rather that system of practising upon others which I have endeavoured to describe, and in reflecting upon the state of mind which this species of practising indicates, we arrive at a more clear and decided idea of integrity, as directly opposed to this system, than we can by any other process of thought. There is in fact no means of giving a positive definition of integrity, so as to make it fully understood. We may call it a straightforward and upright mode of conduct; but it will still remain, as before, to be considered by young ladies a sort of thing which belongs to servants and trades people, but not to them.

It is a matter of surprise to some, and ought to be a subject of universal regret, that in our public seminaries for the training of youth, integrity should occupy so small a share of attention. Even in our popular works on education, it holds no very important place; and yet I am inclined to think, that a want of strict integrity is the greatest of all wants to a social, moral, and accountable being. In this opinion, I doubt not but many of my readers will cordially agree, because all are more or less inclined to restrict the meaning of integrity, to a conscientious abstaining from fraudulent practices. Thus, when a man has never been known to cheat in his business, it is said of him, that his integrity is unimpeachable; and a woman is dignified with the same character, when she is strict in keeping her accounts, and discharging her pecuniary debts. So far, both are entitled to our respect; but there are innumerable modes in which integrity operates upon character and conduct, besides what relate to the management of pecuniary affairs.

Simplicity of heart is perhaps more generally understood and admired than integrity, if we may judge by the frequent and eloquent manner in which it is expatiated upon by those who describe the attractions of youth. Simplicity of heart is unquestionably a great charm in woman; yet I cannot think it superior to integrity, because it consists more in ignorance of evil, and consequently of temptation, than in principle, which would withstand both. It consists chiefly in that unruffled serenity of soul, which suspects no lurking mischief beneath the fair surface of things in general—which trusts, and confides, and is happy in this confidence; because it has never been deceived, nor hag learned the fatal mystery of deceiving others. It is like the dew on the untrodden grass, the bloom of the flower, the down on the butterfly's wing, the purity of newly-fallen snow, before even a breath of wind has swept over it. Alas! what has it to do in this world of ours, where so many rude feet tread, and where so many rough winds blow? Consequently we find but little true simplicity of heart, except in early youth; or connected with a dullness of perception as to the nature and condition of the human race; or in situations where a very limited knowledge of the world is admitted.

But integrity we may find in every circumstance of life, because integrity is founded on principle; and consequently while not a stranger to temptation, its nature is to withstand it. Integrity is shown in a straightforward and upright line of conduct, on trifling, as well as on great occasions; in private, as well as in public; beneath the eye of God alone, as well as before the observation of men. It is a shield of protection under which no man can make us afraid; because when actuated in all things by the principle of integrity, no unexpected event can bring to light what we are afraid or ashamed to have known. The woman who walks through the world with unstained integrity, is always safe. No fear then of whispering tongues; or of those confidential revealings of friendly secrets, by which the creature of artifice is ever kept in a state of dread; no fear then of a comparing of evidence by different parties; of the treachery of private agents; of the mal-occurrence of contingent events; above all, of that half-implied suspicion which can with difficulty be warded off, except by an entire falsehood. The woman of integrity fears none of these. Her course is clear as that of the sun in the heavens, and the light she sheds around her in society, is scarcely less genial and pure.

Let us ask then, how this integrity may be preserved, or rather—for I fear that Will be more to the purpose—how it is most frequently, and most fatally destroyed.

There is reason to fear, that even home education is defective enough on this point; but if every one who has been educated at a public school, would tell one half of the many arts of subterfuge, trickery, and evasion, which she learned to practise there; and if all who are advanced in life would also trace out the consequences upon their subsequent conduct, of having learned in early life these lessons in the school of deception, I believe an amount of moral culpability, and of offensiveness in the sight of God, would be unfolded, which some of our early instructors would shudder to contemplate. On looking into the dark past, they would then see how, while they were so diligently and patiently—yes, and meritoriously too, teaching us the rules of grammar, arithmetic, and geography; expending their daily strength, and often their midnight thought, in devising and carrying out improved schemes for making us learn more languages, and remember more words; we had been almost equally busy in devising schemes to promote our own interest, to establish ourselves in the favour of our instructors, or to escape their too frequently well-merited displeasure.

And women from their very infancy are apt at all this; because to the timid, and affectionate little girl, it is so sad a thing to fall into disgrace—so pleasant a thing to be approved, and loved. Her young and tender spirit sinks like a broken flower, when she falls under condemnation; but springs up exulting like the lark, when commended by the lips she loves.

What, then, shall we say, when it is this very sensitiveness and tenderness of her nature, which so often, in the first instance, betrays her into ingenious, indirect, and too frequently unlawful means, for warding off blame, or obtaining praise. There is but one thing we can say—that in common kindness, in Christian charity, her education should be studiously rendered such as to strengthen her under this weakness, not to involve her more deeply in its worst consequences—the loss of her integrity.

Few persons are aware, until they have entered into a full and candid examination of this subject, how very minute, and apparently insignificant, are those beginnings, from whence flow some of the deepest channels of deception. Falsehood makes a serious beginning at school, when the master helps out a drawing, and the pupil obtains the praise, as if the whole work was her own. The master has most probably added only a few effective touches, so extremely small as not to be detected by an unpractised eye; and while the proud and triumphant mother exhibits the drawing to her flattering friends, it would be difficult indeed for the little girl to say it was not her own doing, because all the patience, all the labour, and a great deal of the merit, were unquestionably hers. Yet, to let it pass with these unqualified commendations bestowed upon her as the author, is a species of lying to God. Her young heart knows it to be so, and she feels either humbled, or confirmed in the deception. Happy! thrice happy, if it be the former!

Nor is home-education by any means exempt from its temptations to falsehood. There are many little deceptions practised upon unsuspecting mothers and absent fathers, which stain the page of youthful experience, and lead to farther and more skilful practice in the school of deception. There are stolen sweets, whose bitter fruit has been deliberate falsehood ; excuses made, and perhaps wholly believed, which were perhaps only half true; and sly thefts committed upon household property, to serve a selfish end; all which have had a degrading effect upon the character, and which in their worst consequences have led to one falsehood made use of to conceal another, and a third or a fourth to cover both.

But if childhood is beset with these temptations, how much has woman to guard against, when she first mixes with society, and enters the disputed ground, where, to be most agreeable, constitutes the strongest title to possession. She is then tempted to falsehood, not in her words only, but in her looks; for there is a degree of integrity in looks, as well as in expressions; and I am not quite sure that the woman who can look a falsehood, is not a worse deceiver than she who only tells one. All sweetness of look and manner, assumed for the purpose of gaining a point, or answering a particular end, comes under this description of artifice. Many persons who cannot conscientiously assent to what is said, assume a look of sympathy or approval, which sufficiently answers the purpose of deception, and at the same time escapes all risk of discovery as such. Thus, an implied assent by a smile and a nod, to what we do not believe, often spares us the trouble and pain of exposing our real sentiments, where they are unpopular, or would be likely to meet with inconvenient opposition.

Still I should be sorry to set down all persons who smile, and nod, and appear to assent to two different sides of a question, as intentional deceivers; because I believe that much of this sort of double-dealing arises out of the habit so many women indulge, of never making up their minds decidedly on any point of general interest, or viewing any subject in a distinct and determinate manner; so that they may almost be said really to think for the time in two different ways; at any rate, during the time they listen to each speaker separately, they are sufficiently convinced for them.

Thus it becomes the first act of integrity to endeavour to see, hear, and believe the truth, and then to speak it. A grateful woman, regardless of this rule, speaks of all persons as good, to whom she is indebted, or who have in any way served her purposes. Another, and a far more serious instance of the same kind of practice, consists in pretending not to see, or not to understand vice, where it is not convenient to believe in its existence; and this is often done by the same persons, who are quick to detect and expose it where such exposure is suited to their purpose.

And thus women in general become habituated to an indefinite way of thinking, and a careless mode of speech, both which may be serviceable to the mean-spirited, by preventing the detection of error in sentiment, or unsoundness of principle; though I believe neither of them were ever yet found available in assisting the cause of truth or righteousness.

Again, in the act of doing good, there is a manner of speaking of what we have done, which, though not directly false, is certainly at variance with strict integrity. I mean when young ladies talk especially about *their* schools, *their* poor women, and *their* old men; as if their individual charities were most benevolent in their operation, and unbounded in their extent; when perhaps they have but recently begun to be exercised in these particular channels. This is speaking the truth in such a manner, as to produce a false impression; and the consequence not unfrequently is, when really zealous and devoted people hear the speaker give this account of her good deeds, and when they take up the subject, and address her upon it, according to the impression her words have produced; that, rather than descend from the false position she has assumed, and lower herself in the opinion of those with whom she wishes to stand well, she goes on to practise farther artifice, or possibly plunges into actual falsehood. And it ought always to be borne in mind, that these little casual, but sometimes startling turns in common conversation, produce more actual untruths than the most trying circumstances in life, where we have incomparably more at stake. If we were all to take account each night of the untruths we had told in the course of the day, from an exaggerated description designed to make a story more amusing, down to the frequent case of receiving credit for an original remark, which we knew was not our own, I imagine few persons would find themselves altogether clear of having done violence to the pure spirit of truth. And if we add, also, to this list of falsehoods, all those unfair or garbled statements, which may tend to throw a brighter colouring over some cause we wish to advocate, or cast another into shade, I believe we should find that we bad indeed abundant need to pray for the renewed assistance of the Holy Spirit, to touch and guard our lips, so that they should utter no more guile.   Besides these instances of the want of integrity, in which our own consciences alone are concerned, there are others which demand a stricter attention to the claims of justice, as they relate to our friends, and to society at large. Under which head, I would notice the duty of doing justice to those we do not love, and especially to those who have injured us. Instead of which, how frequently do we find that young women begin to tell all the bad qualities of their friends, as soon as they have quarrelled with them. How often do we find, too, that such disagreements are related with conscious unfairness, their own evil being kept out of tight, as well as their friend's good, where there has been a mixture of both.

There is a common practice, too, when our own conduct is in any way called in question, and our friends kindly assign a plausible reason for what we have done, to let that pass as the real one, though we know, within our hearts, it is not so; or to let persons make a favourable guess respecting us, without contradicting it, though we know their conclusions, in consequence of our silence, or apparent assent, will be false ones.

Now, all these things, how insignificant soever they may appear to man, are important between the soul and its Maker, and must be deeply offensive in the sight of that Being who is of purer eyes than to behold iniquity. They are important, as forming parts of a whole, items of a mass, links in a chain, steps in a downward progress, which must lead away from a participation with the blessed, in a kingdom, whose enjoyments consist of purity and truth.

We have now come to that consideration of the subject of integrity, which relates to pecuniary affairs. And here what a field of operation opens before us, for the development of those principles of good or evil, of benevolence or selfishness, of uprightness or artifice, which I have endeavoured to describe, less by their own nature, than by their influence upon the manners and general conduct of women.

I believe there is nothing in the usages of society more fatal to the interests of mankind, to the spiritual progress of individuals, or to the general well-being of the human soul, than laxity of principle as regards our pecuniary dealings with each other. It is a case which all can understand—the worldly, as well as religious professors; if, then, the slightest flaw appears in the conduct of the latter in this respect; the interests of religion must be injured in consequence, and the cause of Christ must suffer.

"But it is impossible," say the fair readers of this page, "that this part of the subject can have any reference to us, we have so little to do with money;" or, perhaps, they say, "so little in our power to spend." Perhaps it is the very smallness of your supply according to the ideas you have formed of its inadequacy to meet your wishes, which is the cause of your want of integrity; for no one can act in strict accordance with the principles of integrity, until they have learned to practise economy. By economy, I do not mean simply the art of saving money, hut the nobler science of employing it for the best purposes, and in its just proportions.

In order to act out the principles of integrity in all their dignity, and all their purity, it is highly important, too, that young women should begin in early life to entertain a scrupulous delicacy with regard to incurring pecuniary obligations; and especially, never to throw themselves upon the politeness of gentlemen, to pay the minutest sum in the way of procuring for them gratification, or indulgence. I do not say that they may not frequently be so circumstanced, as, with the utmost propriety, to receive such kindness from near relations, or even from elderly persons; but I speak of men in general, upon whom they have not the claim of kindred; and I have observed the carelessness with which some young ladies tax the politeness— nay, the purses of gentlemen, respecting which it would be difficult to say, whether it indicated most an absence of delicate feeling, or an absence of integrity.

I am aware, that, in many cases, this unsatisfactory kind of obligation is most difficult to avoid, and, sometimes, even impossible; yet, a prompt and serious effort should always be made—and made in such a way that you shall clearly be understood to have both the wish, and the power, to pay your own expenses. If the wish is waiting, I can have nothing to say in so humiliating a case; but if you have not the means of defraying your own charges, it is plain that you have no right to enjoy your pleasures at the expense of another. There are, however, different ways of proposing to discharge such debts; and there is sometimes a hesitancy in the alternate advance and retreat of the fair lady's purse, which would require extraordinary willingness on the part of the gentleman, were his object to obtain a repayment of his own money.

It is the same in the settlement of all other debts. Delicacy ought seldom, if ever, to form a plea for their adjustment being neglected. Indeed, few persons feel their delicacy much wounded, by having the right money paid to them at the right time; or, in other words, when it is due. The same remarks will apply to all giving of commissions. Never let such affairs stand on and on, for want of a suitable opportunity for arranging their settlement; especially, never let the payment of a debt be longer delayed, because it is evidently forgotten by the party to whom it is owing.

All matters of business should also be adjusted as fairly, and as promptly, with friends and near relations, as with strangers; and all things in such cases should be as clearly understood. If the property transferred be intended as a gift, say so; if a loan, say that the thing is lent; and if a purchase, either pay for it, or name the price you expect. How many lasting and lamentable misunderstandings amongst the nearest connections would this kind of integrity prevent! how much wounded feeling, disappointment, and chagrin!

It is a mistaken view of economy, and evinces a great want of integrity, when persons are always endeavouring to obtain services, or to purchase goods, at a lower rate than their *just* value. But if the vender of an article be indebted to you for a kindness, it is something worse than mean, to ask, for that reason, an abatement in its price.

In many cases where our claims are just, it is easy to press them in an unjust manner; and we never do this more injuriously to the interests of society, than when we urge work-people beyond what is necessary, by telling them that a thing will positively be needed at a certain time, when we do not really believe it will. There is a general complaint against dressmakers, shoemakers, and many other makers of articles of clothing, that they are habitually regardless of punctuality and truth. But I am disposed to think the root of the grievance in a great measure arises out of the evil already alluded to, on the part of the ladies by whom they are employed.

Let us imagine the case of a young dressmaker, one of that most pitiable-class of human beings, whose pallid countenances, and often deformed and feeble frames, sufficiently attest the unnatural exertions by which they obtain their scanty bread. A young lady wishes to have a dress elaborately made, and for the sake of having it done expeditiously, names the precise day on which it must be finished, adding as a sufficient reason for punctuality, that it must then be worn. The poor dressmaker sits all night long in her little joyless room, working by the light of a thin candle, while the young lady sleeps soundly in her bed. The Sabbath dawns, and the dressmaker is still at work; until passing feet begin to be heard in the street, and shutters are unclosed; and then, with aching head and weary limbs, she puts away her unfinished task, doubting whether the remainder of the day shall be devoted to the sleep which exhausted nature demands, or to wandering abroad to search for purer air, of which that nature is equally in need. The day arrives at last on which the dress must be taken home, according to appointment. This time the dressmaker is punctual, because she believes that delay would be of consequence. She knocks at the door of the lady's mansion. The servant coolly tells her that her young mistress has gone to spend a few days in the country. Is it likely that this poor workwoman should be equally punctual the next time her services are required? or need we ask how the law of love has operated here?

The habit of keeping strict accounts with regard to the expenditure of money, is good in all circumstances of life; but it is never so imperative a duty, as when we have the property of others committed to our care. Unfaithfulness in the keeping and management of money which belongs to others, has perhaps been the cause of more flagrant disaster and disgrace, than any other species of moral delinquency which has stained the character of man, or woman either. Yet, how easily may this occur, without an extreme of scrupulous care, which the young cannot too soon, or too earnestly learn to practise. Even in the collecting of subscriptions for two different purposes, small sums, by some slight irregularity, may become mixed; and integrity is sacrificed, if the minutest fraction be eventually placed to the wrong account.

I cannot for an instant suppose that a Christian woman, under any circumstances, even the most difficult and perplexing, could be under the slightest temptation to appropriate to her own use, for a month, a week, a day, or an hour, the minutest item of what she had collected for another purpose, trusting to her own future resources for its reimbursement; because this would be a species of dishonesty, which, if once admitted as a principle of conduct, would be liable to terminate in the most fearful and disastrous consequences. It is the privilege of the daughters of England, that they have learned a code of purer morals, than to admit even such a thought, presented under the form of an available means of escape from difficulty, or attainment of gratification. Still it is well to fortify the mind, as far as we are able, against temptation of every kind, that if it should occur—and who can be secure again it?—we may not be taken unawares by an enemy whose assaults are sometimes as insidious, as they are always untiring.

One of the means I would now propose to the young reader, is to turn with serious attention to the case of Ananias and Sapphira, as related in the Acts of the Apostles; nor let it be forgotten, that this appalling act of moral delinquency, originating in selfishness, and terminating in falsehood, was the first sin which had crept into the fold of Christ, after the Shepherd had been withdrawn, and while the flock remained in a state approaching the nearest to that of perfect holiness, which we have reason to believe was ever experienced on this earth, since the time when sin first entered into the world.

Yes, it is an awful and impressive thought, that even in this state, temptation was allowed to present itself in such a form, accompanied with a desire still to stand well with the faithful, even after integrity was gone. The words of Peter are most memorable on this occasion. *Whiles it remained, was it not thine own? and after it was sold, was it not in thine own power?* Evidently implying, that it was better not to pretend to act upon high and generous principles, than not to do so faithfully. He then concludes in this emphatic language: "*Thou hast not lied unto men, but unto God.*" By which we learn, that every species of dishonesty practised between the soul and its Maker, is equally offensive in the sight of God, as that which is evident to men; and that there is no clear, upright, and faithful walk for any human being in this world, whether young or old, whether rich or poor, whether exalted or lowly, but that which is in strict accordance with the principles of integrity.

CHAP. XII.
DEDICATION OF YOUTH.

 Without having made any pretension in this volume to class it under the head of a religious work, I have endeavoured to render it throughout conducive to the interests of religion, by pointing out those minor duties of life, and those errors of society, which strictly religious writers almost universally consider as too insignificant for their attention. And, perhaps, it is not easy to interweave these seeming trifles in practice, with the great fundamental principles of Christian faith.

I cannot but think, however, that, to many, and especially to the young, this minuteness of detail may have its use, by bringing home to their attention familiar instances upon which Christian principle may be brought to bear. For I am one of those who think that religion ought never to be treated or considered as a thing set apart from daily and familiar use, to be spoken of as belonging almost exclusively to sabbaths, and societies, and serious reading. To me it appears that the influence of religion should be like an atmosphere, pervading all things connected with our being; that it ought to constitute the element in which the Christian lives, more than the sanctuary into which he retires. When considered in this point of view, nothing can be too minute to be submitted to the test of its principles; so that, instead of our worldly and our spiritual concerns occupying two distinct pages in our experience, the one, according to this rule, becomes regulated by our spiritual views; and the other applied to our worldly avocations, as well as to our eternal interests.

In relation to this subject, it has been remarked, in the quaint language of an old writer, that no sin is "little in itself, because there is no *little* law to be despised; no *little* heaven to be lost; no *little* hell to be endured;" and it is by this estimate that I would value every act, and every thought, in which the principles of good and evil are involved.

The great question, whether the principles of Christian faith, or, in other words, whether the religion of the Bible, shall be adopted as the rule of conduct by the young, remains yet to be considered, not in relation to the nature of that faith, but as regards the desirableness of embracing it at an early period of life, willingly and entirely, with earnestness, as well as love.

I am writing thus, on the supposition, that, with all who read these pages, convictions of the necessity and excellence of personal religion have at one time or other been experienced. The opinion is general, and, I believe, correct, that the instances are extremely rare in which the Holy Spirit does not awaken the human soul to a sense of its real situation as an accountable being, passing through a state of probation, before entering upon an existence of endless duration. Nor amongst young persons born of Christian parents, and educated in a Christian country, where the means of religious instruction are accessible to all, is it easy to conceive that such convictions have not, at times, been strong and deep; though, possibly, they may have been so neglected as to render their recurrence less frequent, and less powerful in their influence upon the mind.

Still it is good to recall the time when the voice of warning, and of invitation, was first heard; to revisit the scene of a father's faithful instruction, and of the prayers of a lost mother; to hear again the sabbath- evening sermon, to visit the cottage of the dying Christian; or even to look back once more into the chamber of infancy, where our first tears of real penitence were shed. It is good to remember how it was with us in those by-gone days when we welcomed the chastisements of love, and kissed the rod that was stretched forth by a Father's hand. How blest did we then feel, in the belief that we were not neglected, not forgotten, not overlooked! Has anything which the world, we have too much loved, since offered us, afforded a happiness to be compared with this belief? Oh! no. Then why not hearken, when the same voice is still inviting you to come? and why not comply when the same hand is still pointing out the way to peace ? What is the hinderance which stands in your way? What is the difficulty which prevents the dedication of your youth to God? Let this question be seriously asked, and fully answered; for it is of immense importance that you should know on what grounds the invitations of the Holy Spirit have been rejected; and why you are adopting another rule of conduct than that which is prescribed in the gospel of Christ.

I repeat, it is of immense importance, because this is a subject which admits of no trifling. If it is of importance in every branch of mental improvement, that we should be active, willing, earnest, and faithful, it is still more important here. When we do not persevere in learning, it does not follow of necessity that we grow more ignorant, because we may remain where we are, while the rest of the world goes on. But, in religion, there is no standing still, because opportunities neglected, and convictions resisted, are involved in the great question of responsibility; so that no one can open their Bible, or attend the means of religious instruction, or spend a Sabbath, or even enter into solemn communion with their own heart, as in the sight of God, but they must be so much the worse for such opportunities of improvement, if neglected or despised.

I have dwelt much in this volume upon the law of perfect love, as well as upon the sincerity and the faithfulness with which that law should be carried out; and never is this more important, or more essential, than in our religious profession. The very groundwork of the Christian faith is love; and love can accomplish more in the way of conformity in life and practice, than could ever be effected by the most rigid adherence to what is believed to be right, without assistance from the life-giving principle of love.

Still the state of the Christian in this world is always described as one of warfare, and not of repose; and how, without earnestness, are temptations to be resisted, convictions acted upon, or good intentions carried out? As time passes on, too, faithfulness is tried. What has been adopted, or embraced, must be adhered to; and in this, with many young persons, consists the greatest of their trials; for there is often a reaction on first learning to understand something of the realities of life, which throws them back from the high state of expectation and excitement, under which they first embraced religious truth.

But let us return to the objections which most frequently operate to prevent the young surrendering themselves to their convictions of the importance and necessity of personal religion. "If I begin, I must go on." Your mind is not then made up. You have not counted the cost of coming out from the world, nor honestly weighed the advantages of securing the guidance, support, and protection of personal religion, against every other pursuit, object, or idol of your lives. Perhaps it is society, amusement, or fashion, which stands in your way. Be assured there is society of the highest order, where religion is supreme; and if not exactly what is popularly called amusement, there is a heartfelt interest in all which relates, however remotely, to the extension of the kingdom of Christ—an interest unknown to those who have no bond of union, founded upon the basis of Christian love.

Is it possible, then, that fashion can deter you—fashion, a tyrant at once both frivolous and cruel—fashion, who never yet was rich enough to repay one of her followers, for the sacrifice of a single happy hour—fashion, whose realm is folly, and who is perpetually giving place to sickness, sorrow, and the grave? Compare for one instant her empire with that of religion. I admit that her power is extensive, almost all-pervading; but what has her sovereign sway effected upon the destinies of man? She has adjusted ornaments, and selected colours; she has clothed and unclothed thousands, and arrayed multitudes in her own livery—but never has fashion bestowed dignity or peace of mind upon one single individual of the whole family of nan.

It would be an insult to the nature and the power of religion to proceed farther with the comparison. Can that which relates merely to the body, which is fleeting as a breath, and unstable as the shadow of a cloud, deter from what is pure, immortal, and divine?

Still I am aware it is easy, in the solitude of the chamber, or in the privacy of domestic life, to think and speak in this exalted strain, and yet to go into the society of the fashionable, the correct, and the worldly-minded, who have never felt the necessity of being religious, and to be suddenly brought, by the chilling influence of their reasoning or their satire, to conclude that the convenient season for you to admit the claims of religion upon your heart and life, has not yet arrived. I believe the most dangerous influence, which society exercises upon young women, is derived from worldly-minded persons, of strong common sense, who are fashionable in their appearance, generally correct in their conduct, and amiable and attractive in their manners and conversation. Young women guardedly and respectably brought up see little of vice, and know little of   "The thousand paths which slope the way to sin."

They are consequently comparatively unacquainted with the beginnings of evil, and still less so with those dark passages of life, to which such beginnings are calculated to lead. It follows, therefore, that, except when under the influence of strong convictions, they may be said to be ignorant of the real necessity of religion. It is but natural then, that those correct and well-bred persons, to whom allusion has been made, who pass on from the cradle to the brink of the grave, treating religion with respect, as a good thing for the poor and the disconsolate, but altogether unnecessary for *them*, should appear, on a slight examination of the subject, to be living in a much more enviable state, than those who believe themselves called upon to renounce the world and its vanities, and devote their time, and their talents, their energies and their affections, to a cause which the worldly-minded regard at best, as visionary and wild.

I have spoken of such persons passing on to the brink of the grave, and I have used this expression, because, I believe the grave has terrors, even to them; that when one earthly hold after another gives way, and health declines, and fashionable friends fall off, and death sits beckoning on the tomb-stones of their newly buried associates and relatives; I believe there is often a fearful questioning, about the realities of eternal things, and chiefly about the religion, which in idea they had set apart for the poor, the aged, and the disconsolate, but would none of it themselves.

Yes, I believe, if the young could witness the solitude of such persons, could visit their chambers of sickness, and gain admittance to the secret counsels of their souls, they would find there an aching void, a want, a destitution, which the wealth and the fashion, the pomp and the glory of the whole habitable world, would be insufficient to supply.

It is often secretly objected by young people, that, by making a profession of religion they should be brought into fellowship and association with vulgar persons: in answer to which argument, it would be easy to show that nothing can be more vulgar than vice, to say nothing of worldly-mindedness. It is, however, more to the purpose to endeavour to convince them, that true religion is so purifying in its own nature, as to be capable of elevating and refining minds which have never been either softened or enlightened by any other influence.

All who have been extensively engaged in the practical exercise of Christian benevolence; and who, in promoting the good of their fellow-creatures, have been admitted to scenes of domestic privacy amongst the illiterate and the poor, will bear their testimony to the fact, that religion is capable of rendering the society of some of the humblest and simplest of human beings, as truly refined, and far more affecting in its pathos and interest, than that of the most intelligent circles in the higher walks of life. I do not, of course, pretend to call it as refined in manners, and phraseology; but in the ideas and the feelings which its conversation is intended to convey. That is not refined society where polished language is used as the medium for low ideas; but that in which the ideas are raised above vulgar and worldly things and assimilated with thoughts and themes on which the holy and the wise, the saint and the philosopher, alike delight to dwell.

It is no exaggeration then to say, that the conversation of the humble Christian on her death-bed—her lowly bed of suffering, surrounded by poverty and destitution—is sometimes so fraught with the intelligence of that celestial world on which her hopes are fixed, that to have spent an hour in her presence, is like having had the glories of heaven, and the wonders of immortality, revealed. And is this a vulgar or degrading employment for a refined and intellectual being? to dwell upon the noblest theme which human intellect has ever grasped, to look onward from the perishable things of time to the full development of the eternal principles of truth and love? to forget the sufferings of frail humanity, and to live by faith amongst the ransomed spirits of the blest, in the presence of angels, and before the Saviour, ascribing *honour, and glory, dominion, and power, to Him that sitteth on the throne, and to the Lamb forever and ever?*

In turning back to the world, from the contemplation of such a state of mind, we feel that vulgarity consists neither in religion itself, nor in its requirements, but in attaching undue importance to the things of time, and in making them our chief, or only good.

If young people are often deterred from becoming religious by seeing a great number of genteel, correct, and agreeable persons, who, for anything they can discover to the contrary, are doing very well without it they are still more forcibly deterred by feeling no want of it within themselves.

Perhaps you are so protected by parents, and so hemmed in by domestic regulations, that you feel it more difficult to do what is positively wrong, than what is generally approved as right. But do not be so blind and presumptuous as to mistake this apparently inoffensive state, for being religious; and remember, if it is difficult to do wrong now, it is the last stage of your experience in which you will find it so. Obliged to quit the parental roof, deprived by death of your natural protectors, required as years advance to take a more active part in the duties of life, or to incur a greater share of culpability by their neglect; thrown amongst strangers, or friends who are no longer watchful or solicitous for your temporal and spiritual good; involved in new connections, and exposed to temptations both from within and from without, how will your mind, lately so careless and secure, awake to a conscious feeling of your own weakness, and a secret terror of impending harm. For woman from her very feebleness is fearful; while from her sensitiveness she is peculiarly exposed to pain. Without religion, then, she is the most pitiable, the most abject, the most utterly destitute of all created beings. The world—society—nay, even domestic life, has nothing to offer on which her heart in its unregenerate state can rest in safety. Each day is a period of peril, if not of absolute agony; for all she has to give—her affections, which constitute her wealth—are involved in speculations, which can yield back into her bosom nothing but ashes and mourning.

It is not so with the woman who has made religion her stronghold—her defence—her stay. Unchecked in the happiest and most congenial impulse of her nature, she can still love, because the Lord her God has commanded that she should love him with all her heart, and with all her strength, and that she should love her neighbour as herself. Thus, though disappointment or death may blight her earthly hopes; or though a cloud may rest upon the bestowment of her affections in this vale of tears, the principle of love which fills her soul remains the same, and she is most happy when its sphere of exercise is unbounded and eternal. And is it possible that any of the rational beings whom I am addressing would dare to rush upon the dangers and temptations of this uncertain and precarious life, without the protection and support of religion? Oh! no, they tell me they are all believers in religion?all professors of the Christian faith. But are you all religious? Deceive not yourselves. There is no other way of being Christians, except by being personally religious. If not personally religious now, are you then ready to begin to be so? Delay not; you have arrived at years of discretion, and are capable of judging on many important points. You profess to believe in a religion which expressly teaches you that it is itself the one thing needful. What then stands in the way? If, after mature and candid deliberation, you decidedly prefer the world, injure not the cause of Christ by an empty profession, nor act the cowardly part of wearing the outward badge of a faith which holds not possession of your heart and affections. It is neither honourable nor just to allow any one to doubt on whose side you are. If, therefore, your decision be in favour of religion, it is still more important that you should not blush to own a Saviour, who left the glory of the heavenly kingdom, inhabited a mortal and suffering frame, and finally died an ignominious death, for you.   Nor let the plea of youth retard the offering of your heart to Him who gave you all its capacity for exquisite and intense enjoyment. If you are young, you are happy in having more to offer. Though it constitutes the greatest privilege of the Christian dispensation, that we are not required to bring anything by which to purchase the blessings of pardon and salvation; it surely must afford some additional satisfaction to a generous mind, to feel that because but a short period of life has passed away, there is more of health and strength, of elasticity and vigour, to bring into the field of action, than if the decision upon whose side to engage, had been deferred until a later period.

What, for instance, should we think of the subjects of a gracious and beneficent sovereign, who maintained a small territory in the midst of belligerent foes, if none of these subjects would consent to serve in his army for the defence of his kingdom, until they had wasted their strength and their vigour in the enemy's ranks, in fighting deliberately and decidedly against the master, whom yet they professed to consider as their rightful lord; and then, when all was lost, and they were poor, decrepit, destitute, and almost useless, returned to him, for no other reason, but because he was a better paymaster than the enemy, under whose colours they had fought for the whole of their previous lives? What should we say, if we beheld this gracious master willing to receive them on such terms, and not only to receive, but to honour and reward them with the choicest treasures of his kingdom? We should say, that one of the most agonizing thoughts which could haunt the bosom of each of those faithless servants, would be regret and self-reproach, that he had not earlier entered upon the service of his rightful lord.

There is besides, this fearful consideration connected with the indecision of youth, that in religious experience none can remain stationary. Where there is no progress, there must be a falling back. *He who is not with me, is against me*, was the appalling language of our Saviour when on earth; by which those who are halting between two opinions, and those who are imagining themselves safe on neutral ground, are alike condemned, as being opposed to the Redeemer's kingdom. It is but reasonable, however, that the young should understand the principles, and reflect maturely upon the claims, of religion, before their decision is openly declared. Much injury has been done to individuals, as well as to society at large, by a precipitate and uncalculating readiness to enlist under the banners of the Cross, before the duties of a faithful soldier of Christ have been duly considered. It is the tendency of ardent youth, to invest whatever it delights in for the moment, with ideal qualities adapted to its taste and fancy. Thus has religion often—too often—been decked in charms more appropriate to the divinities of Greece and Rome, than to the worship of a self-denying and persecuted people, whose lot on earth, they have been fully warned, is not to be one of luxury or repose.

The first and severest disappointment to which the young enthusiast in religion is subject, is generally that of finding, on a nearer acquaintance with the devout men and honourable women who compose the religious societies into which they are admitted, that they have faults and failings like the rest of mankind, and even inconsistencies in their spiritual walk, which are still more unexpected, and more difficult to reconcile. The first impulse of the young, on making this discovery, is often to give up the cause altogether; 'for if such,' say they, 'be the defects of the Christian character, after such a season of experience, and while occupying so exalted a position, it can be of little use to us to persevere in the same course.' They forget, or perhaps they never have considered, that the highest attainment of the Christian in this world, is often that of alternate error and repentance; and that it is the state of the heart before God, of which he alone is the judge, which constitutes the difference betwixt a penitent, and an impenitent sinner. Besides which, they know not all. The secret struggles of the heart, the temptations overcome, the tears of repentance, which no human eye beholds, must alike be hid from them, as well as the fearful effects upon the peace of mind which these inconsistencies so seriously disturb, or destroy. A wiser application of this humbling lesson, would be, for youth to reflect, that if such be the defects in the character of more experienced Christians, they themselves enjoy the greatest of all privileges, that of profiting by the example of others, so as to avoid stumbling where they have fallen; and instead of petulantly turning back from a path which will still remain to be right, though thousands upon thousands should wander from it, they will thus be enabled to steer a steadier course, and to finish it with greater joy.   Another great discouragement to the young, consists in finding their efforts to do good so feeble and unavailing—nay, sometimes almost productive of evil, rather than of good. In their charities, especially, they find their confidence abused, and their intentions misunderstood. On every hand, the coldness of the rich, and the ingratitude of the poor, alike repel their ardour. If they engage in schools, no one appears the better for their instruction. If they connect themselves with benevolent societies, they find their individual efforts so trifling, in comparison with the guilt and the misery which prevail, as scarcely to appear deserving of repetition; while, in the distribution of religious books, and the general attention they give to the spiritual concerns of the ignorant and the destitute, they perceive no fruit of all their zeal, and all their labour.

I freely grant, that these are very natural and reasonable causes of depression, and such as few can altogether withstand; but there is one important secret which would operate as a remedy for such depression, if we could fully realize its supporting and consoling power. The secret is, are we doing all this unto God, or unto man? If unto man, and in our own strength, and solely for the sake of going about doing good; but especially if we have done it for the sake of having been seen and known to have done it; even if we have done it for the sake of the reward which we believe to follow the performance of every laudable act; or with a secret hope of thereby purchasing the favour of God; we have no need to be surprised, or to murmur at such unsatisfactory results, which may possibly have been designed as our wholesome chastisement, or as the means of checking our farther progress in folly and presumption.

But, if in every act of duty or kindness we engage in, we are actuated simply by a love to God, and a sense of the vast debt of gratitude we owe for all the unmerited mercies we enjoy, accompanied with a conviction, that whatever the apparent results may be, our debt and our duty are still the same; that whatever the apparent results may be, our heavenly Father has the overruling of them, and is able to make everything contribute to the promotion of his glory, and the extension of the Redeemer's kingdom, though in ways which we may neither be able to perceive nor understand; then, indeed, with this view of the subject, we are enabled to persevere through every discouragement, rejoicing only in the ability to labour, and leaving the fruit of our labour with him who has appointed both.

I must yet allude to another cause of discouragement with which the young have to contend, and that is, their own spiritual declension, after the ardour of their early zeal has abated. Perhaps I ought rather to say, their imagined declension, because I believe they are often nearer heaven in this humbled, and apparently degraded state, than when exulting in the confidence of untried patience, fortitude, and love. The prevalent idea under this state of mind is, that of their own culpability, in having made a profession of religion in a state of unfitness, or on improper and insufficient grounds, accompanied with an impression that they are undergoing a just punishment for such an act of presumption, and that the only duty which remains for them to do, is to give up the profession of religion altogether. Perhaps no delusion is greater, or more universal, than to believe, that because we have been wrong in assuming a position, we must, necessarily, throw ourselves out of it, in order to be right. This principle would, unquestionably, be just, in all situations where any particular qualification was needed, which could not immediately be acquired; but, if the regret be so great on discovering that you are deficient in the evidences of personal religion, surely you can have no hesitation in choosing to lay hold of the means which are always available for obtaining that divine assistance, which shall render your profession sincere, rather than to give up the duties, the hopes, and the privileges of religion altogether.

It becomes a serious inquiry on these occasions, whether the inclination is not wrong, and whether a plea is not even wished for, as an excuse for turning back, after having laid the hand on the plough. If not, the alternative is a safe, and easy one. Begin afresh. Make a fresh dedication of the heart to God. Commence the work as if it had never been undertaken before, and all may yet be well—perhaps better than if you had never doubted whether you stood upon the right foundation.

It should always be remembered, for the consolation and encouragement of youth, that in making the decision in favour of religion in early life, there is comparatively little to undo; while if this most important duty is left until a later period, there will be the force of long established habit to contend with on the side of wrong, meshes of evil to unravel, dark paths to travel back, and all that mingled texture of light and darkness, which originates in a polluted heart, and a partially enlightened understanding, to separate thread from thread. And, oh! what associations, what memories are there! what gleaming forth again of the false fire, even after the true has been kindled! what yawning of the wide sepulchre in which the past is buried, though it cannot rest! what struggling with the demons of imagination, before they are cast out forever! what bleeding of the heart, which, like a chastened child, would kiss the rod, yet dare not think how many stripes would be commensurate with its delinquency! Oh! happy youth! it is thy privilege, that this can never be thy portion!

Yes, happy youth! for thou art ever happy in the contemplation of age; and yet thou hast thy tears. Thou hast thy trials too; and perhaps their acuteness renders them less bearable than the dull burden of accumulated sorrow, which hangs upon maturer years. Thou hast thy sorrows: and when the mother's eye is closed, that used to watch thy infant steps so fondly; and the father's hand is cold, that used to rest upon thy head with gentle and impressive admonition; whom hast thou, whom wilt thou ever have, to supply thy parents' place on earth? Whom hast thou? The world is poor to thee; for none will ever love thee with a love like theirs. Thou hast thy golden and exuberant youth, thy joyous step, thy rosy smile, and we call thee happy. But thou hast also thy hours of loneliness, thy disappointments, thy chills, thy blights; when the hopes on which thy young spirit has soared begin for the first time to droop; when the love in which thou hast so fondly trusted begins to cool; when the flowers thou hast cherished begin to fade; when the bird thou hast fed through the winter, in the summer flies away; when the lamb thou hast nursed in thy bosom, prefers the stranger to thee.—Thou hast thy tears; but the bitterest of thy sorrows, how soon are they assuaged? It is this then which constitutes thy happiness, for we all have griefs; but long before old age, they have worn themselves channels which cannot be effaced. It is therefore that we look back to youth with envy; because the tablet of the heart is then fresh, and unimpressed, and we long to begin again with that fair surface, and to write upon it no characters but those of truth.

And will not youth accept the invitation of experience, and come before it is too late?—and come with all its health, and its bloom, and its first-fruits untainted, and lay them upon the altar; an offering which age cannot make? Let us count the different items in the riches which belong to youth, and ask, if it is not a holy and a glorious privilege to dedicate them to the service of the Most High?

First, then, there is the freshness of unwearied nature, for which so many millions pine in vain; the glow of health, that life-spring of all the energies of thought and action; the confidence of unbroken trust—the power to believe, as well as hope—a power which the might of human intellect could never yet restore; the purity of undivided affection; the earnestness of zeal unchilled by disappointment; the first awakening of joy, that has never been depressed; high aspirations that have never stooped to earth; the clear perception of a mind unbiassed in its search of truth; with the fervour of an untroubled soul.

All these, and more than pen could write or tongue could utter, has youth the power to dedicate to the noblest cause which ever yet engaged the attention of an intellectual and immortal being. What, then, I would ask again, is that which hinders the surrender of your heart to God, your, conduct to the requirements of the religion of Christ?

With this solemn inquiry, I would leave the young reader to pursue the train of her own reflections. All that I have proposed to her consideration as desirable in character and habit—in heart and conduct—will be without consistency, and without foundation, unless based upon Christian principle, and supported by Christian faith. All that I have proposed to her as most lovely, and most admirable, may be rendered more, infinitely more so, by the refinement of feeling, the elevation of sentiment, and the purity of purpose, which those principles and that faith are calculated to impart.

THE END.

Made in the USA
Middletown, DE
22 October 2021